RELATIVELY FAMOUS

FAMOUS BOOK I

Heather C. Leigh

Third Edition, License Notes

QUOTES

With fame, you know, you can read about yourself, somebody else's ideas about you, but what's important is how you feel about yourself - for survival and living day to day with what comes up.

Marilyn Monroe

It is dangerous to let the public behind the scenes. They are easily disillusioned and then they are angry with you, for it was the illusion they loved.

W. Somerset Maugham

We're constantly striving for success, fame and comfort when all we really need to be happy is someone or something to be enthusiastic about.

H. Jackson Brown, Jr.

Many thanks to my very understanding and supportive husband, who let me spend hours and hours with Drew and Sydney while I ignored everything else in life.

CHAPTER I

The sudden screech of tires to my left makes me reflexively turn my head toward the sound, so when my foot hits a patch of ice on the sidewalk, I don't see it coming.

"Ooof!"

I hit the ground, hard, and my right arm takes the brunt of the impact. *Ow.*

"Are you alright?"

A kind, well-dressed older man is walking around a black sedan to crouch beside me, his breath puffing out in soft wisps from the bitter cold.

"I don't know." I lift my arm and see that my long sleeved thermal jacket is ripped open. Blood is already dripping from a two inch gash showing through the brand new hole.

"Oh my." He holds out a hand with a smile on his kind face. "Here, let's clean you up." The man helps me to my feet and leads me to a battered metal door that says *GYM* across it in red lettering.

Everything I was taught about strangers as a child comes rushing back. I don't know this man and this place looks a little rougher than I'm accustomed to. Digging in my pocket, I pull a napkin and show it to him.

"No worries. I'm okay. I can just use this."

He chuckles at my sad attempt to refuse his kindness and gracefully plucks the napkin from my hand.

"Miss, you have blood running down your arm and dripping onto the sidewalk. What kind of man would I be if I let you leave in this condition? Come on. I know for a fact they have a first aid kit inside and can get you fixed up quick." He holds up his hands to show he means no harm. "I promise."

My initial hesitation evaporates with this compassionate man's words. For some reason, he makes me feel safe in a fatherly way. A way I haven't felt in a long time.

"Okay, I guess I do need a little help."

He opens the door and as I pass through he grins, the fine lines around his eyes scrunching up into the grey hair on his temples. "I'm Bruce by the way."

He's so genuine, I can't help but give him a small smile back. "Sydney. Nice to meet you Bruce. Thanks for taking pity on me and my clumsiness. I'm usually much better at staying upright."

"It happens to the best of us," he chuckles.

Once inside, I take in my surroundings. Surprised, I glance back over at Bruce. I'm finding it hard to believe that a guy like Bruce, in his dress pants and impeccably pressed shirt, frequents this gym. For one thing, it smells awful, like old sweat socks and industrial strength cleaner. Second, it's quite obvious that this isn't the type of gym that people use to stay in shape.

Taking in the huge room, I quickly notice that I'm the only female in this place. Not very comforting.

The remaining ten or so people I can see are half-naked men grappling or punching bags or beating each other up with their fists like the two guys in the huge center ring.

Mixed martial arts training, that's what they do here according to the UFC banner that spans the back of the room, covering up the dreary, chipped cinderblocks that make up the walls.

"Damien!" Bruce calls out, waving someone over.

The two men in the cage immediately stop fighting to stare at us. Both of them hop down the small set of stairs and trot over. I have no idea which one is Damien, but I can't take my eyes off of the fighter in the black and red shorts with the green eyes. He is beyond attractive—he's positively stunning.

I feel the prickly heat creeping up my neck and face. I wish I could disappear. It's humiliating to be standing here in front of these two hot, sweaty men while my blood drips on the floor. Not to mention the rest of the gym, which has gone silent to watch.

"Can you grab the first aid kit?" Bruce asks. "She fell on some ice out front. Cut her arm pretty bad."

The man with the buzz cut and tattoos wearing black and yellow shorts nods and hurries off to fetch it. That must be Damien.

The other guy, the too-beautiful one, is eyeing me warily. Which, in turn, makes me even more uncomfortable.

"I'm sorry to interrupt," I blurt out awkwardly.

The man says nothing. Instead, he stares at me as if he's afraid of me! I have no idea what to make of that, so I stand there bleeding since it's all I can do.

"Here." He hands me a small towel. "So you won't drip everywhere."

His voice is deep and smooth. When his hand brushes against mine to hand me the towel, a shiver goes up my spine. Fumbling from nerves, I wrap it around my arm the best as I can.

"Thanks." I stare at the ground, glancing up to take a peek at his handsome face. He's acting really odd, wary, like me. But I'm the one in the strange situation surrounded by men I don't know. Why would he be uncomfortable?

Not knowing what else to do, I go for mindless pleasantries. "I'm Sydney."

The beautiful man gives me another strange look before introducing himself… albeit reluctantly. "I'm Drew. So you fell?"

Either I'm so inept that he's dying to get away from me, or this guy is really off his game. There's no way a man who looks like that isn't smoother at making small talk with women.

I shrug, which sends a burning hot spike of pain down my arm. "I fell. It's no big deal, really." I wince from the sensation, my voice coming out strained. "Nice to meet you, Drew."

Bruce and Drew exchange a look. "Have we met before?" Drew asks hesitantly.

I pull down my brows, trying to place him. I don't think I know him. Do I? *Oh my god!* What if he recognizes me because of my resemblance to my mother?

I need to get out of here before one of them figures it out.

"No. I don't think we've met."

Now Drew looks absolutely dumfounded. His perfect lips fall open in shock.

Let it drop, please let it drop.

I can't have this guy to figuring out who my parents are, who *I* am. I'm pretty sure we've never met. There's no way I would forget his unbelievable face and body if we had.

Damien jogs up to us with a large white box. "Got it."

"I'll do it," Drew says, his green eyes penetrating mine as he snatches the kit from Damien's hands. He doesn't look away, that powerful gaze trapping me in place. "Bruce, thanks for bringing her in. I'll be out in a few minutes."

Bruce must be his driver, now everything makes sense. He's most likely waiting for Drew to finish his workout.

"You sure?" Damien asks. Drew turns to scowl at him, Damien shrugging his shoulders in response, "Okay man, I'll see you later?"

"Yeah, I'll be here." Drew has that intense stare aimed back at me as he speaks. The noise of the gym starts back up, a cacophony of grunts and punches. Suddenly, I'm alone with this beautiful man.

"Here, sit down." He points to a nearby bench.

Mesmerized, I do as he says and watch as he kneels in front of me. Still shirtless, I track his lean, sinewy muscles as they stretch and flex in front of me in a tantalizing dance. He's close enough to touch. I want to lean in and lick every hard ridge of his body. It's literally torture to sit this close to him.

Drew places the kit on the bench and opens it up.

"Let's see what you did." His gruff tone has been replaced with kindness. It helps to relax me, but only somewhat. I'm still nervous to have this very intimidating man so close. I watch those intelligent green eyes flick up to mine before he focuses back on my injury. Drew puts one of his large, tape wrapped hands around my wrist and I gasp when a heart-stopping rush of heat travels up my arm.

Wow!

Drew pauses before carefully removing the towel to assess my wound.

"It isn't that bad. It's big, but not deep, so it shouldn't leave a scar or anything." Drew looks at me and smiles, "Wouldn't want to ruin that perfect skin."

My heart stops when he smiles at me. He has brilliant white teeth and full lips, light stubble covers his angular jaw. I notice that his eyes aren't the green I originally thought, but green with a dark ring of brown in the center. What does me in is the single dimple that appears on his right cheek when he smiles.

The heat I felt in my arm has taken root and begins to grow. What started as a small burn is rapidly building into a smoldering fire. I shift uncomfortably on the bench, hoping to rein in the urge to tackle him to the ground and grind on his hard body.

Sydney, whatever has gotten in to you needs to stop right now.

"Take off that jacket while I get what I need."

Aren't we bossy.

I finally stop my gawking and do as he asks.

When Drew turns away to rummage through the first aid kit, I let out the breath that I'd been holding in an attempt to keep him from noticing how heavy my breathing has become.

"Here." His deep, calm voice wraps around me like a warm blanket. "This may sting. I'm sorry Sydney." Drew's eyes look pained as he presses a cold, wet gauze pad to my arm.

I flinch, unable to stop myself from hissing when the antiseptic hits my skin.

"I'm sorry," he says again.

"It's okay." It seems that Drew feels genuine remorse for hurting me even though he's the one helping me. He's sensitive, caring. A contradictory quality for a man who hits other people for fun.

Drew reaches back into the kit and pulls out a large bandage and some gauze. Laying it on my arm, he wraps it up quickly and efficiently.

"Looks like you've done this before." I grin at the professional job he did on my wound.

"Yeah, a few times…." Drew glances up at me and stops. I watch as his eyes dilate and his lips part. The smoldering fire grows larger, turning into a raging inferno inside me.

Drew shakes his head and looks away, putting back everything he took out of the kit.

I'm about to pull away from his grasp when he sucks in a pained breath and clutches my wrist a little tighter. Drew trails a long, rough finger from my thumb to my elbow, following along the jagged pink path of a very old scar.

"What happened?" he whispers.

Instinctively, I yank my arm away, swallowing down the lump that has formed in my throat.

"Nothing, I'm fine." Without any explanation, I jump up and wrap my arms around my stomach to keep from falling apart. "Thank you for fixing me, I really appreciate it."

Memories I've repressed for years come flooding back. I bolt for the door, keeping my head down so Drew won't see the unshed tears that threaten to fall. I don't discuss that scar, not with anyone.

"Wait!"

I stop right before I get to the door, but can't bring myself to turn around. I don't want to go to pieces in front of this beautiful stranger.

"Your jacket." Drew holds out the torn and bloody remains of my coat. "It's pretty much ruined though."

"Thanks. Yeah, it is." Pulling myself together, I glance at him and take my coat. Certainly, after that display he thinks I'm crazy.

Drew's handsome face is furrows with concern. "Is that all you have to wear? It's freezing outside."

I shrug. He saw what I came in here with.

"Wait here." Drew holds up a finger to show he'll be back in a minute. Fascinated, I watch him jog over to the ring as he grabs a shirt and tugs it over his head. I think about what a shame it is to cover it up such perfection and manage a smile. He stuffs his feet into a pair of shoes, throws on a ratty old hat and hurries back over to the door.

"Come on." He takes my hand as if it's the most natural thing in the world, his large, calloused fingers curling around mine.

We go outside and the biting cold January air pierces right through my thin shirt. He's right, it's much, much colder without my jacket or the benefit of being heated up from running. I have to fight the urge to curl up against his large, warm body.

Drew opens the back door of the same black sedan that Bruce stepped out of when I fell. "Get in."

I stare at him suspiciously. I can't get into a strange car.

Drew gives me an exasperated look. "Sydney, I'm going to have Bruce bring you home. It's too cold for you to walk like that." He sticks his head in the open door, "Bruce, take her home and then come back here. I'll be ready to go when you return."

Hesitant, I fidget on the sidewalk. I don't know if I should accept the ride. Drew seems like a genuine guy, but this *is* New York and people here rarely do things simply out of kindness.

"Please." Drew puts his hands on my shoulders, the contact warming me up a few degrees. "I couldn't sleep knowing I sent you out on the street to freeze."

Intrigued to see who would care about a total stranger, I study his face. There's something about his eyes, an honesty I see that makes me give in. That, and the fact that I'm already shivering violently and I'm still pretty far from home.

"Okay." With a small smile, I climb into the back seat of the car. "Thank you, for everything."

Drew leans down toward me, his purely masculine scent overpowering my senses. God, he smells good. "Take care Sydney." That honeyed voice sends my hormones into overdrive.

He shuts the door and as I give Bruce my address, I catch a glimpse of Drew. He's deep in thought, rubbing a finger over his lips as he stands alone on the empty sidewalk. Knowing he can't see me through the blacked-out windows, I watch as we drive away until he's out of sight.

CHAPTER 2

"Do you need me to get you a cab this morning?" Richard, my doorman asks as he follows me out into the freezing morning air.

I laugh at the kind man who I've known for years. "I must be a glutton for punishment since I'm walking this morning Richard, but thanks." My idea that the icy air will help wake me up probably isn't a good one, but I start walking.

I wave, turn right, and effortlessly merge into the crowded city sidewalk. Hustling through the congested sidewalk as fast as I can without twisting an ankle or crashing into someone, I make it to the Village Coffee Bar on Bleecker Street in less than ten minutes.

Arriving just before the end of my nose goes numb, I fling open the door to the café and am surrounded by two of my favorite smells—coffee and cinnamon. Happy to be out of the bitter cold, I make a beeline for the long serving counter where my best friend Leah is waiting on an older woman who seems to be having difficulty deciding on her order.

After an eternity of waffling between a cranberry and a blueberry lemon croissant, the woman pays for her pastries and her drink and leaves the café.

Stepping up to the register, I give my best friend a sweet smile. "How's it going Leah?"

Narrowing her eyes as if there's something different about me, she assesses my appearance. She must not find anything, because she breaks into a huge grin. "Going great. Busy. Your usual?" She starts getting my order without waiting for my answer.

"Were you up late last night working on the Warren Hotel project?" She smirks, lowering her voice into a seductive purr. "Or were you thinking about your handsome, MMA-loving, white knight?" Leah laughs as she hands me my coffee and croissant.

I roll my eyes. I shouldn't have told her about my encounter with Drew yesterday. She'll push me to date him. She pushes me to date anyone with a pulse.

"The presentation, Leah." I don't feel a single bit guilty for lying to my friend. In actuality, I *was* up all night thinking about Drew and his hot body and honest eyes. But she would make me miserable if she knew. "Wait, how did you know I was up late?"

"Syd, first, I've known you for a long time. Second, I know you have a deadline coming up, and third," she points at my face, "the bags under your eyes have bags."

I relax and laugh at her honesty. "Yeah, you're right. I do look like something the dog dragged home."

Leah cackles loudly, her blonde ponytail swishing behind her. "You're still more gorgeous with your overtired, baggy-eyed face than most girls are on their best day, Syd. No wonder the guy at that gym helped you out."

Smiling, I turn and sling my bag onto my favorite table in the back corner. Leah is always complementing me, but she's quite the looker herself. Sometimes I wonder how many of New York's finest young businessmen come in for the great pastries, and how many come in to hit on Leah.

Probably fifty-fifty.

Settling into a chair, I pull my huge stack of files and my laptop from the messenger bag and spread them out on the table to get started. This presentation has to be perfect; it's the highest profile project I've been given and the executives at the Warren hotel are going to decide if the concept I came up with is suitable for the image they wish to convey for their rebranded nightclub.

After letting my mind fill with visions of Drew's hot body all night and the electricity I felt when he touched me, I have a lot of work to get done.

An hour and a half and two cups of coffee later, I'm startled when a chair is dragged back from my table and a tall man with a huge to-go cup of coffee and a napkin-wrapped croissant sits gracefully across from me.

"Sydney, how are you Sweetheart?" he asks as he shows me his perfect white teeth.

"Adam, how have you been?"

Adam is what I like to think of as an acquaintance, not a friend. I don't let people into my inner circle so I have very few friends. Well, one friend actually. Leah. But I know several people well enough in passing to hold a semi-personal conversation. Adam has been a frequent customer of the Coffee Bar over the last three months, and whenever he comes in and sees me, he tends to sit and chat.

I like Adam, he's perpetually happy and makes me feel good, but mostly I like him because he never asks questions I find too invasive to answer. Plus, it seems as though he has similar reasons to protect his own personal life. Adam even sits as though he's protecting his space. Hiding in the corner with his back to the door, using me as a human shield.

He's is also super easy on the eyes, so spending a few hours with him each week is no hardship. Plus he's great at letting me bounce ideas off of him when I feel conflicted about a design element. He has a unique perspective on design that makes me think that he's a very creative person overall.

"I'm brilliant," Adam says in his smooth British accent. "I've had quite a bit on my plate so I haven't been able to get here in a while. When I woke up for work much earlier than should be allowed, I decided I really wanted a good cup of coffee, so I knew I had to pop in here. Plus, this week's croissant is espresso chip, and you well know I can't pass that up." He breaks out that million dollar smile again as he sips from his coffee. "Getting to chat you up is just the icing on the cake, Sweetheart."

He sounds exhausted. I take a good look at Adam, but he looks as good as usual. From his short, almost black hair that sticks up on the top of his head in a sexy just-out-of-bed way, his stubble-covered angular jaw and perfect lips, to his obviously toned body shown-off under form fitting t-shirts. Then there's my favorite, that mysterious dark tattoo that peeks out from his left sleeve. Of course today, most of him is hidden under a hat, scarf and winter coat, but still, he's very attractive.

I start mentally comparing him to Drew as he's regarding me curiously.

"Well, everyone knows that if you want a good cup of coffee, this is the only place in the city to get it." I lace my words with humor.

Narrowing my gaze on Adam, I think about a problem I'm having that he may be able to help me with. "Actually, since you're here, I'm working on the design for the new Verve nightclub at the Warren Hotel in Midtown that I told you about. I have the barstools narrowed down to these two choices."

Clicking a few times on the laptop, I spin it around to show him the screen. "Which one says young and fun, but only if you have tons of money?" Adam looks up from the computer, confused. I purse my lips and wink at him. "Strange, right? The Warren execs want to convey an exclusive feel, but also want young trendy people to frequent the bar."

Smirking, Adam's lively hazel eyes meet mine. "Okay, I'll have a go." He stares at the screen and within seconds points to the chair on the left. "Chrome is high maintenance and expensive looking. Dark distressed leather is fun and young. I would go with that one."

I turn the laptop back to face me and scowl at the two photos as if one of them would jump off the screen and into my lap.

He's good, really good.

"You're right. It fits perfectly." I let my stressed out features relax into an expression of relief and rest back in my chair. "Thanks Adam, I've been working so much lately that even the smallest decisions seem overwhelming. All I needed was a break and a fresh set of eyes." I nudge his arm playfully and close the laptop.

"Well, my work here is done." He stands up to leave, leaning over to give me a chaste peck on the cheek. "See you later, Sweetheart. Don't stress so much, your design is great. I'm sure all of the rich young elites in New York will be queuing up at The Warren's new club soon enough. Just remember me when you have that big opening night bash to attend."

"Bye Adam, and thanks for being my sounding board. I think I'll take your advice and call it a day." I smile and start packing up my things as Adam ducks his head and leaves the café.

Leah comes bounding over, gathers up the dishes and gives the table a quick wipe down. "I never get sick of looking at that fine man" She waggles her perfectly plucked eyebrows suggestively.

"I know what you mean," I mumble as I gather up the rest of my wayward files and stuff them into my bag.

Leah grabs my arm and stares at me. "I don't think you do, Syd." Her tiny face hardens as she lectures me *again* on my lack of a social life. "You're going to have to let someone in eventually. You can't keep secrets from everyone forever. I'm your best friend, and I love you, but the extremes you go to for privacy are ridiculous. I get it, but it's still ridiculous. You can't let your past dictate your life.

"You should have gotten yourself a piece of Adam by now. You've spent who knows how many hours sitting next to him and you don't even know what he does for a living! And what about this Drew guy from yesterday that you're obsessing over? Did you get his number?"

Trying my hardest not to get angry, I tell her what she doesn't want to hear. "No, I didn't get his number and I'm not obsessing over him." *I so am.* "I appreciate your concern. I know you're right but I just don't feel that way about Adam. He's hot and he's nice and he might be into me." I sigh. "You know it would only be a one-night stand and I just don't want to go there with him. I like talking to him about useless, unimportant stuff. The second I get involved deeper; I get asked questions about my life. It would ruin everything. It's the same with Drew, I just can't risk it right now." I pull back the frustration I feel rising in my voice. "Call me tomorrow. If I need a break from work we can grab dinner."

Leah stares hard into my eyes, as if silently willing me to see things her way. I watch as her resolve melts away. "Definitely. Dinner sounds great."

The next few days consist of work, sleep, and breaks to eat and hang with Leah. That's it. Adam hasn't reappeared at the café, so

I've avoided having that conversation with Leah again and she let the Drew thing drop since I have no way to contact him.

Not that I've stopped thinking about him and his gentle touch and scorching hot gaze. Such a contradiction, a man so strong and fierce that he fights other men in his spare time, but so tender and kind that he wrapped up my injury and made sure I got home okay.

It's Tuesday afternoon and I have to show the Warren Hotel's final presentation to my mother for approval. Sitting in my home office, I stretch my arms over my head, drained from work.

I love my mom, but sometimes dealing with her is exhausting, even if it's only on the phone. When your mom is also your boss, it gets even more stressful, and Evangeline Allen is a force of nature. I decide to rest on the comfy couch by the huge office window before calling her.

My mom packed her bags at age nineteen and moved to LA. Her innate talent, natural good looks and unwavering work ethic brought her near instant success in Hollywood, landing her the tabloid title of "America's Sweetheart".

Within a year, she accepted her Best Actress Oscar for her portrayal of a pharmaceutical company CEO turned patient activist. My mom is still comforted years after her parents died in a car crash in upstate New York by the fact that they got to see her best moment and didn't have to see her very public disgrace.

Young, rich and famous, my mom married Hollywood's "Bad Boy", my dad, Reid Tannen. Rugged, masculine, and an A-list fixture in Hollywood circles, he broke hearts all over town when he and my mom exchanged "I do's". My mom and dad were a tabloid reporter's dream come true. The fresh faced and sweet Evangeline landing Hollywood's biggest player meant they were hounded by paparazzi and fans everywhere they went.

My dad had been known to get into bar fights in his early days in L.A., and his "Bad Boy" image resurfaced several times in my childhood. Usually rearing its ugly head when he would beat down photographers that threatened my mother or me. I remember having to be surrounded by bodyguards just to go to school every day. It got so bad that my parents couldn't even drop me off themselves because it caused too big of a scene.

I stare at the ceiling in my office, thinking about how lonely my childhood was. If there's one thing I learned from my parents, it's to be cautious of anyone and everyone, because they just want to use you to get something for themselves. When I was twelve, it made my world turn upside down.

****

My best friend Tara and I are hanging by her pool after school on one of a string of perfect days in L.A. in early September. Her mother, a producer that had worked with my mom several times, comes out of the house and down by the pool where we're sunning ourselves and gossiping about classmates at our elite private school.

"Sydney, your mom is sending a car for you early, you need to get home."

Tara and I exchange looks and roll our eyes at the drama that always seems to surround my parents, constantly bleeding over into my life.

"I'll see you tomorrow at school, Tara." I grab my stuff and leave the backyard, not knowing that I'd never see my friend again.

My mom's silver Range Rover with the blacked out windows is sitting in the driveway when I leave the house. Robbie, Mom's bodyguard jumps out of the back seat and holds the door open for me to climb in then follows suit behind me.

"Miss Tannen, sorry to interrupt your fun."

My eyes widen in surprise at his apology. I notice his normally serious face has softened. He puts a large, dark hand on my shoulder, patting me awkwardly.

I wrinkle my nose and look at Robbie like he's crazy. "No problem, Robbie. I'm sure mom has some *super important* stuff going on." I use my pre-teen sarcasm to make me sound confident, but as we drive through the hills to the house I have a nagging feeling that something is very wrong.

By the time the SUV turns up the long drive to my parents' massive house, I've worked myself into a full out panic. There are reporters all over the street in front of our private gate, screaming at the Range Rover as it passes them, banging on the sides, not possibly knowing who's inside the SUV because of the dark windows.

I press my sweaty palms to legs and sit up as straight and rigid as a board, swallowing so hard I swear that our driver Brett could hear it from the front seat. I'm used to the press hanging around, but this many of them at once isn't a common occurrence.

The Range Rover pulls up to the side of the garage and now it's quite clear that something is off. There are at least six cars in the driveway that don't belong to my parents, only one of which I recognize. That one belongs to mom's head of public relations, Devin Arnette. He's a nice enough guy, but why is he here?

Notably absent is Daddy's sleek, black Bugatti Veyron. My dad might be gone a lot, but he rarely takes out the Bugatti since he had it rebuilt after the accident. He loves that car, but hates the attention he gets when he drives it and the memories it holds.

Robbie jumps out and helps me down from the Rover. He turns and grabs my bag from the seat and follows as I weave through the vehicles in our eight car garage and into the house.

When I climb the stairs from the garage and come out into the foyer, a ripple of fear runs down my neck. There are people all over the house with clipboards and earpieces and they're tossing things into boxes all around me.

Standing, shaky and confused, I forget about Robbie until he whispers in my ear. "Your mom is up in her room, you need to go see her."

At some point I must have moved because somehow I make it up the stairs and down the hallway to my parents' room, but I don't remember doing it. The closer I get to the enormous master suite, the louder the thudding in my chest becomes.

Nervously, I peek into the room. Mom is standing in her giant walk-in closet barking orders to a disheveled looking young man with yet another clipboard.

"Sydney! You're here."

I turn around to see Devin sitting on one of the oversized leather chairs by the fireplace. He jumps up and hugs me to his perfectly pressed, Prada-clad chest, his expensive cologne surrounding me.

"W-w-what's going on, Devin?"

"Sydney, I'm going to let your mom tell you most of what's happening. What I can say is that the two of you are going to live in New York."

I let out a cry and take a step back from Devin. "Are you insane? We can't go to New York! I live here! *We* live here! What about my dad?"

Devin's face falls when I mention my dad. Quickly, he composes himself, rearranging his features back into that perfect Hollywood pleasantry. I know that look, I've seen my parents use it. Whatever is going on is bad. Really bad.

"Your dad's not going Sydney. Your parents are getting divorced."

Whether it's the long day, the dehydration from lying in the sun, or the hysteria building up inside me, I, Sydney Tannen, have my very first panic attack and black out.

****

Trembling all over, I wake up, not quite sure where I am. It's pitch black in the room. It takes me a full minute of fumbling around to realize I fell asleep on the couch in my office. I sit up and frown, trying to push the past that continues to plague me out of my head.

Why does my mind keep going back there?

For the second time that day, I'm shaking and freaking out. When the panic begins to overtake me, I stand up and press my forehead against the cool glass of the massive picture window behind my desk. Breathing in deep and taking in the enormity of the city stops the shaking in my hands. The feeling I get from the view—that I'm small, invisible, and anonymous, knowing that no one can find me—that's what slows my racing heart.

A few minutes later, I let out a huge breath and drop into the desk chair to call my mom.

"Sydney! How are you sweetie?" Mom's soothing voice floats out of the phone after the third ring.

"Great mom, how's Belize?"

My mom spends every winter on a private island off the coast of Belize. She designs her custom décor and furniture line from her winter home, running Allen Deconstruction from her home. I have at least thirty employees at my beck and call at the New York office, so it's pretty much my fault when I get overwhelmed on a project, since I never call any of them. Very few of them know who I am. I don't need them judging me or worse, trying to befriend me. Only three employees know that Evangeline Allen is the Allen behind the company name and they've signed non-disclosures.

"It's beautiful darling. If I didn't need you in New York, I would have you stay here with me for a month."

I suppress the urge to respond with a laugh, instead rolling my eyes. Mom always talks about needing me in New York, but I know she could easily have someone else to do the presentations. Including me is my mother's way of making me feel necessary to the business, and I appreciate it.

"So you received the Warren project? Did you look over everything?"

On edge and unable to sit still, I get up and pace back and forth in front of the big window, watching the headlights crawl down the street in front of my building.

"I did sweetie, and they're great. I love what you did with the VIP area, incorporating our new line of low-rise loveseats and the glass and chrome tables. It's genius."

I can hear my mom's fingers flying over the keyboard of her computer as she speaks, making changes and sending them back to me. "I tweaked one little thing with the table sconces but the rest is a go. I'm sending it back to you right now. I've cc'd Bethany Williams at the office so don't worry about that." The typing sounds stop. "Good luck tomorrow Syd, but I know you don't need it."

I can feel my mom smiling through the phone as we chat a little about the weather in New York and the diving in Belize, as well as next year's designs. When we hang up, I'm relieved. That went better than expected. Maybe she trusts me more after my last two projects were so well received.

Tired, I take one last look through the huge office window and into the night. Breathing deep, I turn back to the desk and shut down my MacBook, plug in my phone, and leave the office to get ready for bed.

As I scrub my weary face I look in the mirror. At five foot seven inches, I'm tall enough, and my near religious devotion to yoga and running keep my body lithe and athletic, although sometimes I'm almost too thin. Probably because the exercise is more to keep me too tired to think, which is why I take it to extremes sometimes. Touching my mouth I know I look exactly like my mother except I have my dad's eyes and too-full lips.

The circles under my large blue eyes are becoming darker than ever. I also notice how dull they seem; joyless. As much as I blame the stress on work, I know that my anxiety issues and lack of sleep from never facing down the trauma of my past play the biggest part in my haggard appearance.

I'm twenty-four going on fifty.

Sighing, I turn from the mirror and head into my bedroom.

I devoted an entire corner of the room to my bookcases, stacked high with all types of novels and design books. Since I don't watch or even own a TV, the shelves are overflowing.

Too tired, I skip reading tonight and climb into bed. Thankfully, I fall asleep before a single worry can come back into my fragile mind.

CHAPTER 3

"Well Miss Allen, this is perfect. It is exactly what the Warren was looking for in our nightclub redesign." I smile and stand up from the conference table to shake hands with Jeff Talley, the project manager for the Warren Hotel remodel.

"Yes, it's definitely what we want Verve to portray to the city," chirps Natasha Lin, head of the New York location. "I think that the hotel chain president will want to redesign all of our nightclubs with your firm once he sees what you've done."

As I reach out to shake Natasha's small hand, I look at her beautiful, put-together appearance. Her shiny black hair is cut blunt at her pointy chin and her dark eyes are radiant. I silently thank my under eye concealer for keeping me from looking like a zombie this morning.

"Thank you both so much. Mr. Talley, I'll arrange for the shipments of materials for your workers to begin the install, and you can tell me the dates that you choose so I can be there to oversee the design."

After exchanging goodbyes, I pack up my presentation and head home, smiling genuinely for the first time in several weeks.

With the pitch done, I feel as if a huge weight has been lifted from my shoulders. Unfortunately, the weight of being Sydney Allen still presses down on me relentlessly. I had thought that at age fourteen, when I asked my mom to let me change my name from Tannen to Allen some of the anxiety I suffered would have vanished with my dad's famous name. And it did bring me some degree of anonymity. Everyone knew who Sydney Tannen was, but few put the pieces together when I was introduced as Sydney Allen.

But there is no erasing my memories, no matter how hard I try to pretend they didn't happen. I refuse to dwell on the fact that my dad betrayed me and my mother very publically and hasn't bothered to contact us since. I asked my mom about Reid Tannen when they broke up. I cried and threw a fit and missed him every single day, but I was just too young to understand and eventually too afraid of opening wounds that had taken my mom years to heal.

Ultimately, it was easier to cope if I just stuffed the pain down and didn't think about it at all. As much as I want to ask all of the questions that plague me to this day, I'm deathly afraid to find out the answers.

So here I am, in this unending limbo of denial. It doesn't take a genius to ascertain that this is the root of all of my problems.

Once I get home, I turn to my usual therapy to work through my issues, running. I throw on my Nikes, strap my iPod to my arm, pull on a knitted skullcap and head back into the city to sweat out my problems before the winter brings a very early nightfall.

I'm on my 4th mile when I think about what Leah had said the other day in the café. Leah was my first friend when I moved to New York twelve years ago, and she knows *everything* about my past. She knows why I refuse to own a TV, why I won't read entertainment magazines, why I haven't seen a movie since moving to the city, why

I don't listen to any music made after 2001, why I avoid real relationships, and even *she* thinks it's time for me to let people in.

Is it time to let someone in?

Maybe, but I'm afraid that anyone I let in would eventually sell me out to the tabloids when they find out who I am. The thought of reliving that nightmare sends a paralyzing spasm through my chest, making it difficult to breathe. Leah hasn't sold me out, but not everyone is as loyal as my best friend.

People also weren't camping out on her front walk, threatening to kill themselves if they couldn't meet her dad.

Wanting to get rid of the anxiety I have rushing through my veins, I crank up the deep bass of Green Day and push myself to run faster as I contemplate Leah's advice. What is the worst that could happen? Could I lose my hard-earned anonymity and survive? Or is it worse to live without ever letting anyone in? Would letting go stop the anxiety and the flashbacks? Is it time to want more for myself?

After pushing through four more miles I come to a stop in front of the brick and glass exterior of my building. Panting, I bend over and put my hands down on my knees, attempting to catch my breath.

I pull out my ear buds, throw a quick "hello" at Richard and bolt inside. Feeling even more anti-social than usual, I decide to order Thai food to be delivered and spend the night reading until I fall asleep.

****

"Sydney. Sydney! Baby, are you awake?" The stress and panic in mother's voice jolts me awake.

I open my eyes and remember that I'm lying on my parents' bed, with my mother and Devin, her head of PR, leaning over me. They both have deep furrows etched in their concerned faces.

"Don't sit up too fast, baby. You scared us there by fainting." Mom hugs me to her chest and pulls her fingers through my wavy auburn hair. "I know this is overwhelming, Sydney. I'm getting us out of here before it gets worse. Don't worry, I won't let them destroy you."

I'm too tired to know what Mom is talking about so I simply nod my head. I've been through so much these past two months, I don't have the energy for questions right now. Suddenly, I'm so tired I feel as though every last bit of me had been drained out and left hollow.

The next hour is a whirlwind of activity of strangers in my house, so I retreat to my bedroom and collapse on the massive bed. My eyes track the erratic patterns of light on the ceiling. Moments later there's a soft knock on the door. Mom breezes into the room and sits on the bed, putting a hand on my knee.

"Sydney, we're going now. All of your stuff will be sent to New York later this week. The jet is waiting for us at Van Nuys."

Exhausted, I gather all of the strength I have left and sit up to get a look at my mother's face. From a very young age I've been able to tell the difference between *Eva Allen,* my mom and *Evangeline Allen,* the actress. The face I'm looking at across the brand new fluffy pink and white comforter is nothing but an act. This is the composed façade my mom wears to make it seem as though she's strong while inside, she's falling to pieces. This is what makes her a great actress. But even Mom can't hold up the performance for much longer.

"Am I going to see Daddy before we leave?"

Reacting to my question, my mother's face falls for the briefest of moments before the mask snaps back in place.

"No, Syd. He's gone. I've asked him to leave and to never come back."

****

I shoot up out of bed clutching at the covers to get to my rapidly beating heart. Wiping the sweat off of my brow with a trembling hand, I take a quick look at the clock on the nightstand.

3:07am

I sigh and fall back, punching my pillow in defeat. Running to exhaustion is supposed to keep the memories away for the night but it isn't working anymore. Rage and resentment course through me, flooding my skin with heat.

I'm angry. *Beyond* angry. I'm furious.

Why can't I sleep peacefully without exercising myself to death? I'm so sick and tired of pretending my past didn't happen, that I didn't care my dad abandoned me. Years of therapy and I'm still an untrusting, anxiety-ridden, shell of a girl.

Too wound up to sleep, I throw back the covers and stomp down the hall to the kitchen. Flicking on lights as I enter each room, I stomp over to cabinet, yank out a shot glass and bottle of Patrón and throw down a large gulp of the liquid, letting the fire burn my throat as I swallow. I slam the glass down on the counter and step over to the full sized wine cooler, pull out a bottle of my favorite Cabernet and pour a huge glassful.

If running won't work, I know for sure that alcohol will calm my nerves.

I turn on my heel and stalk back down the hall, fuming as I head into my office and fall into the desk chair in a heap. Taking a huge gulp of wine, I flip open my laptop and tap my fingers impatiently as I wait for it to start up.

Ugh! Still vibrating with nervous energy, I spin the chair around and stare out the window. One more giant mouthful and the alcohol coursing through my body will begin to numb the pain.

Turning back to the computer, I bring up Google and hesitate as my hands hover over the keyboard. Determined to see this through, I throw back the final gulp, emptying the glass of my liquid courage. Shaking, I type a name into the search engine that I haven't looked for in the last twelve years.

Reid Tannen

As cold as I it is in my apartment in January, I can feel sweat beading on my furrowed brow. "I can do this," I say out loud to myself.

The last twelve years of my life have been carefully structured to avoid situations like this one. No Hollywood, no gossip rags, no TV shows, no Google, no celebrity—all to prevent repeating the overpowering heartache I had suffered through when I was just a kid.

I can't even name the latest hot young actor. Newest blockbuster? No clue. Biggest TV show? Nope. Top 50 songs? No idea.

After seeing the hurt my mother felt at the hands of fame; hands that would rip you to shreds five minutes after holding you aloft for your achievements, I feel nauseous at the entire concept of their ivory tower of hypocrisy and livid at Americans for buying into all that celebrity obsessed garbage.

But I'm even more sick of worrying, sick of being alone, sick of not trusting anyone, sick of sleepless nights, sick of pretending my dad didn't leave. It's time to take the past and confront it. My finger hovers over the key, I take a deep breath, squeeze my eyes shut and hit

Enter

Afraid to look at the results, I press the heels of my hands into my tired eyes, inhale deeply, and peek up at the screen. Along with several photos of dad, my eyes bug out as I scan link after link of articles relating to his life and work: *150,000,000* results to be exact. *Holy cow.*

Reid Tannen – IMDB
Reid Tannen: Actor, producer. Filmography, biography, awards, personal life…

Reid Tannen - Wikipedia, the free encyclopedia
Arthur Reid Tannen (born March 20, 1966) is an American actor and film producer. Tannen has received four Academy Award nominations and five Golden Globe nominations. Winning one Golden Globe for….

Reid Tannen fan site
Find all the latest news, images, videos and more. Click…

News for Reid Tannen
Reid Tannen Breaking News, Photos, and Videos | RoxyFan
1 day ago – Top Hollywood hunks Maxon Sundry and Reid Tannen show-off their sculpted abs while filming a movie at an undisclosed beach in Hawaii. The ever hot Reid grabbed a paddleboard between scenes and hit the surf……

Bad Boy Reid Tannen Angry Again

CelebWeekly- Reid Tannen lashes out at fans and photogs that get too close and personal to the star on the set of his current movie, *Anti-Hero*, filming in various locations around Hawaii. The long time "Bad Boy" was....

Reid Tannen admits in Walters interview that he screwed up with Evangeline Allen

abcnews.com- The notoriously tight-lipped Tannen sat down with Barbara Walters for her "Most Fascinating Person of the Year" interview and shed a little bit of light on his relationship with his ex-wife, Evangeline Allen, and his estranged daughter Sydney. What small bits of information he revealed....

Hollywood buzzes with Oscar fever, Reid Tannen a sure thing?

Entertainment 8- Insiders say that Reid Tannen is not only a shoe-in for an Oscar nomination for his portrayal of tormented painter Vincent Van Gogh in his movie *House of Auvers*, it is said he is all but guaranteed the win. After four nominations and zero wins, is it finally Tannen's time to shine? Academy....

My eyes are drawn to the hundreds of tiny thumbnails of my dad. I click on each one and study it intently before moving to the next. Hot tears fill my eyes as I look at the face of a man I loved and looked up to as a child. He doesn't look a whole lot different than I remember. Maybe there are a few more lines around the face and his piercing blue eyes a little less lively in photos than in person.

My dad is clearly still gorgeous. His light brownish-blonde hair is tousled in that care-free way he always had, his trademark lopsided smile shows a hint of his perfect, white teeth. One eyebrow is always arched slightly above the other, making you think he knew something that you didn't, but desperately wanted him to share with you. His chiseled jaw is covered in just the right amount of five o'clock shadow to make him seem dangerous and the full lips I inherited are ones that women literally used to scream over.

Doubling over, I'm winded from the sharp pain of the loss of my dad. My habit of shoving down every horrible situation in my life and acting as if they didn't happen isn't working for me anymore. Yes I'm still angry, but I miss my dad like crazy.

I glance through the articles, not quite brave enough to click on any of the links. I'm too afraid to find out that he's moved on, has a new wife, kids, a family that doesn't include me. My heart stops when I reach a link for an interview with Barbara Walters.

Hyperventilating, I put my head down on the desk and take deep, even breaths to calm down. I feel lightheaded from the oncoming panic attack.

Maybe facing reality isn't any better than the denial.

With my head still down, I stick out my hand and slam the laptop shut. Call me childish, call me the queen of denial, I don't care. I'm just not ready to read about my dad's point of view from that terrible time in my childhood.

CHAPTER 4

Since I still haven't heard from Jeff Talley at the Warren Hotel, I'm free to spend my days as I wish. I chat with Mom every few days about upcoming designs and potential projects she'll eventually need me to pitch. None of it is urgent right now.

The custom furniture pieces are being made for the Verve nightclub. My job consists of I'm for the deliveries so the project can start.

Leah's advice to open up to people keeps nagging at the back of my mind. I know that a random one night stand here and there isn't going to bring me any happiness. I'm lonely for human contact. I'll know I'll have to let someone else past my walls… eventually.

Regret pierces through me as I think about Drew for the millionth time and know that I missed a perfect opportunity to get to know someone.

I could just go back to that gym and find him.

I snort. Like I'd ever do anything that bold. I shake my head. No, he wasn't meant to be.

After an invigorating five mile run on a frosty January morning, I decide to visit the cafe and finally talk to Leah about her advice.

Sweaty yet somehow frozen at the same time, I hop in the shower and wash away the sweat and city streets. Even though I have no meetings today, I resolve to take the time to put myself together, drying my hair and wearing makeup. Slobbing it for the last week hasn't done me any favors in helping my sour mood. Hopefully looking good will help me believe I'm okay.

Feeling attractive for the first time in a *long* time, I grab a charcoal gray wrap shirt, pair it with my super soft broken-in low-rise jeans and pick my four inch, black Louboutin suede ankle boots from the rows of designer shoes in my closet. Totally over the top for a coffee bar, but they're pretty and who wouldn't feel good in such gorgeous shoes?

I step over to the full-length mirror smile at the girl who, for the first time in a long time, looks twenty-four years old even if life has made her feel much, much older.

As I approach the Village Coffee Bar, I realize something is off. There are crowds, literally *a horde* of people crammed inside the café. I pull open the door, stunned, and politely weave through the people that are just standing around cluelessly, neither drinking coffee nor eating pastries.

Confused, I push past the patrons that stand between me and Leah, and notice that my normally perky and sweet friend looks frazzled and harassed.

"Leah, what is going on around here today?"

I give her a good once over. Her blonde hair is disheveled and falling out of her ponytail, her shirt is stained and untucked, and her usual bright smile is notably absent.

Leah barely has time to acknowledge me as she juggles two cups of coffee and narrowly avoids colliding with Ben, her assistant, who looks equally put out by the crowd.

"We got a little bit of free publicity, so everyone that read about us came to check us out," she huffs as she turns back to her order. "I'll catch up with you later and bring you your usual as soon as this dies down."

I groan. *Of course* my timing to discuss a major life change would be terrible. It doesn't look as if she'll be available for girl talk anytime soon.

What free publicity is Leah talking about?

I turn to sit in my usual seat and stop abruptly. Someone is sitting at my table. Not just that, but there are *someones* sitting at every table in the café. The man at my table is alone, bent over and facing the corner. Similar to how Adam sits when he comes in.

On a whim, I decide that this guy would be a good test for me to branch out and meet more people. I don't know him, he doesn't know me, plus, he's sitting at my table, so it makes sense to see how it goes.

Approaching the table from behind, I flick my eyes over him, taking inventory—winter coat, scarf, hideous baseball hat pulled down low, scruffy beard that's a tad longer than the usual sexy stubble that men favor. The way his body is hunched over his coffee, it seems as if he's trying to become all but invisible. I recognize the posture because I look just like that when I'm uncomfortable being out in a crowd.

Well, here goes nothing ...

To give him some semblance of a warning, I sling my huge purse up onto the table with a loud *thunk* and sit in the familiar chair. Smiling brightly, I start babbling nervously.

"I'm sorry to intrude, you don't have to talk to me if you want privacy, there's just nowhere else to sit." I make a vague motion with my hand indicating the full room. As I get situated, I look up at him. What little I can see of him under the brim of his filthy Boston Red Sox cap, and my mouth falls open.

It's *him*. I mean Drew, from the gym. The same Drew who has been plaguing my every waking thought over the last few days, and quite a few of my nights.

The heat of a deep blush prickles under my skin, no doubt staining my cheeks as every single feeling he brings out in me surges through my body at once. The sensation has me both embarrassed and excited at the same time. I try my hardest to keep a smile pasted on my face. It falters when he stares back at me, saying nothing.

Does he not remember me?

After what feels like an eternity, Drew breaks the silence. "Sydney." His voice is just as comforting and sexy as I recall. "What are you doing here?"

Speechless, I continue staring until I realize that my lack of a response has become incredibly awkward. The corner of his lip quirks up. He's holding back a laugh at my embarrassment. My eyes drop down to the table. The familiar humiliation from the other day surfaces. I'm once again mortified by my lack of social skills when he's around.

"My best friend owns this café. I can give you a proper introduction later." I glance around the near capacity room. "It's not usually this crowded in here."

Unable to stop myself, I flick my gaze up to meet his and groan at the shameless way my body reacts to him. He is just as beautiful as I remember. Stunning if you were to get rid of the week old stubble, the ratty ball cap pulled almost all the way down over his gorgeous green eyes, and the massive winter coat that is zipped up to his chin.

His shoulders are shaking, clearly trying not to laugh at my distress. My eyes narrow at his mocking.

Composing myself so I won't look even more like an idiot, I decide that if Drew is going to laugh at me then I can laugh at him. Who knows, maybe humor is his thing. My eyes leave his face and stray down over his interesting choice of clothing.

"What's with the repellant outfit?"

His lip quirks up again and his green eyes sparkle with humor. My body tightens in response. "Repellant…" he says slowly, as if he's testing the way the word sounds, rolling it around in that sensual mouth. "Interesting description, but accurate in a way." Drew winks at me as he sips his coffee.

Thank god, he has a sense of humor. I laugh at his ability to be self-deprecating. "Obviously not repellant enough since I'm sitting here with you."

He grins, liking our playful banter.

"Yes, but you're only sitting here because there were no other tables free and from the looks of it," Drew glances under the table, "Your shoes are probably uncomfortable. I'm apparently just shy of being repellant enough to make you suffer blisters. I must be losing my touch. I'll have to step up my game and find a more offensive outfit next time."

Casually, Drew takes another sip of his coffee and meets my eyes for brief second before smiling and looking back down at the table.

Now I'm really enjoying his teasing. So different from the intense and serious man I met a few days ago. I'm also finding his faint New England accent to be quite adorable. I can't believe he's here with me.

"True, the comfort of my feet will always trump avoiding repellant men in coffee shops." I giggle at my own joke. "Plus, you did save me from freezing to death the other day, so that counts for something." Did I actually giggle?

When Drew looks up he shakes his head and gives me a brilliant grin, trying and failing to hold in his own deep chuckle. Just like the last time I saw his smile, I stop in the middle of a laugh and suck in a breath. He really is stunning. My memory didn't do him justice. That dimple on his right cheek comes into view, his eyes light up with joy, and I can see the rings of deep brown around the center of his irises. His eyes are framed by the darkest, thickest lashes that any woman would be jealous of.

At that moment, I realize I'm feeling something I haven't experienced in a while. Something besides the obvious desire that zings through me. I've only ever had one-night stands when I want male company, not willing to risk my anonymity for a real relationship.

But this? This is different. Of course I *want* him physically. What's unnerving me is that I want him as in want to *know* him. That never happens to me. Ever.

"Sorry, Syd. It's just nuts in here today." Leah breaks me from my little epiphany as she places a large Kona and an orange croissant on the table in front of me. Her eyes flash over to Drew, who has gone back to ducking his head and staring at the table.

"What's with this guy?" She mouths, pointing at the top of his hat.

I give her a stern look that clearly says *"leave, now, I'll tell you later"*.

Like the good friend she is, Leah takes the hint. "Well, I gotta get back behind the counter. These ladies are eating Ben alive!" She laughs and bounces back to the front counter.

I nervously smooth my hair down and turn back to Drew. "That's my friend Leah. The one I said owns this place. Like I said, it's never this crowded in here." I watch Drew as he adjusts his hat even lower over his eyes and picks at his napkin with his long, dexterous fingers.

Feeling socially awkward again, I swallow a giant gulp of coffee and decide to go for it and start my test. I'll ask him a personal question.

"So, you're new here, like a lot of these people. What brings you here this lovely morning?"

Drew continues fingering his napkin, destroying it bit by bit. It must be a nervous habit. He shrugs. "I had time to kill, wanted a cup of coffee, and walked past this place. It looked good, so I stopped in. It wasn't this crowded when I got here." He stops picking at his napkin and meets my eyes, smirking. "I didn't slip on the ice out front and come in bleeding if that's what you're wondering."

His piercing green gaze is holding me captive once more. Then it falls to look at my lips briefly before he meets my eyes again. His stare is so smoldering, it penetrates all the way down to the base of my spine where it heats up into a tangle of hormones. Neither of us is willing to look away, but it doesn't feel weird. It's as if we're both trying to read each other.

I smile shyly and drop my eyelashes as I break eye contact first. "Well, I'm glad you stopped by."

I feel the mortifying heat creep up my neck from my confession. I peek back up at Drew. Unable to help myself, my own gaze drops down to his mouth. Full and sensual, I start wondering what it would be like to taste it. *What that mouth could do as it moves across my skin ...*

I press my thighs together as I start to overheat. Those long nights fantasizing about him have made me a desperate, hormonal mess.

Drew sips his coffee and speaks, breaking my little fantasy. "I'm glad too. Maybe I'm not so repellant after all, huh?" His mouth twists up wickedly, as if he knows he caught me daydreaming about him.

"No, I don't think you are. So …" I can't finish my thought, because Leah chooses that moment to bound over and unceremoniously plop a thick magazine onto the table with a loud *thwack!*

I hold my hands up defensively and bristle up while cautiously eyeing the issue of GQ.

"Leah, what are you doing? You know I don't read magazines like that." I glance at Drew to see his reaction. I don't want him knowing about me or my neuroses. He'll think I'm a freak.

Thankfully, he isn't paying attention. Instead, he's looking back down at the table, intent on picking his napkin apart again.

Leah grabs a chair from a neighboring table and yanks it over, intruding shamelessly on our intimate conversation. "I know Syd, I'm sorry for interrupting but I wanted to show you something and the counter is a little slower right now, so Ben can handle it alone." She looks at Drew cautiously. "Sorry, I don't mean to be rude. I'm Leah."

"Drew. Nice to meet you." He peeks from under his hat to introduce himself, then resumes fiddling with the remnants of his napkin.

Leah is stunned speechless when she sees his face. She flicks her eyes to me, then back to Drew, trying to compose a response. I would laugh if I weren't so uncomfortable. I know exactly what she's thinking—he's hot, and yes, he's the same Drew from the gym.

"Yes, well, like I said, I'm … I'm sorry to intrude but I've, uh, I've been waiting for Sydney to get here to uh … show her this."

Ha! Leah can barely speak! It's not just me that becomes a bumbling mess around Drew.

Familiar racing panic wells up as Leah pushes the magazine toward me. I hope like crazy that my fear isn't obvious on my face. I don't want Drew to think I'm crazy by showing him my hang-ups in their full glory. Honestly, what the heck is Leah doing?

"Leah!" I whine.

I swear, there'd better not be anything about my parents in that thing.

She holds up a hand. "I know, I know. But you have to see this, it's why we're so busy today, and I thought it was time you knew something." Leah spins the magazine around to face me. "Trust me, please." She sneaks another sideways peek at Drew, tilts her head and frowns, then focuses back on me.

I observe Drew, who seems as bewildered as me, a blank look on his handsome face. He pulls his hat down again and shrugs.

What is with that hideous old hat?

Unable to stall any longer, I take a deep breath and force myself to look at the cover. I look, blink, and look again.

"W-what?" I stutter. "I don't ... What the ...? I'm not sure I ..." I can't seem to form a coherent sentence. "What the heck, Leah! Adam?"

Sure enough, the gorgeous man in a beautifully cut, custom Armani suit on the cover of GQ magazine is Adam. Adam from the coffee shop Adam. Adam of the helpful, creative, sounding board Adam. Cute British Flirty Adam. Adam. On. GQ.

What. The. Heck.

This revelation seems to grab Drew's interest. He leans over to stare at the magazine cover. I notice that he's so close that I can smell him, masculine and inviting, as I try to control my racing thoughts. I also realize that my mouth is gaping open and shut like a fish. My teeth together in a useless bid to stop.

Drew sticks out a finger and pokes photo of Adam, "You know him?"

I arch an eyebrow at him. Is it just me or does he kind of sound annoyed?

"Yes. No. Kind of. I don't know. I don't understand." How can I explain what I don't understand myself? "He comes in here a lot. We sit together when we're here at the same time, maybe a dozen times over the last few months. I only know him from the Coffee Bar. I've never seen him outside of here. And I guess I never asked enough personal questions for me to know that he would appear on the cover of freaking GQ magazine!"

I look to Leah for help, but she just sits there as I become increasingly agitated, alternating between staring at me and shooting odd looks at Drew. Leah isn't helping me at all!

Drew scowls. "You had no idea that the man you have been chatting with for several months was Adam Reynolds? Grammy winning lead singer of *Sphere of Irony*, Adam Reynolds? That's crazy? Everyone knows who he is," he hisses with a look that says he thinks I'm full of it.

Before I can respond, Leah jumps in to save me.

"Look, Sydney doesn't own a TV. She doesn't read gossip rags, or follow celebrity bullshit, okay?" Leah's voice gets heated as she spits out the word 'celebrity' and gestures wildly in Drew's stunned face. "She doesn't care about that crap, so trust me, no, she had no clue who he was."

"Leah!"

Oh my god! She's going to make Drew think I'm a shut-in or a lonely cat lady or something! My face flames up as I turn to Drew. "I just don't care for that whole scene, you know? I'm not interested in famous people's lives, and everything on TV sucks so I just don't bother with it." I wave my hand in a way that I hope conveys that this isn't a big deal, even though it is a big deal. *Huge.*

Drew stares into my eyes and studies me. It's as though he's trying to see into the deepest part of my soul and figure out if I'm being honest. Without warning, his mouth quirks up into a smile as if he thinks this entire scenario is funny.

"Ok, I believe you. I've just never met anyone who wasn't at least familiar with most famous faces, let alone held multiple conversations with one on a first name basis and still didn't recognize them."

He nods and averts his gaze, continuing to speak softly. "I think it's great. People *do* spend too much time obsessing over celebrities and in front of the TV. It's nice to know that not everyone is like that." He leans back in his chair and resumes casually drinking his coffee from under that decrepit hat.

Leah gapes at Drew openmouthed again before slowly turning back to me. "I wanted to show you his interview, Syd." She takes the magazine and flips open to a page that she has folded over. "Right here, see what Adam says?" She points to a line in what is clearly an interview. Irritated, I shove her hand away and read it out loud.

GQ: So you've been in New York City for the last 3 months recording your new solo album, do you have any favorite haunts in the city?

AR: Well, I've been right busy, and the studio hours are really early, but Galaxy, a nightclub in SoHo is brilliant. And there's a neat little café, the Village Coffee Bar, in the West Village that makes the best specialty croissants you've ever had.

GQ: Who knew you were a croissant lover?

AR: I know, (laughing, he smacks his abs with his hand) I can't eat too many, it's too painful to sweat off later in the gym. I'm hoping to make it back to New York again soon, because a friend of mine is

redesigning Verve, the nightclub at the Warren Hotel. I've seen some of
her work and she's quite the talent. I'm keen on checking it out.
GQ: I'm sure the Warren will send you an invite to the opening.
AR: Hopefully. (Crosses fingers and laughs)

"Oh my god." I know I must look as though I'm falling to pieces. I'm not. I'm completely freaking out. I feel like throwing up onto my beautiful stiletto booties.

"I know, Syd. I know." Leah looks back in sympathy. "But think of all the publicity the Warren is getting. If they didn't already love you, they really love you now. This is why it's so crowded in here today. And I know Adam thought he was helping you and me out. He doesn't know about you, Syd."

I close the magazine and throw it onto the table, wanting it far away from me. Rubbing my temples, I shut my eyes in frustration, the churning nausea of an oncoming panic attack building in my gut. I'm losing it and don't want to do it here.

"I can't talk about this now. Call me later?" I stand up and hug Leah.

She picks up the GQ, gives Drew yet another pinched look, "Nice to meet you, Drew," and goes back behind the counter without waiting for his response.

Drew jumps to his feet, suddenly part of the conversation again. "Are you leaving?" He sounds as frantic as I feel.

"Yes, I need to get out of here." I grab my coat and throw it on.

"I'm going with you, you're upset. I can walk you home if you like."

I stop and stare at him. "Drew, you're being very nice considering I nearly had a nervous breakdown right now. Just because you saved me once doesn't mean you have an obligation to do it again." My words don't reflect how I feel. Inside, I have butterflies deep in my belly that flutter and send electric pulses to every extremity. As stressed as I am, I admit I don't want to say goodbye to Drew.

He puts a gentle hand on my arm and once again, it tingles with heat from his touch. "First of all, you're not a psycho, well, maybe a little for sitting with a strange, pseudo-repellant man who gives really good first aid and rides home to bleeding women." He smiles, but it doesn't reach those captivating eyes. "Second, I know I'm not obligated to walk you home, but I don't think you should be alone when you're upset. Plus, I like talking to you and was hoping we could talk more."

He shocks me the way he lays his feelings out there. I study his face and find he has the same sweet and sincere look as the other day. I can't bring myself to say no to that face. And I *like* talking to him. I feel different with him than everyone else, safe, protected.

I nod my consent and head for the door. Drew pulls down that ratty Red Sox hat and places his hand on my lower back to guide me out. My body vibrates with electricity when he touches me so possessively. Even through my coat, his warmth causes my heart to start pounding. Between the anxiety and the racing hormones, I'm so confused. It's not until we're outside that I realize I have absolutely no idea what to do next.

We walk out of the café and onto the packed New York sidewalk. I stand there cluelessly, not sure what to say or where to go. Drew, a take-charge kind of guy, recognizes my bewilderment and speaks first.

"So which way is your place? I'll walk you home and we can talk if you want." Drew looks so hopeful that I manage a smile.

"Okay. That sounds great." I give him my address. He nods and once again puts his hand on my lower back. My breath catches from the contact. I shiver in pleasure, glad it's too cold for Drew to notice. He affects me way, way too much to be good for me.

"So, how long have you lived in Manhattan, Sydney?"

Uh oh, here go the personal questions that I hate so much. At least this is an easy one. I'm sure I can manage to answer a few general questions without going all nuclear crazy on him. Baby steps, right? "Twelve years, you?"

Now I know my thoughts are all tangled up. Asking him questions is a sure way to get him to expect me to answer more of his. I mentally slap myself in the forehead for my recklessness by deviating from my strict adherence to the rules.

"I've been here for ten years. Funny how the island is only thirty-three square miles but we can both live here for a decade and never meet and then suddenly run into each other twice in a week." He glances over at me from under that God-awful hat and grins. The adorable dimple on his right cheek nearly makes me trip over my own feet.

"That's what I love about New York. You can be invisible if you want to."

Crud! Again! Me and my big mouth! What is it about this guy that makes me want to spill my guts to him?

Drew grasps my arm lightly and stops me to face him. His green eyes darken as he speaks. "Sydney, you might be a lot of things, but you could never be invisible." He lets go of my arm and keeps walking, leaving me gaping and running to catch up to him.

Okay, this is going somewhere beyond just talking. Being with Drew is different. I haven't felt this way about someone before. It would feel wrong to just use him for sex and kick him out like I'm used to doing. Unbelievably, I want more.

What do normal people do?

For the first time, I realize that I'm so messed up I haven't got a single clue as to what normal people do after meeting someone they find attractive besides have sex.

When we walk up to my building a few minutes later, I still haven't figured out what to do next. Richard greets us warmly. "Miss Allen, welcome home."

I stand on the sidewalk, not knowing anything except that I don't want to part with Drew yet. Especially since I regretted not getting to know him better the first time we met and I know once he leaves I'll have to deal with the fall out from seeing Adam on GQ.

"Do you maybe… would you want to come in and continue talking? I mean, well …" *Ugh!* I sound so inexperienced.

I must not sound as ridiculous as I feel, because Drew flashes me that sexy dimple and accepts my invitation. We cross the lobby and take the elevator up to my floor.

"This place is great." Drew enters my loft and checks it out with an appreciative eye.

"Thanks. Let me take your coat and your, ummmm, hat." I wrinkle my nose as I ask for it. I pray that he takes off that revolting hat. Drew doesn't hesitate to hand me his coat, but he takes off the hat and tosses it onto my coffee table.

"That's pretty old and sweaty. I wouldn't want you to have to touch it." His eyes sparkle with mischief as he runs his hands through his silky brown hair in an attempt to fix his hat head. So he has his suspicions that I hate his hat. Who wouldn't?

I put his coat next to mine in the closet by the door and head toward the kitchen. "Would you like a drink? I know it's not five o'clock, but I have no shame in indulging in a beer this early."

"A beer would be great, thanks, Sydney."

My pulse roars in my ears and I lick my dry lips. Hearing my name caressed by Drew's deep baritone does wicked things to me. Blowing out a breath, I need to calm down. Man, it's been a while if a man's voice is getting me turned on. Either that, or Drew really is different somehow.

Eager to say goodbye to the underlying anxiety from the whole Adam revelation, I pull out a shot glass and my trusty bottle of

Patrón and quickly throw one back, putting the glass in the dishwasher and the Patrón back in the cabinet. The welcome fire burns its way down my throat and settles in my nervous belly.

Hoping for the alcohol to work it's magic, I head over to the fridge and remove two bottles of Sam Adams, pop the tops off, and gather my courage to head into the living room.

I enter to find Drew examining some of the photos I have on the mantle above my fireplace. He turns as I hand him his beer.

"You've been to a lot of places." Drew motions with his bottle at the pictures of me posing in front of various European landmarks.

Of course he picks out the only personal items in the entire loft to ask me about. Thankfully, I learned a long time ago not to put any pictures of my mom on display where visitors could see them. They would always recognize her right away and the super-fan *I love celebrity can you introduce me to your mom* excitement would instantly kill any conversation I tried to have after that.

"Yes, I've traveled a bit. How about you? Ever been to Europe?" Deflection, I've learned, is a great way to avoid talking about yourself. Most people love discussing themselves, so steering the questions back to them could keep some people entertained for hours. It's a skill I've perfected over the past few years.

"Yes, I've been to most of Europe." He takes a long swig of his beer and sits down on the couch, eyeing me appreciatively. "I hope your arm is better."

Shoot, he isn't going to fall for the deflection technique.

Uneasy, I shift on my feet. "It is. Thanks again."

I take a seat on the other end of the couch and down a third of my beer to squelch my nerves. Looking over at Drew, his six foot plus body slung gracefully back on the couch, he appears as comfortable as if he were in his own home. I notice that he did manage to fix his hair after taking off that gross hat. It has that tousled, just fucked look that only works on guys like him. My fingers are itching to run through it. I really want to touch his hair.

"I noticed that you were telling the truth at the café. You really don't own a TV, unless you've hidden it somewhere. So– why don't you like the entertainment industry, Sydney?"

My mouth is suddenly parched, my tongue thick and heavy. Drew went right for the jugular with that question. He's very perceptive.

"I … I don't feel like answering that right now, if that's okay with you?" I look away, feeling like a sideshow freak and nervously gulp down another third of my beer.

The cushion next to me dips. I turn to see Drew has shifted closer to me on the couch. I twist to face him. His lips are within inches of mine, his warmth inviting me in, making my hormones run wild. Drew puts his free hand on top of mine and wraps his fingers around it.

The contact sooths my frazzled nerves. The frantic worrying in my mind quiets down.

"Sydney, I don't want to make you uncomfortable. You don't have to tell me anything you don't want to. Maybe someday you'll feel like you can trust me enough to tell me. I'm patient." He squeezes my hand and gives me a kind smile.

He wants there to be a someday? I'm not sure if I should be excited or scared to death, so I file it for further thought later.

"Even though I barely know you, I do feel like I can trust you, Drew, but that's a part of me that I don't like talking about. I'm not able to go there. Not yet." I give him a feeble smile and shrug my shoulders as I finish my beer.

When I glance down I notice that his beer is gone too, so I gather both bottles and head back into the kitchen. Since I seem to be aware of his presence at all times, I sense Drew following behind me. I set the bottles in the sink and spin around to find him right there, hands on either side of my hips, trapping me against the counter. I'm surrounded by his raw, rugged masculinity.

Afraid I'll do something impulsive if I stay too close, I place my hands on the sink for support and lean back.

"Are you hungry? We could order in, hang out. What do you think?" Drew's voice is husky and seductive, drawing me nearer. He's so close all I have to do is lean in and our lips would touch.

I shudder and take in a shaky breath. If I don't get some space I won't be able to think. "Sure. Why don't you start a fire? Everything you need is in the wood box next to the fireplace. I'll just order the food, is sushi okay?"

My rambling is embarrassing, but Drew doesn't seem to mind. He pushes off the counter and grins, his dimple making another sexy appearance.

"Sure thing, Sydney. Sushi sounds great." I gaze at his tight, jean-clad backside as he leaves the kitchen wishing I hadn't. My body is vibrating with desire. He looks just as good in clothes as he did half-naked at his gym. Releasing the huge breath that I had been holding to prevent myself from combusting on the spot, I attempt to distract myself by ordering food.

Can you die from lust?

I'm not sure, but I don't want to find out.

Drew manages to have a big, crackling fire going by the time I finish ordering dinner. I retrieve a big soft quilt from a chest at the end of my bed and spread it out on the floor by the hearth so we can eat picnic style.

As we talk and eat, he discovers that I hate wasabi and I find out that Drew piles it on as if it were the last food on earth. We crack up trying to feed each other from our chopsticks and just about die laughing when a piece flies out of my grasp and goes bouncing under the couch.

Between us we manage to finish an entire bottle of my favorite Italian Pinot Blanc and best of all—we avoid a single awkward moment. It is by far the greatest date I have ever been on. Honestly, it's the *only* date I have ever been on that didn't begin and end with no-strings attached, no names necessary, sex.

Drew helps me clean up, then walks over to the closet and gets his coat. "I'd better be going, Sydney. It's pretty late."

Disappointment makes my stomach do a nervous twist. I don't want tonight to end, but I don't want to ruin it with sex either.

While I'm thinking of a way to see him again, he moves into my space. In fact, he gets so close that I find myself backed up against the front door, my head hitting gently with a quiet thud.

Drew reaches up, dragging a finger down my cheek all the way to my collarbone. The path he traces leaves my skin scorched as though he's singeing me with an open flame. I'm going to burn to death from his touch if he doesn't stop.

He leans in close, our mouths almost meeting. His warm breath caresses my cheek. "Can I see you again?"

I can't take it. He's so close and he smells so good. I inhale deep and close my eyes, waiting for his mouth to cover mine. And ... nothing happens. My eyes open to find Drew hovering an hairsbreadth from my face, his intense green eyes fixed on mine.

"What? Am I wrong to expect a kiss goodbye?"

Maybe I am wrong, I honestly have no idea how dating works.

Drew tilts his head and brushes his lips against my ear. "I'll kiss you. As soon as you say that you'll see me again." He pulls back to wait for my response. His eyes mirror mine, filled with lust and longing.

My body is strung as tight as a bow, ready to snap at any moment and beg him to take me.

"Yes," I pant, drawing in quick breaths. "I'll see you again Drew. Now please, kiss me."

I hardly finish speaking and Drew is on me, his large, hard body pressing me to the door, his mouth moving against mine sensually. He skims his wet tongue over my lips, asking me and let him in. My mouth parts and he takes full advantage, plunging into my mouth with sensual strokes.

A quiet moan vibrates in my throat. The soft sound sends Drew into a frenzy. His hands slide around my backside pulling me against him. I gasp when his erection grinds down against my stomach.

Our kiss never breaks. It's as if Drew can't get enough. Long slow licks of his tongue delve into every part of my mouth in on of the most erotic kisses I've ever experienced.

Desperate for air, Drew reluctantly breaks away and runs his teeth along my neck, nipping and kissing as he makes his way from my shoulder to my ear.

"Give me your phone, Sydney," he growls, his deep, rumbling voice caressing my ear, sending chills down my spine. The desire pulsing through my veins has me unable to respond with more than a whimper. A rush of air where Drew was just pressed against me leaves me cold.

Opening my eyes, I find him staring down at me with pure, carnal need. His pupils are blown wide, the black nearly eclipsing the green. His face is flushed and his lips swollen from our kisses.

Drew holds out his hand. "Your phone. Please."

I reach over to the small table next to the door and feel for my purse. Somehow I'm able to dig through it and find my phone without ever breaking eye contact. I drop it in his open palm.

Quickly, Drew expertly manipulates it while I lean against the heavy wooden door, catching my breath.

He gently places my phone back on the table and I hear a quite *beep* from his jeans. Drew's eyes alight with mischief. "Well, well." He removes his own phone from his pocket. "You sent me a text and asked me to dinner tomorrow night." He swipes the screen and I hear my own phone *beep* as he slides his back into his pants. Drew brings his hand to my chin and tips my face back until we're eye to eye again. "I said yes."

Dear god that's hot.

He slides his hands along my jaw, cupping my face in his huge hands. Leaning in, Drew brushes his lips against mine. "I should go, Sydney. It was great seeing you again. I'll see you tomorrow?" His low, seductive tone is laced with the promise of things to come. The way he looks at me has my heart throbbing in my chest, my pulse pounding behind my ears.

I nod. "Yes. Tomorrow." I'm so caught up in wondering what tomorrow will bring, I'm surprised I remember to move from in front of the door.

Drew gives me a stunning, full out, panty-dropping smile, complete with that dimple—the one that is begging for me to lick it.

"I can't wait," he says, pressing one last peck on my cheek. The door shuts behind him with a soft click.

Dazed and more turned on than I can ever remember being, I stand in the foyer and put my hand up to my swollen, slightly stubble-burned lips. I smile as I think about how Drew tasted and how that impressive bulge in his jeans felt when it pressed against me. Wandering back into the living room I slump down on the couch, exhausted. I close my eyes and try to etch the wonderful memories of the last few hours onto my brain permanently. The only reason I'm sure it all wasn't just a dream, is because I can still smell Drew's scent on my skin.

Sighing, I stand to get ready for bed. As I pick the up quilt off the floor, something catches my eye. I see it and laugh, and I mean *really* laugh. Bent over, clutching my stomach, tears in my eyes laugh. There, sitting on my coffee table, is Drew's hideous, filthy, beat up old Red Sox cap.

I'm halfway through my nightly yoga routine, dutifully avoiding the monsters in the next room that are Reid Tannen and Google, when my phone chirps from my nightstand. When I see who's calling, I scoop up the phone.

"Hey Leah, I know you said this morning that you'd call me later, but 11:30 is *way* later."

"I know, I know, the café was a freaking mess today! It took me all day to clean up and get ready for tomorrow after all of Adam's *fans* tore the place to pieces." She spits out the word fans so scathingly, I swear I shrink back from her hostility.

Laughing humorlessly, I respond. "What, so I'm not the only one who's not very appreciative of a little publicity in GQ? I thought you'd love such adoration from a such a *huge* celebrity!" The sarcasm in my voice will most likely piss Leah off, but she deserves to be poked fun of after months of hiding Adam's identity from me.

Leah's parents are quite well-known in Manhattan. Her mom is a top billed Broadway singer and her dad is a Tony Award-winning playwright. We met at our Manhattan private school when I was brought to New York, not knowing a soul and carrying the weight of public scandal around with me. Leah didn't care about my parents or their problems, and while she isn't celebrity adverse like I am, she doesn't suffer from bizarre celebrity hero-worship either.

"Yeah, right! Adam has made my life hell. I mean, I hate to sound ungrateful, but the next few weeks are going to be awful. I've had to hire an extra person on the fly to get through until the wow-factor dies down a little. But really, it's pretty awesome that Adam likes my place enough to name drop it in an interview. It makes my Coffee Bar seem cool or something."

"About Adam…"

I hear a long sigh through the phone. "I know what you're going to say, Sydney, and yes. Yes I knew who he was this whole time. I figured if you didn't know, then what difference did it make that he was a celebrity? You wouldn't have given him the time of day if you knew, and you liked hanging with him, getting to know him as a person, right?"

I know Leah is trying to make a point, and what makes me angry is that she's right. I do enjoy Adam's company and I am glad that I got to know him, something I wouldn't have allowed if I knew he was famous.

"I'm not mad. He *is* a cool guy. I guess I just hate that I could have been sucked into some kind of tabloid feeding frenzy. What if he had asked me out? I might have said yes, Leah."

"Yeah, Sydney ... what *if* he asked you out? He's just a guy with a weird job. You of all people should know that it doesn't make him a bad person, and it doesn't make him your dad."

I press my hand to my forehead to push the building anxiety out of my head. "No Leah, it doesn't make him my dad, and of course he's not a bad person. What it does is it makes me a target for the media. If they started digging, they would find out who I am and who my parents are, and then the feeding frenzy I've been avoiding starts all over again. I'm trying to deal with my issues, really I am. But the thought of letting anyone know about my past, let alone hang out with someone who has tabloid reporters digging around them all of the time, is just too much for me."

"Sydney, do you really think it's worth living your life this way? Hiding forever because of the *possibility* of a media frenzy? The more you hide, the worse it's going to be when it happens. And yes, I said *when* it happens. They're eventually going to find you. Your dad is still in the news all the time and ..."

"Stop!" I shout louder than I intended. "I don't want to hear about my dad." Leah doesn't know about my brief flirtation with

Reid Tannen on Google the other night, and I'm not quite ready to tell her. She'd want to psychoanalyze that for hours. The thought makes me shudder. "I know that I was just a kid, but you can't be naïve enough to think that there isn't still fascination as to where I went? People haven't forgotten. I mean, my mom just up and left Hollywood with me, and we never went back. When it comes out, it's going to be ugly. I'm not ready for that yet Leah. I'm just not."

I can hear Leah exhale in frustration. "Sydney, the point is, is that if you like a guy, he's eventually going to find out who you are. I just think that this huge betrayal you're waiting for isn't going to come from the one you love. You are not your mom. Live your life and stop worrying about your parents' mistakes."

"I'm trying. It's just … complicated. It was awful Leah, I can't explain how bad it was."

"I know, Syd, I know. I just don't want to you to wake up one day and realize you missed out on life because of something that might never happen, and honestly, doesn't matter in the huge scheme of things. You can't let tabloids dictate your life."

I know this. I've always known this. It's impossible to accept after seeing what happened to my parents, to me.

"I'm tired, Leah. I think I'll hit the sack." Between Adam, GQ, Leah, Reid Tannen, Google, and Drew, I have too much to process on my own to talk about it anymore.

"Okay, see you tomorrow. And hey, don't think I've forgotten about the hottie you left the café with today. I want a full update next time I see you."

I smile as I think of Drew and his scruffy chin and adorable dimple, not to mention how hot I got when he pressed against me. "Okay, bye Leah."

"Bye Syd."

Physically and mentally exhausted, I get up off the floor and throw the phone onto my bed. Today was great in some ways, meeting Drew and having an actual date and enjoying myself, but the whole "Adam is famous" thing on top of obsessing over Googling my dad the other night, and Leah lecturing me to get over my past, made today pretty depressing too.

I dread sleep tonight. I know my anxiety level is somewhere around DEFCON 1, the memories inevitable. I drag myself into the closet and change into a tank top and sleep shorts and flop into bed.

****

"Hello class, we have a new student starting today. Miss Sydney Tannen just moved here from California, I hope everyone will welcome her kindly."

The older woman with the severe hairstyle and glasses dangling from a chain holds onto my arms with her cold, bony hands as she humiliates me in front of my new peers.

"Sydney, take the empty chair in the back row, dear." She looks down and smiles a little too wide to be sincere. I notice a big glob of lipstick on her front tooth and cringe.

Staring at my shoes I try to ignore the whispers as I make my way down the aisle. In L.A. I was used to being the cool girl, the one everyone wanted to know. Dropped in a city where I don't know anyone, I have to bear the burden of being the target of gossip and stares and pity. Going from popular to pariah overnight isn't easy when you're twelve.

When I reach the empty seat, I throw my bag onto the desk and slump down into the chair, determined to become invisible. I thought I was doing a pretty good job of disappearing until a balled up piece of paper pelts me a few minutes later. I glance over and see the girl next to me grinning widely, her teeth swallowed up by huge metal braces. I choke back a laugh, not wanting to be rude, and unfold the note.

Don't worry about what all of these stuck up jerks think. I'm cool. I'll be your friend. Leah Eliza Quinn-Slade

I crumple the note back up and stuff it into my bag. *"Thanks,"* I mouth at Leah. Apparently, perky little blonde New Yorkers with braces have no problem hanging out with the depressed daughter of L.A. tabloid super-stars. My horrific week got a tiny bit better. But that small moment of happiness only lasted until the end of first period.

"Hey Tannen! I heard your dad banged everyone in L.A.!"

"Sydney, I saw your dad's newest movie! You know, the secret one?"

"Sydney, if your mom is lonely, bring her over to my house!"

The first three months of school are the worst. Most days consist of kids taunting me with rumors about my parents and me removing tabloid photos that have been taped all over my locker. Leah tries to get there first and take them down, but she can't protect me from everything. I love her for it though.

Grainy pictures of my dad and *her*. Photos of my mom and dad from their wedding, my parents at the Oscars. Every single picture of them happy or angry over the last fifteen years regurgitated for the world to see due to the latest scandal.

They find photos of my dad punching the paparazzi that have apparently been hounding him since my mom left. Pictures of *her* being followed everywhere, like she's someone special. And my personal favorite, pictures of me and parents from when everything was still good and we all loved each other.

My life, my broken family, nothing but entertainment for the world. It feels as if someone is pulling my heart out of my chest as I rip them off of my locker and stuff them in the garbage.

****

The shrill ring of my iPhone brings me out of my fitful sleep. I feel around my nightstand, searching for it. Unable to find it, I sit up and look around spotting it on my bed where I tossed it last night.

Snatching it up, I answer for no other reason than to stop the ringing.

"Sydney! I'm on my way to your place. I'll be there in five with coffee and croissants."

Leah hangs up before I can respond. What time is it? I peer down at the clock on my phone.

9:55am

Falling back on my pillows, I groan. She's going to want to know everything about Drew. What should I tell her? That I like him? *Do* I like him? Obviously, the answer is yes. How much will I tell him about myself?

Leah will push me to spill my guts on the first date, like a test to see if Drew can handle it. I'm leaning toward less is more and not address my personal life until we see if we're compatible. The loud buzzer at my door means I'm out of time. Hurricane Leah just made landfall.

"Hey Leah." I move to let her breeze past me and into my loft.

"Did you just get up? Wow! You never sleep this late Syd. Come, I brought the Nectar of the Gods" She holds up a huge cup of coffee as she makes her way to my kitchen. She is way to perky in the morning.

I trail behind, dragging my feet. I may be tired and not in the mood for girl talk, but I'm not going to turn down the best cup of coffee in the city.

"Here, I brought croissants too. Today is lemon crème." She pulls two pastries from out of a brown bag and places them on plates that she retrieved from my cabinet.

"Let's go sit on the couch where it's more comfortable." Leah is already halfway down the hall. I follow along, my head spinning, clutching my beloved Kona in one hand and a lemon crème croissant in the other.

"Mmmmm. I may feel human in a few minutes. Thanks." I inhale the perfect scent of coffee as I sip from it gratefully. We nibble our croissants in silence and drink our coffees. Leah waits a few blessed minutes for the caffeine to take effect before starting the third degree.

"So. The cutie from the café, did he walk you home?"

Here we go.

"Drew, and yes, he did." I take a huge bite of lemon croissant just to annoy Leah when my mouth is too full to elaborate.

"Drew. Okay, *Drew* then," she says playfully. "And is he the same Drew who rescued you the other day?" Leah stares at me expectantly, bouncing on the couch as if she were a kid on a pogo stick.

"Yes, he is. I invited him up and we ordered sushi. And please stop jumping around. If you make me spill my coffee I may never forgive you." I give her the evil eye and place a hand on her shoulder to stop the dizzying movement.

"And ...? Did you two, you know?" Her wide grin is going to split her face in half.

"Leah! No! Jeez." I'm sure I'm blushing at the thought. "But, we are going out again tonight."

Leah's eyes practically pop out of her head. "*You* are going on a second date. You. Dating. Drew from the gym. Your white knight." She shakes her head. "I can't believe it. Are you sure about this?"

"I think I really like him." I nervously pull my croissant apart.

"Like him enough to tell him about yourself?"

"No. I'm not ready for that yet. But... I do have a confession." I see Leah staring at me as I bite my lip. "I Googled my dad the other day."

"Holy cow Syd! That's huge!" She grabs my shoulders and goes in for a hug.

"Wait! Stop!" I hold up my palm, halting her mid-embrace. "I didn't read any articles or click any of the links. I was too nervous. All I did was look at a few photos and read some of the headlines." My heart is beating so fast it might fly out of my chest. I remove Leah's hands from my arms and take another sip of coffee. Inhaling deeply, I steel myself to tell her the rest. "There was one article that terrified me. Did you—did you watch my dad on Barbara Walters last month?"

Leah's mouth twists into a frown and she pauses a moment before answering me. "No. I didn't watch it, Syd. But I do know some of what it was about." Her eyes shine with sympathy.

I throw my hand up again. "Don't tell me! I'm getting there, Leah. Slowly. But I don't think I want to know anything about my dad. Not yet."

"Okay. I'll just say it was kind of sweet. When you finally do check out your dad, watch that interview first." She pops the last bit of croissant in her mouth and relaxes into the cushions, casually scanning the room. In the blink of an eye, Leah is pointing at something and screaming, coiling back in fear on the couch. "Holy hell Sydney!"

Fear shoots though me. "What! What! Is it a rat? Do I have a rat in my house?" I leap up onto the sofa and scan the room for the offensive creature.

Leah jumps to her feet, runs over to my fireplace, and snatches up the fire tongs. With a pained expression, she whips around, walks back over to the coffee table, and uses the tongs to pick something up, making sure to hold it as far away from her body as possible. "What on God's green earth is this?"

Hanging from the end of my fire tongs while my best friend makes a face, is Drew's nasty old baseball hat.

CHAPTER 5

Right on the verge of hyperventilating in my bathroom, I'm taking deep breaths to calm myself down before my second date with Drew. "You can do this" I keep repeating the mantra over and over in my head.

I stand up straight and do a final assessment in front of the mirror. As bad as I feel, I have to admit that I look pretty good. Leah arm-twisted me into spending the day with her at the spa to relax for tonight. We had every service you could think of. I was buffed, waxed, plucked and massaged. My hair is now hanging in perfect auburn waves down my back. My skin is dewy and clear. The aesthetician even managed to get rid of my ever present under-eye circles.

Drew said to dress up, so I put on a short black dress. It has a loose long-sleeve top and a tight miniskirt. Okay, I'm ready. Except for the fact that I'm on the edge of a major panic attack because I'm going way out of my comfort zone with this date.

With a few minutes to spare, I walk over to my bedroom window and watch the busy city, using the distraction to forget about my nerves. I'm seriously contemplating having a few shots of Patrón when the buzzing of my phone nearly causes me to fall over in my stilettos. I grab it to read the text.

Drew—Waiting for you outside. Same black Town Car. Can't wait to see you.

I fetch my coat and keys, swallow down my insecurities, and head out to hopefully enjoy my night.

As I exit the elevator, I spot the same sleek black car from Drew's gym idling by the curb. Approaching the sedan, the driver's side opens and Bruce comes around to open the door. "Thank you so much." I give him a small smile. "For your help the other day that is."

"My pleasure Sydney." He gently helps me inside. When I slide across the seat, I'm hit with the same enticing smell from yesterday. The one I associate with Drew. Body wash scented like grapefruit, some faint, spicy cologne, and the purely masculine scent of pure Drew. It saturates every surface of the car. I inhale deeply and turn to see him sitting next to me with a wickedly carnal expression on his handsome face.

"Sydney, you look stunning". His greedy eyes look me up and down. Drew takes my face in his hands and presses a soft kiss to my lips.

A prickly, heated blush creeps up my neck under his intense scrutiny.

"Drew, you clean up rather well yourself."

His thick brown hair is styled so that it looks as if he ran his hands through it all day. His face is clean shaven for the first time since I met him, and I can see that sexy dimple quite clearly. I wonder what it would be like to taste that tiny indentation and decide to file that image for later.

Drew is wearing a beautifully cut, expensive looking, dark gray suit and black shirt with a black tie. I'm having a hard time reconciling this sleek, beautiful man with the unshaven, nasty hat-wearing guy from yesterday.

"Shoot. I forgot. You left your hat at my place."

His mouth quirks up in the corner. "My hat. Yes, I'll need to get that back. It's sort of my lucky charm." Drew reaches out and casually puts his hand on my knee. My body tenses, my heart stopping before it flips around in my chest. Intense heat spreads over my skin, humming like a live wire.

Oh god, I'll never make it through dinner without incinerating.

I'm able to choke out a sentence, even with his overwhelming presence and my racing hormones. "Lucky charm? Why is it lucky?" I look at his hand on my knee, then back up into his brilliant green eyes.

"I was wearing it when I bumped into you at the coffee shop after I was convinced I'd never see you again." He says it so simply, and so honestly, that my breath hitches. Surely this fascinating man isn't as taken with me as I am with him? I swallow and hold his gaze.

"Sydney, we're here." Drew takes my hand to help me out of the car. I step onto the pavement and find myself pressed against him. Time slows down as I revel in the warmth from his body seeping into mine. His eyes fall to my mouth and his lashes drop in a hooded gaze. "We'd better go in, it's cold out here," he whispers as his thumb brushes across my lips.

"I hadn't noticed."

The cold cruelly rushes in when Drew turns to walk into the building. He takes my hand just as naturally as he did yesterday. I glance around the small parking lot. Surrounded by tall buildings, it's well-lit, but secluded, as if hiding from the prying eyes of Manhattan.

"What is this place?"

"This is Sunset House, on 76th. We're using the back entrance. I've reserved us a private dining room."

He continues leading me to a non-descript red door located in the middle of a brick building.

"Oh. Why a private dining room?"

Drew opens the door and speaks softly as I enter, his rich, warm voice both heating me up and giving me chills. "So I can spend time with only you, of course."

Of course. I swallow down my nerves as Drew reaches for my shaky hand. Oh god. I can hardly be near him without turning into a quivering mess of hormones.

Drew holds my gaze, his eyes unwavering as he continues. "Plus, you're too sexy for your own good. I don't like to share, Sydney. And every man in the restaurant would be watching you."

Before I can say anything about his high-handedness, a young man in tailored black dress pants, shirt and tie, welcomes us in the small foyer. "Mr. Forrester, Miss Allen, welcome to Sunset House. I'm Chase and I'll be taking care of you tonight. We have your room ready, please follow me."

I stiffen when Chase uses my last name, pretty sure that I never told Drew what it was.

We go up a flight of stairs to a short hallway with three doors, all located on the same side of the hall. Chase opens the first door and ushers us inside.

I have been lucky to have seen some spectacular things in my life. I come from money, I have famous parents, I've been to many upscale restaurants in many different countries. But I have never, ever seen anything like the private dining room at the Sunset House.

The space isn't small but it feels cozy and intimate. It's an inviting mix of steel and cable and warm woods, most likely African Zebrawood, I think, noting the bold striations on the buffet by the door. A table for eight, but set for two sits in the middle of the room, low light emanating from industrial-style Edison pendants hanging from overhead.

That's all well and good, but what makes the room so special is the far wall, which is made entirely of glass. Looking out, you can see the restaurant below. Everything is visible, from the busy open kitchen in the center of the room to the cozy tables surrounding it.

The interior designer in me is impressed. The girl on a second date is a little overwhelmed. And now, on top of everything else, I'm nervous that people will be staring up at me from the main dining room, like an animal in a cage.

"Don't worry," Drew whispers in my ear, his breath sending a delicious shiver down my spine. "The glass is one way. No one can see into the private rooms from the main restaurant." I'm about to ask Drew how he knew what I was thinking when Chase interrupts to take our coats, hanging them in a small closet near the door.

Drew pulls out a chair and once I'm settled, he takes the seat next to me. "I hope you like champagne, I ordered some for us."

No sooner has he finished his sentence than Chase is back and filling two flutes, leaving the bottle in a bucket of ice. He exits just as quickly, giving us the privacy the room promises.

"So, I'm impressed, Mr. Forrester." I finger my glass of champagne and look at Drew. "I guess I should find it odd that the host knew your last name and I didn't and we're on a date. Or should I be more creeped out that you know mine?"

The corner of his mouth twitches in that sexy way. "Well Miss Allen, if you must know, your doorman used your name yesterday. That's how I know it. I promise I didn't go through your mail to find out."

He leans towards me, lowering his voice. "And you never asked for my last name, so now you know. There's no secret motive behind my actions." Drew sits back. "I just enjoy spending time with you and want to get to know you better." Thankfully, he looks amused. My accusation that he might be a stalker didn't offend him.

"A toast then, Mr. Forrester?" I hold my flute a little higher and arch an eyebrow.

"To getting to know each other better." His darkening eyes meet mine and I lick my lips in anticipation.

"Yes. I'll toast that." *As long as you don't ask questions about my parents.*

The ride back to my loft is filled with intense, thrumming desire. Dinner was perfect. We both enjoyed the food immensely.

The chef even came up to our room to explain his farm to table menu and how he only uses local produce. Drew became very animated speaking with the chef about organic food, his New England accent *Boston, I'm guessing?* getting more pronounced the more excited he got.

We ate and drank while we observed the other diners like voyeurs, spying from our crow's nest as servers scurried around the room below.

Small, brief touches between us during dinner started a slow burn inside me that is now a raging fire. It's bad enough that his warm, rough hand is drawing slow circles on the inside of my leg. I'm so worked up, it's all I can do to stay in my own seat and not jump on Drew's lap to grind down on his mouthwatering body.

We pull up to my building and Drew grabs my hand so I can't get out. His other hand moves from my leg to my face, brushing across my cheek. My tongue darts out to lick my suddenly parched lips and my gaze falls to his perfect mouth.

"Drew."

"Can I come up?" His voice is husky and deep.

I smile, glad he is just as affected by the tension in the car as I am. "Of course, I have to give you your hat."

The corners of his mouth twitch for just a second, then his eyes glaze over again and he leans in and hesitantly kisses me, just a soft brush of his lips across mine. The smoldering embers that have been building up all night ignite into an inferno that I can no longer hold back. I weave my hands into his silky hair, pulling his face closer, and mash our lips together fueled by the need for more.

Breathless, I groan when Drew breaks the kiss, shifting to exit the car. My door opens seconds later when he leans in. His delicious scent assaults me as he growls in my ear. "I don't want to take you in the back of the car, Sydney. And if I don't stop now, I won't be able to." Nodding, I take his hand and we duck across the dark sidewalk and into my building.

The second the elevator doors close, Drew spins to forcefully pin me against the wall with his hard, masculine body. He looks into my eyes as he skims his hand up my thigh stopping just inches from the edge of my panties. He pushes his hard length against my stomach as he leans in and sucks my lower lip into his mouth, nibbling on it gently. The uncontrollable need I felt in the car rushes back full force.

I knot my fingers in that touchable hair of his and give it a sharp tug, drawing a husky growl from Drew's throat. His mouth opens and I shudder as our lips meet messily—wet and hot, with teeth mashing and tongues exploring. My hand drops from his head so I can feel his tight backside. Drew shoves a leg between mine, and I rub against it shamelessly. The groan that he makes in response is the single sexiest thing I have ever heard in my life.

When the elevator stops we break apart, both of us breathless and disheveled. I fumble in my purse for my keys, my head so full of everything "Drew" that I can barely think.

After a few fumbles, I'm finally able to unlock the door. When we step into the foyer, I turn and face Drew while removing my coat and letting it drop to the floor. Drew shrugs out of his and tosses it on top of mine. Reaching out, I take his hand and lead him to my bedroom.

Maybe this is a mistake, maybe it's too soon, but I have to be with him, now. I don't believe in love at first, or even second sight, but there's something between us that I have to explore. But I can't think until I feel his incredible body on top of mine. We have to rid ourselves of the overwhelming desire that hums between us before we can do anything else.

I can't wait to feel those hard muscles and smooth skin beneath my hands, his hot mouth on every part of my body. The need to be with him is almost painful after a week of non-stop fantasizing. I can tell he feels the same way. His body is tense and his eyes are feral. He needs this as much as I do.

The city casts a pale light across the dark bedroom. I sense Drew as he follow me over to the windows. He presses himself against my back when I stop in front of them. I take in the enormity of it all and revel in the feel of his body behind me.

Drew gathers up my hair, carefully placing it over my shoulder. He drags his lips and teeth back and forth across the nape of my neck. It's so quiet all I can hear are the sounds of our rapid, shallow breaths.

I shudder in pleasure and arch against him, feeling his erection hot and hard at my back. The warmth from his body seeps through the thin fabric of my dress, heating up my already blazing hot skin. Inexplicably, I feel calmer than I have in ages—safe, protected when I'm with him. Drew does things to me that no one else can.

"Sydney." Drew growls, turning me around to face him. I reach up with a trembling hand to loosen his tie, pulling it out slowly and dropping it on the floor. He brings his hands up to my breasts, his strong fingers working my nipples into hard buds. My breathing is embarrassingly loud by the time he reaches around my back, smoothly unzipping my dress until it falls in a silken puddle around my feet.

"Jesus, Sydney." The reverence in his voice is unmistakable.

Drew steps back so he can study every inch of me as I stand there in only my black lace bra, matching lace boy shorts, and mile-high stilettos. His eyes betray his composed exterior, alight with a possessive desire. He begins to unbutton his shirt as his eyes continue to devour me. "You're so fucking beautiful."

I step out of the pile of discarded fabric and crush myself against him, my last tiny bit of control shredded by my ability to bring out such a powerful reaction in a man like Drew. Desperate to feel his skin, I help to remove his shirt, impatiently working my nervous fingers over the buttons as fast as I can, praying that I don't lose it and simply rip his shirt off.

My hands finally find the bare skin of his abdomen, gliding down the hard ridges to the light dusting of hair that disappears into his waistband. I take my time running my fingers up and down over every perfect inch of his ripped torso. I revel in the feel of his smooth, warm skin, the steady movement of his chest as he breathes in and out, the rapid beating of his heart under my fingers.

Drew groans and reaches his hands under my backside to lift me up. Somehow knowing what he wants, I wrap my legs around his waist and hang on tight, pressing against him as everything lines up perfectly. Our mouths crash together again while I cling to his strong shoulders.

Drew steps over to the bed and sits down with me perched on his lap, my legs still wound around him, stiletto heels digging into his back. I place my hands on that beautiful, broad chest and take pleasure in the feel of his chiseled muscles, sliding my fingers up to his collarbone and back down again as his skin jumps under my touch.

Giving me a dark look that nearly undoes me, Drew hooks a finger in each side of my black lace bra and tucks the cups beneath my breasts.

"You're so perfect. Do you have any idea what you're doing to me?" he whispers. My nipples are tight and hard as he drops his head to take one in his hot mouth.

The overwhelming sensations are becoming too much to handle. I have to have more, some sort of relief. I shift back and forth on his lap, grinding down to create friction, way too aroused to wait any longer.

"Drew, I need you."

I can feel him smile against my breast as he moves to the other stiff peak and suckles it, gently biting it as I squirm.

"Please," I know I sound desperate, but I'm literally aching to have him inside me after imagining this moment over and over since the day we met.

Drew finally releases my breasts from his torture and picks me up off his lap placing me on the bed. Standing, Drew begins to remove the rest of his clothes. The soft rustle of fabric is the only sound in the room besides our heavy breathing and the loud thrumming of my own pulse behind my ears.

Impatient, I reach out, stroking the obvious bulge through the soft fabric of pants. Drew stops undressing and hisses as he inhales through his teeth. "Jesus, Sydney, you're killing me."

I smile sweetly at him, thinking how he was just teasing me mercilessly as I begged him for more. Determined, I yank down his pants and boxer-briefs, grab his heavy erection in my palm. Drew groans as I move my hand up and down his thick shaft. He begins moaning, thrusting himself back and forth in my tight grip.

When I lean in and lick across the broad head, eager for a taste, Drew pushes me away. "No. I won't last if you do that. I want to be inside you." My body clenches in pleasure at the thought.

Reluctantly, I let go and lie back on the bed, staring at Drew as I try to figure out which one of us needs this the most. He bends down and retrieves a small packet from his pants, grinning, and tosses it next to me. Climbing onto the bed between my legs he suddenly grabs my ankles and yanks me toward him, my body sliding easily across the sheets.

Drew deftly removes each stiletto, placing them on the floor. He bites and kisses his way up one of my legs from my ankle to the sensitive spot on the inside of my thigh. I squirm from the scraping of his teeth and lips, so wound up that I feel as if a soft breeze could make me come apart.

"I don't think you need these either," he growls as he nuzzles me through my lace boy shorts. My hips to shoot up off of the bed from his touch. "Do you?"

Panting heavily, I close my eyes and feel his hot breath on my skin as he slowly peels my panties down. When his tongue lightly makes contact where I need it most, I nearly come.

"Drew," I whisper as I look down. The sight of this gorgeous man, naked between my thighs is so erotic I can barely stand it. He uses his fingers and tongue, massaging and licking until I'm seeing stars.

I can't hold back, writhing wildly on the bed. Drew uses a free hand to force my hips down as I moan and shudder and fly apart, white lights bursting behind my eyelids and pleasure vibrating through my body. Only after I nearly pass out and my loud screams turn into a quiet keening, does Drew finally relent and stop torturing me.

"Sydney, that was the hottest thing I've ever seen." His voice is gravelly as he climbs up over me. I seize his head, pulling on his thick hair and crush my lips to him, loving the taste of my arousal mixed with the sinful taste of Drew.

"That was the hottest thing I've ever felt," I say breathlessly.

I grab the condom from the bed, tearing it open with my teeth. Without breaking eye contact I reach down between us, grasping his hard length firmly. Drew hisses from my touch as I sheath him. When it's done he takes my hands and holds them over my head, effectively pinning me down. Drew kisses me hard, possessively, then pulls back to watch my face as he sinks in deep with one sharp snap of his hips.

"Ahhhh." Drew pauses for a moment. "Fuck, this is going to be quick babe, you feel too good." His forehead is damp with sweat and he scrunches up his face in an attempt to regain control.

After a moment, Drew opens his eyes, staring at me, intense green into cool blue, as he begins to move. The scents in the room assault me, turning me on even more—sweat, sex, and a faint hint body wash. I watch Drew's tight, corded muscles flex and stretch as he moves on top of me. My head is swirling with everything about this moment, about him, wishing it could last forever.

"Wrap your legs around me." I do as he says as his hips snap forward, sinking even deeper inside me than I thought possible. He grinds his pelvis against me with each thrust. Pleasure sparks through every nerve in my body and it's not long before I start incoherently moaning against his increasingly demanding pace. I can feel my orgasm building quickly, and it's going to be absolutely mind-blowing.

Drew shifts and that's all it takes. Shattering, I come, loudly, screaming his name as my body squeezes him tight and I convulse around him. He allows himself to let go, pumping one last time before finding his own sweet release. Drew lets out a string of obscenities and collapses, freeing my hands so he can use them to gently stroke my face.

Overwhelmed, I wrap my arms around his sweaty neck and kiss the spot where his pulse is racing under his skin. Supporting his weight on his elbows, Drew brushes my damp hair from my face then rolls away, leaving me feeling cold.

"I have to take care of this." He gestures to the used condom. Drew gets up, making his way to the bathroom, his chiseled body flexing gloriously with each step. Once he's out of sight and my post-orgasm high is gone, my nerves take over.

Oh my god, I like this guy. I really really like this guy.

I chew on my bottom lip as I think about what this means. The sex part is easy. It's everything else about a relationship that I can't handle.

Drew returns from the bathroom and slips into the bed. He drags the covers up, turning me so my back faces his front, then slides his huge arm around my waist, holding me close against his warm body. I tense up, he smells so good. The emotions I'm feeling are scary. This whole thing is scary. Can I do this? Can I have a normal relationship?

"Is it okay if I stay?"

I'm silent for a moment, thinking about how I usually kick guys out right after sex. No man has ever *asked* to spend the night. It's assumed that they'll want to leave immediately, and I always want them to. He takes my silence as a dismissal.

"I mean, I don't have to if ..."

"I want you to stay, Drew."

Why wouldn't I? Inexplicably, he makes me feel safe, cared for. Somehow, he keeps away the anxieties that have plagued me my entire life. Drew is the first person to get past my defenses, the first one I've *wanted* to get past my defenses.

"Good." He snuggles up closer, kisses my neck and sighs, his warm breath in my hair. God this feels so right.

I am so screwed.

I smell coffee. That's the first thing I notice when I wake up. Then I remember Drew. I allowed a man spend the night in my bed. That's a first for me.

Looking around my room, I can see I'm alone. Next to my bed is a steaming to-go cup of Kona from the Village Coffee Bar. Smiling, I take a sip and get up to use the bathroom.

Feeling much better after splashing water on my face and brushing my teeth, I look at my reflection. My grin is so big my cheeks are actually hurting. My skin is flushed and my eyes are bright. Even the dark circles have faded.

Apparently, great sex makes a huge difference. That and the first good night's sleep I've had in a while, which is odd because I've never slept in a bed with a man before. I would think I'd have more difficulty getting used to it.

Knotting my robe in place, I go looking for sexy Drew.

I find him sitting at my kitchen table. Just like yesterday, he's as comfortable here as if this were his own home. Drew has his own cup of coffee and a copy of the New York Post which he hastily folds up and places out of my reach.

"Good morning." Drew stands to pull me in for a kiss.

How unfair. He's so perfect he even looks good first thing in the morning. His hair is thick and sexy and there's a shadow on his jawline. His lips are still slightly swollen from our kisses and his brilliant green eyes are sparkling with contentment.

I glance around the kitchen. "Well, you've been busy." On the table is a plate holding several of Leah's croissants. As I reach for one, I realize something. "How did you get out of my loft and back in without waking me for the key?"

"Oh, I didn't." Drew's gaze drops to the table, his cheeks flush pink with embarrassment. "I had someone pick up the pastries and coffee and bring them to your lobby. Your concierge brought them up"

"Oh." *Interesting, I'll have to think about this more later. He has people he calls and they bring him stuff?* "Well, thanks." I grab a hazelnut croissant and pop a piece in my mouth. "Did they bring the paper as well?" I point at the Post with my elbow.

"Yes. Did you sleep okay?" Drew looks at me with that sincere expression of his and I melt.

"Except for when you woke me up in the middle of the night like a horny teenager, I slept like a rock. Which is actually unusual for me." Stunned at my rare admission, I see surprise register on his face and realize I just gave him some very personal information.

I twitch and focus on something else. Drew is wearing different clothes from the ones he had on last night. Not an expensive, custom made suit that fits his body like a glove, but jeans and a tight fitting long-sleeved T-shirt.

So he has people who bring him croissants and newspapers and changes of clothes? I want to know who he calls to run these errands but I don't want to start asking a ton of questions. Asking questions means I'd have to answer his.

"You have trouble sleeping?" Drew is regarding me expectantly.

"Ummm, well, yes ..." My anxiety ratchets up. I don't discuss this with people. Ever. Yet those big green eyes suck me right in. "I sometimes have bad dreams, but really, it's not a big deal." Drew cocks his head to the side and smirks as I struggle to explain.

"Hmmm. Maybe we've found a cure for your problem." He gives me a sultry look and slides his finger across his lips. I feel my skin tingling under my thin robe.

My throat feels like sand and my mouth goes dry. All I can do is drop my gaze and drink more coffee, my face heating up.

Drew chuckles at my unexpected embarrassment from his flirting. "Sydney, your reactions always surprise me." He must take pity on me because he changes the subject. "How's your arm? It looks good."

The bloody scrape is now just a small scab, most of the traces of my fall gone.

"It's fine." I duck my arm under the table. I don't want him to ask about my other scar again. The old one.

Drew gets up and crouches down next to my chair, doing another one-eighty on the conversation.

"I have to get going. When can I see you again?"

He takes my hand and strokes his rough thumb across my palm. My body starts responding to his touch. I have no willpower against this handsome, charming man who is literally on his knees, begging to see more of me.

"I have no projects lined up, and I'm just waiting for my current client to call to start work, so I'm fairly open in the next few weeks." I cringe, hoping that my unfilled social schedule doesn't make me sound desperate.

Drew doesn't seem to notice. "I'll call you later today, okay? I need to get home and check some things on my calendar."

He takes my face in his hands and brushes his lips across mine. It's quick, not nearly long enough to satisfy the unwelcome ache in my heart at the thought of him leaving.

Standing, he pulls me with him and kisses me again, deeper. He tastes like coffee and Drew. *Heaven.* Drew steps away, grabs the newspaper off of the table, and a duffel bag from the floor. I follow him down the hall to the foyer.

"Wait here." I hold up a hand so he doesn't leave. It only takes me a second to grab what I need and return. "A gift, I don't want to take a chance losing our luck." I smile as I hand him his revolting hat, making sure to balance it on my palms so it has minimal contact with my skin.

Drew gives me his full out dimple-revealing grin, takes the cap out of my hands, and shoves the nasty thing right on his head.

"Me neither. Sydney, I'll call you later." Turning the brim around so he can kiss me one last time, I sigh and let him out of my loft.

I realize that I may actually love that hideous hat.

Damn.

CHAPTER 6

"What about this one?" I hold up a slinky silver cocktail dress for Leah's approval.

"Ooooh, I'll definitely have to try that one on."

Leah snatches it from me and looks it over as I trail her through Bergdorf's designer dress department. She's obsessed with fashion. Leah could literally shop all day every day. Not me, I grew up with this stuff—the opulence, the pricey designer clothing, and yeah, it's nice and all, but it certainly doesn't fill the gaping hole in my life. I'd take normal over money any day.

Leah is chattering on about her date tonight with a guy she met at the opening night party for her dad's latest Broadway show. Since she refuses to allow a personal shopper to choose dresses for her to try on, I'm subjected to another one of her tortuous days on 5th Avenue.

Luckily, her upcoming date has given her temporary amnesia, so she hasn't remembered to ask about Drew. I know she'll push me to have "the talk" with him, once she knows we've done the deed. Spectacularly. Over and over all night.

"Sydney! Hellooo!" Leah snaps her fingers in front of me to break me from my fantasy.

"Huh?"

"I said, do you think Carter will like this one?" She impatiently holds up a short, tight, black and white color-block dress.

"It's beautiful, Leah. I'm sure any one of these dresses will knock him out. Let's get over to the fitting room so we can see them on you."

I spin her around and nudge her forward, eager to have a few minutes to sit and think. And rest my feet. For once in her life, Leah listens to me, and heads towards the fitting rooms to try on the clothes.

An assistant loads all of the dresses into the huge private room. I immediately drop onto one of the couches to wait. Knowing Leah, we'll be here a while. I retrieve my phone from my purse and wonder once again why Leah won't use a personal shopper, or even allow a sales person to help us when we come here. She says it's because she doesn't like the "snooty attitude" or the "close scrutiny", whatever the heck that means.

My phone shows one missed call and a text from someone at work. No texts or calls from Drew. Is it desperate and needy to text him? We spoke yesterday, and have plans to see each other tonight. He wants me to come over to his place so he can make dinner. Drew said he loves cooking, which explains his enthusiastic conversation with the chef at Sunset House. I decide not to over think anything and go with my gut, typing out a quick text.

Me —Hey, stuck in hell at Bergdorf's with Leah. Can't wait for tonight.

I smile and start to run through my emails, oohing and aahhhing at the various dresses as Leah models each one. One email from a manufacturer says that some of the furniture for Verve will be ready in ten days. That's the fastest rush job for custom furniture ever.

I quickly call Jeff Talley to confirm that the demolition is almost complete. We discuss the remodel and I let him know that the painters will be there next week. Pressing end, I feel satisfied that the Warren project is going well. I'm glad Jeff didn't mention Adam's reference to it in *GQ*.

Maybe he didn't see it?

Not a chance. Who wouldn't want free publicity for their big nightclub launch from a "huge" celebrity in a major magazine?

Just as I start to feel a new round of anxiety from the Adam situation, my phone chirps…

Drew —Only you would think Bergdorf's is hell. Bring your appetite tonight! The car will get you at six.

I can't stop smiling.

Sighing, I lean back on the sofa. I can't do anything about Adam or the article, so it's pointless to worry about it.

When I look up, I suck in a sharp breath. Leah is trying on a shimmering blue-violet, sequined mini-dress and it is stunning.

"Leah, that's the one. Get that one." She grins and twirls for me like a little girl in her first tutu.

"Great. Are we done?"

Leah makes a face. "No, silly. I still need shoes."

The only thing worse than dress shopping with Leah is shoe shopping.

"Yay. I can't wait."

Sitting in the back seat of Drew's Town Car, I nervously smooth down my hair for about the hundredth time. Drew said casual, so I'm wearing faded black skinny jeans and a beaded black t-shirt with black ballet flats. Trying to force myself to relax, my phone scares me when it alerts me to a text.

Leah —Wish me luck! Leaving in 10 for my date! Xoxo

I'm sure she looks gorgeous. After shopping, Leah had an appointment to get her hair done. She could wear a burlap bag and Drew's ugly old hat and still be stunning. I laugh at the thought of that gross hat as I type out a response…

Me —You don't need luck, you're you! Call me tomorrow. Xoxo

The car glides to a stop in front of Drew's place on a shady, tree lined street in Chelsea. I told Drew I would walk, since it's only a few blocks from my loft, but he adamantly refused. He said he'd feel ungentlemanly making me walk in the dark for our date.

I think it's more of a control-freak, bossy thing he has going on, but if he wants to send a car for me I won't argue. It's not worth it when he's only trying to be nice. And, it's kind of sweet.

I giggle. *Ungentlemanly.* Who says that?

Drew's driver helps me out of the car. On the way home from the gym the day we met, Bruce mentioned he's been working for Drew for over six years. I really like Bruce. Not only did he rescue me off of the sidewalk when I fell, he made me laugh on the way over tonight. Now I'm indebted to him twice.

When Bruce releases my hand, I glance up and am momentarily struck dumb. I'm standing in front of a magnificent four story brownstone. Does Drew own the whole thing? He didn't give me an apartment number, so I'm assuming that the brownstone isn't divided into condos.

Wow. Drew is rich. Like really really rich.

Money doesn't usually impress me since I've had it my whole life, but I wonder what Drew does to earn it, and that shocks me. I never want to know personal details about anyone. Distance and denial is so much easier than opening up about myself or letting anyone get close enough to betray me.

Bruce waits for Drew to open the front door before he climbs back in the car and disappears into the thick traffic.

"Hey, you look gorgeous," Drew says standing on the threshold, wearing jeans and a black t-shirt. I sigh. He's beautiful, bright eyes, perfect lips, and his hair is just as messy and touchable as ever.

"Please come in."

"Thanks. This is beautiful, Drew."

I let out a squeak when Drew grabs my hand, wraps his strong arms around my waist, and bends down, capturing my mouth and kissing me deeply. His tongue demands entrance, hungry, forceful, needy. I moan as he nips at my bottom lip.

Reluctantly, Drew pulls back, his green eyes dark and his skin flushed with desire. My nerves have vanished, replaced by an intense vibration humming over my skin. I feel like a live wire, ready to shoot sparks with any small touch.

"Sorry." His voice is husky and deep. "I couldn't wait to do that. I've been thinking about kissing you all day." Drew helps me out of my coat. "Come, I have wine chilling. We can drink while I finish dinner." Intertwining his warm fingers with mine, he leads me up a flight of stairs to the kitchen.

Drew's brownstone is incredible. Dark hardwood floors and high ceilings make it feel huge. The interior designer in me is itching to explore every square inch of this magnificent space. He brings me to a room that must occupy most, if not all of the second floor. The kitchen is bright and open, rustic and industrial. It's masculine, yet everything you could ever want in a kitchen. Drew pulls out one of the twisted wire barstools at the massive island and gestures for me to sit.

"I hope you like filet." He grins as he pours me a glass of red wine, our fingers brushing together as he hands it to me. *That dimple, I really want to lick it.* I hear soft music playing in the background.

"I love it. It smells wonderful in here. What can I do to help?" I start to get up but Drew stops me.

"I've got everything. I want you to sit there and we can talk while I finish up." Hmmm, I was right, he's a control freak. Even in the kitchen.

Drew reaches into a cabinet to remove two plates, placing them on the island. He grabs a bowl from next to the sink, dishing out two arugula and chickpea salads onto each plate. He is damn sexy as he cooks. I sip my wine and watch the sinewy muscles in his arms flex as he finishes making dinner.

We comfortably chat about my day at Bergdorf's with Leah, and the upcoming install at the Warren Hotel nightclub. He tells me about his trip to Chelsea Market to get our steaks from a shop that specializes in buying from small local farms.

Drew has a passion for cooking and I let him know that while I love eating, I will burn spaghetti if allowed near a stove. I don't mention that I actually *did* burn spaghetti once. Dinner is delicious, the filet melts in my mouth and the intense look on Drew's face as I enjoy his food reignites the desire that took a backseat during the preparation.

After dinner, Drew leads me up another flight of stairs to a large but cozy living area. I gasp and hurry over to the windows that span the back wall of the room.

"You have a view of the Empire State Building!" I continue babbling on, even though I know I must sound like a tourist. "I love looking out at the city. It relaxes me. I could sit in this room and look at this view all day."

"Me too," Drew whispers. Turning, I find him staring at *me*, not out the window, and feel the inevitable, hot blush spreading up to my ears.

I drop my gaze and wander over to the bookshelves that flank the slate fireplace. He has a lot of books about baseball, history, cooking, fly fishing… I smile at those, and other fiction novels.

There are a few family photos, a pretty young woman with long brown hair laughing with her arm around Drew, and photos of Drew with the same woman and an older couple as well as Drew alone with the older couple.

A strong arm snakes around my waist as Drew pulls my back to his front, his warm breath caressing my ear. "My sister, Allie, and my parents." He answers my unspoken question, probably aware that I won't ask. His perceptiveness astounds me. Drew kisses my neck and lightly rakes his teeth across my skin, causing a shiver to unfurl down my spine.

There's another photo of Drew, this time on the field of a baseball stadium posing with a player from the Boston Red Sox, both of them wearing sunglasses and smiling.

His mouth brushes against my cheek. "Meeting Red Sox catcher Trevor Caldwell at Fenway Park. That was a great day."

Hoping to change the subject so he won't ask about my own family, I turn and lead him toward the couch. I place my glass of wine on the end table. Drew lets me push him down onto the sofa so I can straddle his lap.

"Sydney," he breathes as I run my hands through that soft, thick hair. I give it a sharp tug, and he unleashes the primal desire I saw in his eyes when I arrived. Drew's fingers dig into my hips, pulling me back and forth across his hard length.

I moan and claw at his shirt, eager to taste his smooth skin. Drew makes me crazy with want, and the look he's giving me suggests he feels the same.

Drew lets go of my hips long enough to help me undress him. I toss his shirt carelessly to the floor and lave his wide chest with my tongue. His scent permeates every molecule in my body and ignites it into a fiery blaze.

"Drew," I murmur as I suckle the skin on his neck.

I want to devour every inch of him. It's frustrating, as close as we are it's not enough. I need more, even though I could taste his skin for hours.

My hands drift up and down his chest and abdomen, the heat between us nearly overwhelming in it's intensity. My body desperately wants to be closer to him, to get to know him. At the same time, my brain is telling me to pull back from the intimacy, that it's too much to handle.

Before I can panic, Drew lifts my shirt over my head, hastily unsnapping my bra and dropping it behind us.

"Christ. So fucking gorgeous, Syd. You drive me insane wanting to be inside you." I'm not one for dirty talk, but hearing those words come out of his sexy mouth, in that raspy tone, has me panting.

Lowering his head, Drew captures a dusky nipple in his mouth, pulling it taut with his teeth. His hair drags across my collarbone, making me shiver from the light touch. He's driving me wild with sensation, easily commanding my body to respond to every one of his caresses, every one of his words.

"I want to pleasure you in every way, Sydney," he says as he takes his time, kneading one breast with his hand and teasing the other one roughly with his mouth, sucking and pulling and biting relentlessly until I'm thrashing in ecstasy.

I shudder, his hot breath against my breast, and can feel the impending orgasm consuming me like an open flame. Arching back I scream his name as the fire rips through my body, exploding out in a torrent of pleasure.

"That was incredible, and a first for me," I whimper against Drew's lips as he kisses me gently.

"I'd like to have a lot of firsts with you, Sydney." He stares into my eyes, that honest expression trapping me.

Then as if a switch were flicked, Drew's pupils enlarge and he curls his fists into my hair. His mouth crashes onto mine, sloppy and wet and so good. Drew thrusts his tongue in deep, in a heated and passionate kiss. Those large hands slide down my back to cup my ass.

He grips me tight and stands up, turning to put me down on the couch.

Before he can take charge again, and I can see in his eyes that he's already planning his attack, I reach up and hook my fingers into Drew's belt loops, yanking him forward until he's standing between my legs. I haven't asserted myself yet, happy to let him lead, but this time, I'm determined to get my way before the control freak takes over.

With a wicked grin on my face, I open my mouth and slowly drag my teeth down the hard bulge in his jeans. "I want to taste you, Drew."

"Jesus," he huffs, squeezing his eyes shut and throwing his head back.

He hasn't tried to stop me so I unzip his pants and reach in to release his gorgeous cock. Licking my lips I lean forward and take him into my mouth, all hot, smooth, and hard, circling around the head with my tongue.

"Fuck, Sydney," Drew hisses in between loud, erratic breaths.

I smile, knowing that I have him at my mercy. I wrap my hands around his backside to pull him in deeper, feeling him hit the back of my throat. I revel in giving him so much pleasure. The sexy, incoherent noises he makes as I take him in and out, swirling my tongue around his cock with each thrust, drive me wild.

"Shit, stop." Drew's eyes are blazing as he pushes me back and moves frantically, his willpower nearly shredded. Drew shoes he pulls my shoes off, discarding them on the floor. In seconds he has my jeans and panties off and has shed his own clothes as well, stopping only to remove a condom from his back pocket and roll it on.

Drew picks me up as if I weigh no more than a feather, twists to sit on the couch and pulls me down onto his lap forcefully, his breath hitching as he buries his thick cock in as deep as it will go.

"Fuck, you're so tight. I love the way you feel." His voice is strained from the control it takes to hold himself in check.

Drew wraps his large hands around my waist, encouraging me to move, driving his hips up every time I slam down. I groan as he penetrates deeper with each thrust, our skin slapping together, the sound barely noticeable under the constant string of filthy words from Drew and moans coming from me.

Hovering on the edge of ecstasy, my nails gouge Drew's shoulders as I hang on tight and grind down one final time. With that, I spiral into another shattering orgasm, calling out his name as white lights explode behind my eyes. Drew punches his hips up a few more times before loudly finding his own climax.

Breathless, I rest my cheek against his chest, listening to his rapidly beating heart as it begins to slow. Drew wraps his arms around me, pulling me even closer, and nuzzles his face against the top of my head.

In this moment, as we hold each other as if we were old lovers instead of new, I realize how deep I'm already in with Drew, whatever it is we're doing. Instead of feeling the fear of letting someone get close, unexpected anticipation fills my heart. I *want* to explore this with Drew, I *want* to see if I can let him in, and as I contemplate that, I can't help but wonder what the heck I think I'm doing.

Bright morning light hits the back of my eyelids. All I want to do is roll over and cover my head with my pillow. Unfortunately, or fortunately depending how I look at it, I can't move. Because Drew's massive, hard body is wrapped tightly around me.

After having mind-blowing sex on the couch, Drew carried me upstairs to his bed and we discovered each other again slowly, thoroughly, before falling asleep in each other's arms.

Enjoying a rare moment of total contentment, I pretend I'm not a screwed up mess with unresolved issues. I gaze past the foot of the bed and out of the tall panes of glass that make up an entire wall of Drew's bedroom. My eyes land on the top of the Empire State Building, jutting up tall and proud from the surrounding buildings. It reminds me of Drew and how his commanding presence would stand out in a crowd.

Normally, looking out at the city diminishes my anxiety, but this morning, I see that one building as it draws focus from everything around it and stress tenses up my muscles.

I don't want to be next to the Empire State Building, with everyone staring and pointing. I want to be in the unnoticed mass of smaller structures, invisible, unexceptional. Can I be with Drew and still remain unseen? Then I think of leaving, stopping this thing before it goes any further, and the panic gets worse.

Overwhelmed, I choke down my fears and burrow further into Drew's chest, inhaling deep and committing his scent to memory. I haven't figured out much, but do I know that I sleep better with him next to me than I have in a long time. No nightmares, no horrific past memories haunting me, no waking up in the middle of the night feeling as if my heart is going to explode.

My wandering thoughts are interrupted when I feel Drew kissing the back of my neck. I decide to file my worries for another day along with everything else I refuse to acknowledge.

"Good morning," he whispers as his wandering hands roam over my curves.

"Good morning yourself," I respond playfully, hoping he doesn't hear the hesitation and anxiety in my voice. Attempting to distract him, I push my backside against his very obvious arousal.

"Is that how it is?" He trails his hand until it's between my thighs. "I think you want me again, Miss Allen."

"I always want you." I press back harder as he deftly finds the small center of my pleasure and begins to circle it tortuously. Drew's hand withdraws and I feel him move away. I'm about to protest the loss, when I hear him rip open a condom.

Drew circles his arm back around me, immediately slipping his fingers back onto me, teasing me to the brink until I'm a panting, writhing mess. I need him as close as possible to erase my fears, to convince me that I'm making the right decision. Impatient, I reach back and grasp his rigid length, and sink back onto it.

"Oh my god," I cry as Drew slides into me.

He continues to torment me with his fingers as he picks up the pace, pounding into me over and over again from behind. I thrust back against him, twisting the silky sheets in my fists as both of us race toward that glorious peak.

"God, Sydney, I can't get enough of you," Drew rumbles as he takes my earlobe into his mouth and sucks on it. Those words combined with his hot mouth on my skin, sends pleasure pulsing out, hurtling through every nerve in my body. I'm too deep in my own orgasm to understand what he whispers in my ear as he stiffens behind me, shuddering through his own release.

Drew rolls over, tossing the condom over the side of the bed. He pulls me around to face him so he can cover my mouth with his.

"Go away with me," he blurts out as his lips roam across my mouth and neck.

"What?"

I stiffen in fear. I've never gone anywhere with a man that involved luggage and overnights. At least one of us knows what he wants. Well, that's not true, I *want* him, us, this… I just don't know if I'm capable of following through without falling to pieces and screwing everything up.

Drew stops kissing me to look in my eyes. Will he see the fear in them? He's so observant, he must, but if he does notice, he doesn't let on.

"I have time before my next project, you have time before the nightclub needs you, let's go away. A friend of mine has a home in the Caribbean and has offered it to us for this coming weekend." Drew's green eyes are shining with excitement as he makes that sweet, sincere face that I find so endearing.

It's simple in his mind, and for everyone else, it probably *is* exactly that simple. Two people meet, they enjoy each other's company, they spend nights together, they go away for the weekend, they find out everything about each other, and they live happily ever after.

Not me, I can't accept anything at face value, there's always an ulterior motive.

Why am I so messed up? I'm twenty-four and I've never even had a real boyfriend. Well screw that! I'm so sick of not taking chances.

"Okay. I'll go," I say shyly, lowering my lashes in embarrassment. Desire has overridden my ridiculous logic and for the first time in my life, I've allowed myself to go with my heart and ignore my irrational fears.

When I glance back up, Drew is doing his full out, dimple-showing grin. I return his wide smile, then lean in and lick that delicious little dent on his cheek. He gives me an amused look and I can only shrug. "I've just been dying to do that." Impulsivity rules the day apparently.

He grins again. "You can do that anytime, babe. Absolutely anytime."

Drew insisted that I take his car back to my loft even though it's only a ten-minute walk. "I'm not having you do the *walk of shame* back to your place," he said as we had coffee in his kitchen earlier this morning. I told him that it's only a walk of shame if you feel shame, which I don't. He laughed and called Bruce to come get me despite my protests. He's kind of bossy sometimes and most definitely a control freak. I kind of like it. For the first time in my life someone makes me feel completely safe and taken care of.

When I get home, Richard opens the door and greets me warmly. "Good morning, Miss Allen. You look radiant today." He's smiling as if he's genuinely happy that I've finally found a social life.

"Hi Richard, and thank you for being so sweet."

Halfway to the elevators, I remember that Richard is seeing me return from a date that started last night and feel weird. Then I realize Richard is probably happy that I've gotten a life. I've lived here for six years and he's never actually seen me date anyone. I'm sure he thought I was a cat lady or asexual or something. I giggle at the thought as I step into the elevator.

I have three whole days to freak out about how much I'll have to share on this upcoming trip. Drew doesn't seem to be the prying type, but in all honesty, I want to know more about him and I just don't see how I can do that without giving him more of myself.

Once inside my loft, I wander into my bedroom to change and clean up.

I've just finished brushing my teeth and applied a little makeup when my phone chirps from my purse in the hall. Rummaging through my bag I see a text from Leah.

Leah —Call me when you can! I'll be off at 3

I tap out a quick response.

Me —Come over later and we'll get dinner, doing a little work first. Need to talk too.

There, that will get Leah's attention; I need to bounce some stuff off of her before this weekend.

Leah —OK. WTH is going on??? See u after work

I bring my phone into the home office and plug it in to charge. Opening my laptop, I answer some emails, coordinating the arrival of all of the different elements needed for Verve. I call Jeff Talley at the hotel and get his voicemail, so I leave a message updating him on the project and let him know I'll stop by early next week to receive the hardware as it begins to arrive.

Having time to kill until Leah will be here, I decide to Google St. Bart's, where Drew's friend has a home. I've never been there, and it's always good to know a little about other countries before you go. I note that they speak mostly French, which I barely speak. But they also speak English, so I won't be totally lost. There's an airport, so I assume that's how we'll get there. It's expensive and exclusive.

Frowning, I remember that Drew's brownstone alone puts him in the exclusive category as well. I'm no real estate expert, but that home is worth at least somewhere around the mid eight figures.

I don't know why it makes me uneasy that Drew has money. I've grown up with money. I've never had to want for anything in my life. I'm proud to say I work hard and earn a living, but I know my life has been infinitely easier with my parents' wealth behind me. I mean, my mom put me through design school and bought this loft for me.

The problem is that I can't rationalize his money because I have no earthly clue how he earns it. It's my own fault. I know he works, he's mentioned it several times. In fact, this morning he referred to a project he has coming up.

Dear God please let him earn a living legally.

I've never asked what he does. Drew hasn't offered, as if he knows I have an aversion to certain types of conversations. Well, I'll have four straight days to find out what kind of job Drew has, so I decide I can't worry about it for now. More denial, I think wistfully, before closing down the page for St. Bart's. I bring Google up again, and swiftly type before I chicken out.

Reid Tannen

Most of the same links from last time pop up again. I swallow hard and feel sweat beading up on my brow. Spinning the chair around I press my forehead to the glass and look out onto the cold, gray afternoon. No, my life is going really well right now. I can't do this today.

I spin the chair back to the desk and close the browser, flipping the lid down to prove some sort of point, I guess. What point? As with most everything else in my life, I have absolutely no clue.

CHAPTER 7

After getting stuck late at the café, I agree to meet Leah for Italian in the Flatiron district. It's a good thing she knows people in the restaurant business otherwise we'd never get a table without reservations.

My cab pulls up in front of Cevasco's just in time to watch Leah duck through the front door. I hand the cabbie money and hurry in to get out of the frigid cold that is biting right through my clothes. The restaurant smells unbelievable, basil, parmesan, and seafood cling to the air and I realize I haven't eaten all day.

Leah orders a bottle of wine for us to share and goes right for the kill. "So, what's going on? Did you watch that Barbara Walters interview or something?"

My muscles stiffen and I cringe reflexively. "No, Leah. I didn't watch that." I have to force myself to look more relaxed as I desperately sip my wine. "Let me hear about your date with Carter first, I need to let the alcohol work through my system before I can even think about my issues."

Leah starts gushing about her night out and doesn't come up for air. I find out that Carter works for his father, who owns one of the largest communication companies in the country. I'm not super happy to find out that includes over 700 radio stations, including a huge one here in New York City, but it's not like paparazzi are chasing radio station owners around or that I'm the one dating him so I'll deal with it without complaint.

He's taking her out again Friday night to some sort of charity gala. Better her than me. Those functions are always attended by Manhattan's elite. They set up a red carpet and bring the press there to snap pictures for the New York Post and various tabloid magazines. I'd rather just write an anonymous check to the charity and call it a day. Leah is excited though, and wants me to go with her again, to look for a dress.

"I'm not going to be in the city this weekend, so you'll have to tackle Bergdorf's alone this time," I choke out somewhere between bites of my seafood stuffed paccheri.

Leah's fork stops halfway to her mouth. She places it on her plate and wipes her mouth delicately. "Where will you be this weekend? I know you're not going to Belize to see your mom. You're not are you?" She narrows her eyes in suspicion, awaiting my answer.

"Well, ummmm, remember the hottie from your café?" I know that I'm probably a lovely shade of scarlet, I can feel it on my neck. Why is this so embarrassing? Leah does stuff like this with guys all the time. I clear my throat. "My white knight as you call him?"

"Drew, yes. He of the hideous hat. Your white knight. Of course I remember him." Her mouth drops open and she's momentarily speechless when she puts the pieces together.

"You're going away with Drew."

I notice that it's not a question.

"Yes. His friend has a home on Saint Barthélemy, he asked me to go for the weekend. I said yes." She looks like she's going to puke, or faint. "Leah, I know it's totally unlike me but—"

"But … you're going away with a guy for the first time in your life, and it's Drew from the café?" Her voice has risen an octave and she's getting kind of freaked out.

"Leah, are you drunk or something? I thought you wanted me to be more open to dating? Remember, the whole speech about Adam? I really thought you'd be, I don't know, happier that I'm taking a chance! You've been pushing for this for years!" Now *my* voice is rising and it's because I'm getting angry.

Leah quickly calms herself down and pastes on a fake smile. "No, Sydney. I am glad you're being more open. I'm happy for you, really. It's just a huge step from going on a date to spending a weekend out of the country with a man you barely know. A man who's going to want to know more about you. Are you ready for that?" She reaches across the table and squeezes my hand gently.

I duck my head guiltily. "I'm not necessarily ready to talk about myself, but honestly, I'm dying to know more about him. I guess I'm going to see what happens. He already said he won't push me to talk about anything that I'm not ready for."

Her eyes open wide with shock. "You're going to ask him about his life? Do you like him enough to accept the answers he gives you, no matter what they are?"

"I haven't thought about it, but yes, I think so." And that scares me.

"Well, then all we can do about it is order dessert," Leah says with that forced smile still on her face, as she clinks her wine glass against mine.

Somehow, Leah's bizarre reaction has me even more confused than I was earlier. And that says a lot.

After spending Monday apart so we can each get some things done, Drew comes over Tuesday to go running together. He says he runs a lot and can keep up with the miles I like to do. Not everyone wants to run eight miles at a time.

It's even colder today than the day I fell outside Drew's gym, so I wear my thermals under my regular winter running clothes and add a bright pink fleece ear warmer.

Drew shows up at my loft looking like a homeless person that raided the floor of a college frat house. He hasn't shaved in a few days, so the scruffy almost-beard is back and he has a navy New England Patriots skullcap pulled down over his forehead and his ears.

Ugly gray sweatpants at least two sizes too big hang off of his hips. I'm praying they don't fall down around his ankles while we run. But the kicker is his sweatshirt. It's a tattered maroon hoodie with fraying cuffs. The Boston College logo on the front is so faded it's difficult to read and the bottom hem is full of holes. He's topped his outfit off with shiny black and red Prada sunglasses.

Okay, so not totally homeless.

"Interesting choice of clothing." I grin as I let him into my loft.

He smiles, bemused. "What? I think I look like a guy who wants to work out."

I bump him with my hip. "*You* look like you crawled out of a sewer and stole from the lost and found at a college student center," I tease, grinning at him.

Drew grabs my waist and swings me around, rubbing his prickly stubble all over my face and neck. "You love it!"

His beard is rough but it still tickles. I giggle and try to squirm out of his tight embrace. "Stop! It tickles! Stop it!" Drew laughs even harder before he releases me from his torture.

"Well, we can't all be as sexy as you when we exercise." He stands a few feet away and checks me out from head to toe. "Even when you wipe out and need to be rescued."

"Trust me, you *are* sexy. It's just hidden under all of that hideous clothing. You know this is New York don't you? Some might take offense at all of that Boston paraphernalia." I wink and he smiles.

"Am I wearing my human-repelling costume again, Miss Allen?" His eyes sparkle with mischief, like a private joke and he's the only one who knows the punch line.

"Why I believe you are, Mr. Forrester. But once again, it's not going to keep me away. Now, let's hit the pavement."

We leave my building and head west over to the Hudson River Greenway and follow it south all the way to the Battery Park Esplanade. Circling Battery Park, which is depressing in the wintertime, we run back the same way we came. It's a good route to avoid car traffic and it's frigid enough to keep away a lot of the regular pedestrians.

We do a good seven and a half miles. I'm impressed that Drew doesn't have any problems with the distance. I mean, his body is unbelievable, so I shouldn't be surprised that he can keep up with me. He's in better shape than I am, that's evident when he takes his clothes off and I can see his long, ripped muscles and lean physique. He can lift me like I weigh nothing and hold me up against a wall as he pounds into me over and over and never get tired.

"Shower?" Drew asks after we get back to my place and each drink an entire liter of water. He's not going to have to ask me twice, especially since I can't wait to get him out of his ugly outfit. I grab his hand and lead the way.

****

My eyes dart around nervously from in front of the big TV in the media room. I pray that Mom doesn't come home anytime soon. I left school, faking a stomach ache so I could have the apartment to myself. Well, without my mom home anyway. We downsized from the twenty-thousand square foot mansion in L.A. to a ten-thousand square foot apartment on Gramercy Park in New York City two years ago, and there are always cooks and bodyguards and housekeepers around. I'm never physically *alone*, even though I pretty much always feel lonely.

My best friend Leah gave me a disc to watch. She didn't want to get it for me, but I begged and cried. I told her I needed to get some answers. Afraid to get caught, I pop open the slot and drop the DVD in. It closes and I wait for the video to appear on the screen.

The opening sequence of a national tabloid television show blasts from the surround sound speakers as I scramble for the remote to turn it down.

"Next, on Backstage Pass!!! A scandal involving Hollywood's most beloved couple! The exclusive video you will only see here!"

The host is dramatically shouting over intense music. A photo of my parents at a movie premiere flashes across the TV. I fast forward past the annoying set up, fumbling the remote in my sweaty palms.

When I find the spot I'm looking for, I stop to watch. A grainy video shot through a handheld camera fills the screen.

"Caught cheating on America's Sweetheart, Reid Tannen has a romantic rendezvous with an unknown woman."

The reporter's irritating voice-over starts as the video plays. I tune him out to focus on what I see. I'm only fourteen and don't know much about cinematography, but this video was obviously taken from pretty far away, so it's hard to see much. It shows the backyard of a huge home, with a pool and an outdoor kitchen. I don't recognize it.

Two people are lounging on chairs near the pool, and the camera zooms in on the man.

"If you look at the man's face, you can clearly make out Hollywood hunk Reid Tannen, and the tell-tale tattoo on his left wrist."

My heart drops into my stomach. That's my dad. Even with the poor quality I can tell that it's him. I don't even need to see the tattoo of my nickname to know who it is.

Dad thought it was so funny that when he put *"Heartbreaker"* on his wrist, the world thought it was a reference to himself. I used to love that it was our little secret. No one knew it was actually his endearing pet name for me. Right now, I'm nauseous to see it on the TV. Was he even thinking of me when he did this to our family?

Swallowing nervously, I keep watching, like a train wreck you can't look away from. I *need* to see this. I have to know why we left everything behind. The footage continues as the shot pans out to show the woman on the lounger next to my dad.

"Who is this mystery woman with the very married Reid Tannen? Our sources say that the home belongs to Gray Sibley, the director of Tannen's latest movie, but this isn't Sibley's wife Leanne, and it clearly isn't Evangeline Allen, A-list actress and Tannen's wife of 13 years."

My world stops as the man on the screen leans in and kisses the woman passionately. They kiss several more times, then stand up and retreat into the house.

I turn off the TV. I can't listen to strangers discuss my family as if they know us. No one knows! Nobody could know what it's like to have millions of people watching your life unravel for entertainment.

I hate them! I hate the reporters who sneak around and film people behind their back! I hate that they follow people to the store and their children to school and call it "news"! I hate my parents for being actors and bringing all this crap into my life! And most of all, I hate my dad for destroying everything I ever loved.

****

I jolt awake, my pulse racing and my skin slick with sweat. Another memory haunting me in my sleep. I lie back down on the bed and close my eyes, focusing to relax. Maybe Drew is right. Maybe he is the cure for my sleep issues. I shouldn't have let him go home last night. Tired and bleary-eyed, I glance at the clock

6:55am

It's too late to go back to sleep so I decide to go ahead and start my day. Getting up early isn't a bad thing. I have a ton of stuff to get done.

I wrap up in my robe and head over to the large windows in my room. The drapes are cracked just enough to see the crimson glow of the sun rising over the city. It's so breathtakingly beautiful that for twenty minutes, I stand there and watch as dawn arrives. Only when the deep orange hues fade to bright streaks of yellow, and then turn a crisp, cloudless blue, do I head into my closet to start packing for my trip.

How can a girl with so many clothes have nothing appropriate for a Caribbean vacation? Probably because I never go on vacation. I never go anywhere to be honest, always too worried about being recognized without the crowds of New Yorkers to blend in with.

I rummage around and find two bathing suits, a maxi dress and a few pairs of shorts. Sitting on the floor of my closet surrounded by piles of clothing, I realize that's all I have that I can bring with me to St. Bart's. Great, I'll have to go shopping and since Leah is working today, she can't go with me.

After a quick run and an even quicker shower, I walk down to the Village Coffee Bar. I'm not one-hundred percent sure that Leah will be glad to see me. After her odd behavior the other night at dinner, I have no idea what to expect. But I need her advice. She's been to the Caribbean tons of times with guys, including with her ex, a loser who was actually named Crash.

"Hey girl!" Leah smiles as she spots me stepping up to the counter. "Usual?"

Awesome, no weirdness. "Not today. Just a coffee in a to-go cup, and some help making a shopping list. If you're not too busy that is." I give her my big, sad-bunny eyes to beg my case.

"Shopping list? Are you cooking or something?" She narrows her eyes. "Because I have to say, after the spaghetti incident, I don't think cooking is such a great idea."

"No, not a list of food," I pout. The *spaghetti incident* refers to the time I attempted to make some spaghetti and then forgot about it on the stove. All of the water boiled off and the spaghetti burned to a giant black clump on the bottom of the pot. It took three days to get the charred smell out of my loft. Leah loves to throw that in my face.

"I have no clothes to bring on my trip, I was hoping you could help me figure out what I need to get."

Her demeanor brightens at the thought of clothes and shopping. "Of course I can help you with that. Give me five minutes."

Four hours later I'm starving and exhausted. Leah was back to her normal self and tirelessly went through each possible scenario that I could be faced with on St. Bart's. Armed with a ridiculous list a mile long, I went to Bloomingdale's, Barney's, La Perla and everywhere else on the Upper East Side that Leah deemed absolutely necessary. I'm tired, but satisfied that I got everything I need to look good this weekend.

Yet another first for me. Worrying about what a man thinks. I know Drew would like whatever I wore, but I want to please him. I want this weekend of firsts to be perfect. In all honesty, I'd give up every last piece of designer clothing just to feel like a normal girl in a normal relationship without any panicking or freaking out.

In my room, I turn on my iPod, singing and dancing around the room as I pack. I pull out my suitcase and toss it on the bed at the exact moment my phone chirps.

Drew —Hey babe. Missing you. Is your day going well?

Grinning so big my cheeks hurt, I respond.

Me —Better now. Miss u 2. Can't wait for tomorrow

It takes only a second for my phone to alert me of his text.

Drew —Me too. Be there at 6am. I'll come up to help with your bags

I roll my eyes but smile. Of course Drew won't let me bring my bags downstairs by myself, he's so sweet. Overprotective and bossy and a control freak, but a very sweet control freak.

Me —OK. See you then

I get another text immediately.

Drew —Yes, yes you will. ;)

I put my phone down and finish packing, singing along with Rob Thomas and the sensual sounds of Santana, smiling as I think about how *"Smooth"* Drew is as I go through the lyrics.

I can only hope my vacation goes just as smooth.

CHAPTER 8

Too keyed up to hide my excitement, I yank open the front door and drink in the sexy sight that is Drew Forrester. I take in his stunning smile, *hello dimple*, and flick my gaze up to his incredible green eyes.

"Hello, Sydney." That husky voice caresses me as six-foot plus of hunky muscle steps inside and pulls me into his arms.

"Hello, Drew," I respond against his mouth as he presses his lips on mine.

Drew snakes his hands around to my backside, pulling me against him as he skims his tongue along the seam of my lips, encouraging me to open. I melt and allow him to kiss me, slow and sensual. The kiss ends too soon and I protest, sucking his bottom lip between my teeth to keep him from pulling away.

Drew groans. "Sydney, as much as I want to throw you down and bury myself in you, we have to go."

He releases me from his embrace and runs a hand through his thick hair, messing it up perfectly. His jaw is clenching in an effort to control his lust. It's cruel and torturous, but I love that I can effect him this way.

"Is this everything?" Drew asks as he bends over and throws my small bag over his body and picks up the huge suitcase as if it weighs nothing.

"Yes, it's everything." I put on my coat and grab my purse and phone. "I'm ready." He meets my gaze and I hesitantly smile. I'm nervous for this trip, for how much sharing I'll have to do, for being unsure if I'm doing the right thing... I avert my eyes and stare at the ground as Drew opens the door.

Drew walks down the short hall to the elevator. I lock the door and follow behind. Drew's perfect, round backside distracts me, wiping away my anxiety. All of my worries fade into the background as I watch those tantalizing muscles shift.

We have to wait for the elevator and it gives Drew a chance to catch me undressing him with my eyes. "Like what you see, Miss Allen?" He smiles, that sexy dimple making an appearance. I stand on my toes and slowly lick it, swirling my tongue into the small divot. I hear his breath catch and feel smug satisfaction at my ability to render Drew speechless.

The elevator pings, intruding on our intimate moment. I pull back reluctantly. Licking my lips, I run my eyes up and down his gorgeous body. "Why yes, Mr. Forrester, I definitely like what I see."

Drew swallows loudly and gives me a raw, carnal look that loosens the tight coil of desire, building at the base of my spine. I have to suppress a groan when he speaks. "Me too, Miss Allen. Me too."

Miraculously, we make it down to the car without ripping each other's clothes off in the elevator and going at it like animals. Bruce loads my luggage as Drew and I duck into the back seat of the Town Car. I snuggle up to his warm body, taking a deep hit of the scent I've come to recognize as purely Drew. Hot, masculine, with that hint of body wash. He winds an arm around my back and I relax into him as the car maneuvers through early morning traffic.

"So, where to? JFK, Newark, La Guardia? Or is it a surprise?" I ask as I look out at the dark city and burrow deeper into his rock hard chest.

His gentle laugh rumbles against my ear. "No, not a surprise, Sydney. We're taking a flight out of Teterboro straight to the Gustave airport on St. Bart's. A car will take us to my friend's house about ten minutes away, and what we do next… is up to us."

He looks right at me, saying the last part so seductively that my breath hitches. I'm never going to make it four hours on a plane if he keeps saying things that make me squirm.

Speechless, I stare at him blankly, captivated by his eyes. After swallowing down my lust, I manage to squeak out a question. "So we're taking a private jet then?"

Drew's previously calm face looks worried. "It's a private jet, yes. There's not really another way to get to the island without a bunch of flight changes. It's the easiest way… is that okay?" His tone is hesitant, guarded, like someone who's afraid of scaring away a nervous animal.

I pull my brows together, confused by his overly-cautious demeanor. "It's fine," I snap.

I chastise myself. I don't want him to think I'm a bitch, and honestly, I *am* so jumpy that I may run away like a nervous animal.

I force myself to relax and put my hand on his knee. "Really, it's wonderful. Thank you for inviting me. I'm excited." I give him a diminutive smile and I feel the tension leave his body as he hugs me tighter.

We cross over the George Washington Bridge into New Jersey and arrive at the airport a few minutes later. My mom always flies in and out of Teterboro, so I've been here many times. Bruce takes us past the sign indicating that the building to the left is the Aviation Hall of Fame of New Jersey. He pulls the car up to a large, corrugated metal structure, coming to a stop in front of a sleek white jet.

Wow.

I'm impressed. It's as large as the plane my dad owned, or still owns, I have no idea.

Drew comes around the car and places his hand on my lower back, guiding me up the carpeted stairway into the cabin. An attractive older woman in a lovely tailored burgundy uniform introduces herself as Gail and greets us as we board. She happily takes our coats and ushers us into the main seating area of the aircraft.

I'm instantly taken with the understated elegance of the interior. The front half of the cabin has an intimate seating area with a gray suede couch flanked by two dark gray leather recliners assembled around a gleaming dark wood coffee table. Across the aisle are two more leather recliners facing each other with a small table in between. The same dark wood is used to form panels that create two bathrooms as well as a partition that separates the back sitting area from the front.

The second half of the cabin has sixteen creamy ivory leather seats, four rows of four, with two seats on each side of the aisle. Each seat has an entertainment center built into the headrest for the guest to use and I can see a luxurious blanket placed on every chair. A shiny mahogany bar spans the back wall of the room, with doorways on either side, probably leading to a bedroom and a private study.

"Please sit anywhere, we'll be departing in a few minutes," Gail says with a bright smile and she strides off to the cockpit area.

Drew stands by the plush couch and gestures for me to sit. I anxiously take my seat and he joins me, reaching over my lap to buckle my seatbelt. "Safety first, Miss Allen," he says mischievously, just inches from my face.

His nearness sends a jolt of delicious anticipation through me. As I'm about to tilt my head in for a kiss, Bruce comes bounding up the stairway with our luggage. He swiftly stows it in a closet near the exit, gives us a quick wave, and heads back out.

I turn to look out the window at the gray winter morning and let out the breath that I hadn't realized I'd been holding. Maybe this was a terrible idea. How will I make it through four days without discussing my family or my past?

Drew shifts to pull his phone from his pocket and checks it. It must be on silent since I didn't hear it ring. His handsome face pulls into a scowl. Drew types out a quick response then slides it into his jacket.

He's upset. I shouldn't ask what's wrong, start the game of twenty questions before we've left the ground. But I can't just sit here and ignore the fact that the text made him unhappy, it would be rude.

I suck it up and go for it. "Everything all right?"

Surprisingly, his annoyed scowl melts away. I'm treated to his full-out, dimple-showing, panty-dropping smile. "I'm with you, everything is perfect."

Wow.

The flight is smooth and comfortable. Gail brings us breakfast consisting of vegetable egg-white omelets and fresh fruit. I gasp when she appears with two huge to-go cups from the Village Coffee Bar. Staring open-mouthed at Drew, he looks a little embarrassed. It's so adorable that I have to stop myself from pinching his pink cheeks.

"I had them stop by the café this morning so we could have it with our meal," he shrugs casually, but I can tell he's apprehensive, waiting to see if his gesture was well received.

I take a big, wonderful sip. "It's perfect Drew. You're the most thoughtful person I've ever met. It's a little over the top, but I can get used to that." I reward him with a huge grin and take another huge mouthful of coffee. "Mmmmm." Closing my eyes I lick my lips to savor the warmth.

When I swallow, I glance back at Drew. He's staring at my mouth with red hot desire burning in his eyes. I freeze mid-sip, trapped like a deer being stalked by a mountain lion. Drew takes the cup from my hand and places it on the table in front of us without looking away for a single second.

I'm mesmerized by his eyes. The brown in the center of the green seems to get darker as I squirm under his heated gaze. Skimming his hand up my side, he brushes my breast with a light touch and continues up to cup my chin gently, tilting his head as he does. The skin he touches sizzles like a live wire, causing me to let out a shaky breath. I lean closer, inhaling to get another hit of my favorite scent, pure Drew.

Lightly teasing my lips with his tongue, Drew speaks softly against my mouth. "I do tend to go big or go home, so you definitely need to get used to me acting over the top." He pauses, measuring my response before continuing. "I cannot wait to get you alone, Sydney. You are driving me insane."

I feel as if I might combust from the combination of delicate touches and arousing words from this insanely hot, yet tender and considerate man. Why have I been avoiding relationships for all this time, again?

Because my parents screwed me up in front of the whole world. And I have trust and intimacy issues, lots of them.

Well, I'm already doing things that the old Sydney would never have done. Maybe it's time to push it a little further since I'm already out of my comfort zone.

Gail breezes back into the cabin to cheerfully clear our plates. She checks to make sure we don't need anything else and lets us know that we have about two more hours until we arrive in St. Bart's, before vanishing to the front of the plane.

Drew shifts over awkwardly and flips open the armrest on his side of the couch, pushing a few buttons. The faint tropical sounds of Caribbean music fill the cabin. I laugh when he sits back and faces me with a self-satisfied smirk.

"I just wanted to prepare us properly for our vacation," he says. "Ambience, you know."

"Trust me, Drew. I'm more than ready to start the weekend, but the music is a nice touch, very smooth. So tell me," I steel myself and garner as much courage as I can manage when I haven't had at least two shots of Patrón. "What kind of work do you do that allows you to take private jets to exclusive tropical islands?" I clench the armrest and wait.

Drew looks shocked, then the corner of his mouth ticks up, as if he's squelching a laugh. "I have to admit, Sydney, I didn't really think you liked personal questions very much."

He's nothing if not direct.

"I don't, when they're directed at me," I say tersely. "I'm a very private person… usually. But I'm finding myself in an odd situation."

"What situation is that?"

He wants me to say it out loud.

"I ummm, well. I-I guess I just really want to know a little more about you. That's rare…for me."

Drew breaks out a huge smile for me and cocks an eyebrow up teasingly. "So what you're saying is, I'm special?"

I roll my eyes and laugh. "You make it sound so dorky, but yes, I guess you are. So...are you going to answer my question?"

Drew hesitates, as if trying to figure out how to word his response.

"I freelance, so my work varies with each project I take on. I'm what you could call an ... independent investor. I invest in projects, sometimes I direct them, sometimes I have a more hands-on role and sometimes I just hand over money and wait for a return on my investment. The amount of input I have over each project varies. It's actually pretty damn complicated sometimes, but fun."

"Huh." I have no idea what that means. "So you're an investor? Like in companies?"

"Sort of." He pauses. "I'll hear about a money making investment, usually through a contact or a previous client, then I research it to see if it's worth the time and money, and go from there. Sometimes it just needs funding to get whatever the client needs off of the ground, sometimes I work on every aspect including marketing. It's a wide range of possibilities."

"That's.... interesting." I must look as lost as I feel because Drew is apologetically amused by my expression.

"It's okay, Sydney. I know it sounds confusing. But that's the best way I know to explain it to you right now. The downside of my work is that I travel quite a bit. Some projects are in different states, some in different countries. That's actually why I wanted to go away with you this weekend. I have to leave for California at the end of next week, and have to be on site for five or six weeks." He looks contrite, and more than a little worried about telling me.

"Oh. I guess I never thought about whether or not you traveled for your job. I mean, I don't usually worry about things like that. Crap, that's not what I mean. I'm sorry. I'm new at this whole *dating* thing. I mean, we are dating, right?" I mentally smack myself in the forehead. "Okay, tell me if I just screwed this all up."

Drew leans over and kisses me sweetly, "I'd like to think we're dating, if that's okay with you?" He has that honest, open look on his face that I find so identifiably *Drew*, so I just nod in agreement. "And you haven't screwed anything up, Sydney. I should have told you about my trip sooner, I just didn't want to scare you away. Plus I hope to be able to come back to New York several times during the six weeks, so with any luck you'll be willing to see me when I'm home."

I feel a painful lump in my throat at the thought of not seeing Drew regularly, but I ignore it and decide to go with what feels right, not what my damaged brain *thinks* is right. "Well, you're not wearing your hat to bring you luck, but I'm sure you don't need it." I smile, then feel shy and avert my gaze. "Of course I want to see you Drew. That's all I seem to think about these days." I glance at him through my eyelashes to see how he reacts. He unbuckles my seat belt and pulls me over to straddle his lap.

"Me too." He silences me, crushing his mouth over mine. We spend the last hour of the flight tasting and exploring each other, savoring every minute. I think about how grateful I am that Gail doesn't bother us until it's time to prepare to land. Then I worry how different everything feels with Drew and how deep in this thing I already am. I'm flying in uncharted territory without a parachute.

Saint Barthelemy is captivating. After flying in over the thick greenery and bright turquoise sea, the plane lands on a frighteningly small runway. We are met on the tarmac by a very tan, very happy, middle-aged man who calls himself Philippe. He enthusiastically shakes our hands, seeming very impressed with Drew, then springs up the stairs to retrieve our luggage. His attitude is quite contagious, and I find myself smiling at everything the man says.

Philippe ushers us over to a weird looking golf cart/Jeep hybrid car called a Mini Moke. I climb in the back as he drops our belongings on the front passenger seat. Drew rummages through his bag for a minute before joining me in the back seat. I burst out laughing when I see him wearing his ratty Red Sox cap.

"What? I know you said I don't need luck, but it can't hurt," he says smiling.

Philippe is a great tour guide, pointing out local attractions and wildlife as he maneuvers the vehicle past the small colorful buildings in town and up toward the hills, where the homes become larger and further apart. We pass a salt pond, and he tells us how the island has no natural source of fresh water, describing how most homes have a rainwater collection system. He explains that they built a more modern desalination plant a few years ago to replace the old, inefficient one, to supply fresh water to the islanders. We see a few peacocks and lots of iguanas sunning on rocks and trees as the Moke climbs up and away from the sea.

It takes less than ten minutes to arrive at the *villa*, as Philippe calls it. Personally, I call it a mansion. I haven't even gotten my bearings in the driveway when Philippe leaps from the car and takes our bags across the white gravel driveway. Drew and I follow him up the short walk to the door of the house.

Philippe unlocks the door and pushes it open with a theatrical flourish, allowing us to enter before following behind. He immediately brings our luggage through the house to the master suite.

"Wait here a minute, I'm going to chat with Philippe." Drew gives me a quick peck and heads toward the bedrooms.

"You're sure you got … it?" I hear Drew's muffled voice from the back of the house, and Philippe agreeing and saying "yes" and something else I don't quite hear. "In the office, correct?" That's all I can make out as Drew and Philippe come back into the great room with Philippe looking quite hassled.

Philippe places the keys on the countertop, shows us maps and phone numbers we may need, and lets us know that the kitchen is stocked and he's available at any time day or night if we have any questions or requests. He shakes my hand, tells Drew how great it is to meet him as he pumps his hand energetically, and then bounds out the door.

"Well, Philippe is…"

"Interesting?" Drew finishes my sentence for me.

"That's one way of putting it, I suppose." We both laugh and decide to take a tour of the house.

The home is beyond spectacular. It's twenty-eight thousand square feet and perched on the top of one of the highest peaks on the island. We find four bedrooms decorated in cheery shades of lime, coral and yellow, each with its own en suite and outdoor shower. The great room has a wall of sliding glass doors that open onto the multi-level tropical hardwood deck as does the master bedroom, effectively opening the entire back of the house to the outdoors.

We step outside and find breathtaking views of the entire island and the aquamarine waters of St. Jean Bay, and an infinity pool surrounded by lush tropical gardens. It reminds me to some extent of my mother's home in Belize.

"This is even better than I imagined," Drew says as he grabs my waist and pulls me down onto a chaise by the pool.

I look at him in astonishment. "You've never been here?"

"No, I haven't. Why?"

"I'm not sure, I just assumed. You said the owner was a friend. I don't know why I thought that."

"The owner is a friend, as well as a business partner in some of my investments. But I work a lot and haven't had the opportunity to just take off and come here. I don't get to take a lot of vacations." Drew sounds wistful at his lack of downtime.

"Yet you're here with me. I assumed you brought all the girls you date here." I poke him in the ribs.

"No, no other girls, Sydney. Just you. You make me want to take time off from work." He lays me back on the lounge and covers me with his hard body. "Miss Allen," he says as he rubs his nose against mine, "I do believe we're wearing too many clothes for this tropical heat. What do you say we fix that?" He buries his head in my neck and drags his teeth along my skin, leaving a wet, hot trail behind.

I shudder with pleasure, arching up into him. "Mr. Forrester, I couldn't agree more."

After skinny dipping in the infinity pool and christening one of the double chaise lounges, I put on one of my new bikinis and start cutting up some mango in the kitchen while Drew grills chicken out on the deck. We have the outer panels of the great room open, so we can chat as we cook.

I pull some spinach and romaine out of the fridge to rinse and pat dry for our salad. Lettuce duty and chopping mango, that's all Drew will allow me to do after I told him about the *spaghetti incident*. He laughed so hard when I told him that story that it took a good ten minutes for him to compose himself. Hmph.

"So, where does Chad live when he's not here?" I ask loud enough for Drew to hear.

Drew wanders back into the kitchen with the chicken on a large glass plate. Barefoot and shirtless, I can't tear my eyes from his body. He really is in perfect shape and must work out *a lot* to maintain his sculpted physique. His shoulders are lean and broad and lead down to biceps that are strong enough lift me against the wall of my shower as he pounds into me like a jackhammer. *Best memory ever.* My eyes skim across his perfect chest and down his rippling abs to the 'v' that peeks above his low slung shorts.

If I threw the lettuce on the floor and licked each side of that 'v' would he stop me?

"Chad lives in L.A."

I snap my head up from my ogling and can barely speak my mouth is so dry. "What? Who's Chad?"

He looks at me strangely for a second, then puts the plate down on the countertop and leans in close. "Were you just eye-fucking me, Miss Allen?"

Busted!

"Ummm, I'm not sure what you mean." The burning heat floods my cheeks as I resume making the salads.

He reaches over grabs a piece of mango, tossing it into his mouth. "Okay, we can play it that way, Sydney." Drew smirks knowingly, takes a knife out of the butcher block, and begins to slice the chicken. "Chad, the guy who owns this house, you asked me where he lives and I said Los Angeles."

Drew slides some chicken onto each salad and I add the mango on top, my pulse still racing from the embarrassment of being caught drooling over his body. I attempt to act casual as I grab both plates and bring them outside to the stylish teak dining set.

"Where in L.A.?"

Drew sets a beer down on the table for each of us and sits next to me. "Brentwood." He takes a huge bite of salad.

I chew my food as I process this information. "Is he involved in the project you have in California?"

Drew takes a deep pull from his beer and I'm enthralled with the movement of his Adam's apple as he swallows. "Yes, Chad is a principle investor as am I. He'll be on site with me most days. That's probably why he let us use his villa, he plans on bugging the shit out of me for six weeks and is just trying to butter me up."

"Not a bad plan if you ask me," I laugh, returning my gaze to my plate so I won't be caught staring again.

Drew laughs with me. "I agree. He's a pretty smart guy."

We spend the rest of the evening lounging by the pool, laughing as Drew tells me stories of his childhood in the Back Bay of Boston.

Soon, he has me laughing so hard I have to hold my stomach. "Stop, stop, there's no way your sister told a girl you liked that you were allergic to deodorant!" I wheeze out between uncontrollable giggles.

He grins and his eyes light up. "She did, believe me. She lied and told everyone that I couldn't wear any because it gave me armpit rashes. It was revenge for the time me and my friends hid a walkie-talkie under her bed and made monster noises."

He looks so gorgeous sitting on a lounge chair by the pool, the dim house lights casting long shadows in the dark night. "She cried every night for a week. We were really mean to her that time."

"We used to tear it up all over that city," Drew reminisces fondly. "Me and my two best friends, Mike and Matt, would get on our bikes and ride over to Kenmore and catch the Sox at Fenway. Sometimes we'd ditch school to get autographs from our favorite players and see batting practice." His accent gets more and more pronounced the more excited he gets as he talks about his hometown.

"That sounds like so much fun. I didn't do anything like that growing up. Do you still talk to your friends from home?" I sit on the edge of the infinity pool so I can dip my feet in the warm water.

Drew shifts his gaze down the hill at the ocean as it shimmers in the moonlight. "I still talk to Mike. Matt died of cancer when we were in high school. They were brothers." He takes a long sip of his beer and looks at his feet. Drew gets up from the chair and sits next to me by the pool.

"I'm sorry," is all I can come up with to say. I put my hand on top of his.

He shrugs like it's no big deal, but I it is. "It was a long time ago." He takes another swig of his beer.

I change the subject to try and bring back some levity. "In the third grade, Denny Hirschler tried to kiss me by the swings at recess." Drew looks at me with interest. "When he puckered up, I reached down and threw a handful of dirt in his face, then ran away."

I frown when I realize that not much has changed. I still run away from any type of connection with people.

"It's your fault for being so kissable." Drew reaches in and tilts my head toward him. He places a soft, tender kiss on my mouth then withdraws, looking out at the sea again.

"You don't have any siblings, do you Sydney?" He asks, still staring at the dark ocean.

"No, I'm an only child."

I know I sound sad, and he picks up on it, twisting his head around to face me. Unnerved by his ability to read me like an open book, I get up and sit in the nearest chair, curling my feet up underneath me.

"You know you don't have to answer anything that makes you uncomfortable?"

Drew won't let me escape into myself. He climbs onto the lounge chair behind me and pulls me back to rest against his broad chest. The warm Caribbean breeze ruffles our hair and rattles the wind chimes on the deck.

"I know. I'll let you know if I'm freaking out. I'm sorry I'm so difficult. I...I don't date much," I admit. "Part of the whole not wanting to talk about myself hang up I have."

I feel bad that Drew is so nice about my neuroses. He shouldn't have to put up with someone so damaged. He's so perfect and gorgeous and agreeable. He deserves better than me, but I'm too selfish to let him go. Drew makes me feel safe from all of the monsters I've been scared of, protected.

Drew winds his arms around me in a comforting embrace. "You're not difficult, Sydney. Everyone is affected by life events differently. When and if you want to tell me what happened to you, I'll be here. In the meantime, I'm happy just to spend time with you."

I blurt it out before I can stop myself. "My parents are divorced. They haven't spoken in twelve years, and I haven't seen my dad since then either."

Wow. I haven't told anyone that. Ever.

Leah already knew my story when we met so she doesn't count. Am I losing my mind? Or maybe I'm healing, a tiny piece at a time, by spending time with Drew.

"That must have been hard. How old were you then?" Even though I feel his body tense behind me, his deep voice is like a calming wave that gently laps at me, eroding my walls bit by bit.

"Twelve. Yes, it was very hard. It made me very untrusting, as I'm sure you can tell."

"I think you're perfect." He nuzzles my ear, poking around with his hot tongue. My body is suddenly coiled up as tight as a spring.

I turn until I'm facing Drew. "I don't think I feel like talking anymore." I slide my hand down his rippled torso, following the light dusting of hair to the front of his shorts, squeezing his hard length.

"Me either." He grabs me in his arms and stands up, carrying me through the open wall to the bedroom.

Placing me down on the massive king-sized four-poster bed, Drew climbs on the mattress, using his arms and legs to hover just above me. I whisper his name as I lift my hips in an attempt to rub against him.

Drew captures my mouth and slowly probes every inch with his persistent tongue, teasing me mercilessly.

"Please, I need you," I beg. I can't connect with words, or by letting Drew get to know me. Sex is easy. It's the only way I know how to be close to him.

I wrap my legs around his waist and try to pull his body down onto me to get some relief from the ache between my thighs, but Drew is strong and he resists, tormenting me by trailing kisses up and down my neck. He never allows our bodies to touch anywhere except our mouths and where my legs are around him. I whine petulantly, groaning into his mouth.

"Patience, Sydney. I want to savor you. I can't get enough of your skin, your smell, the feel of your body. Let's discover everything about each other."

Drew pulls down one side of my bikini top and swirls his tongue around the taut nipple, dragging his teeth across it as I moan and arch back in ecstasy. When he's satisfied, he shifts to the other breast and captures the firm nub in his mouth, sucking hard. Pleasure and pain crash together until I'm desperate to have him inside me, pleading and begging for more. Drew reaches behind me and in one swift move unties my top, tossing it somewhere over my head.

"So beautiful," he whispers as his hands knead my breasts and he returns to take my mouth again. Releasing me, Drew slides off the bed to kneel on the floor and undoes each side of my bikini bottom, yanking it away.

"I need to taste you. You're addictive," he pants as he pushes me further up on the bed and lowers his head to the warmth between my legs. Roughly grabbing my thighs Drew shoves them apart and dives in with a primitive groan, taking what he wants. "Jesus, Sydney." His tongue slips over the tiny bundle of nerves right as he inserts two fingers inside me.

"Oh God, Drew!" My back arches off of the bed from his assault as he pumps his fingers in and out in at a perfect pace. Eyes glazed, I glance down to see him watching me as he flicks his tongue over my most sensitive spot. It's so erotic I can't stand it. His touch sends me over the edge, unable to control my body as my hips buck wildly into his hand.

"Don't stop, I'm going to come!" I cry as the powerful orgasm tears through me. I convulse, squeezing his fingers as he continues punishing me with his hand and mouth. Drew doesn't stop until I collapse in exhaustion, a sheen of sweat covering my body as I close my eyes to catch my breath.

"I'm not done exploring you yet, Miss Allen." Drew grabs my ankles and yanks me to the edge of the bed, my eyes flying open from surprise. His firm, demanding tone reignites the blaze inside and desire punches through me from his bossy behavior.

At some point, Drew lost his shorts and managed to put a condom on, because he's standing next to the bed completely naked.

My gaze drops to his thick shaft as he caresses it teasingly. I lick my lips in hunger, eager to have that perfect cock do very naughty things.

Drew waits, letting me watch him stroke himself before he takes my ankles and puts them up over his shoulders. He meets my gaze, the green of his eyes nearly eclipsed by large, lust-filled pupils.

"Are you ready for me baby? I want to fuck you…hard."

Oh. My. God.

"Yes, take me Drew."

He closes his eyes and tilts his head back, as if savoring my consent. When he looks back down his eyes are black and shining with lust. Drew grips my hips, his fingers pressing deep into my soft flesh, and enters me in one swift thrust. "Ahhhhhh." My eyes roll back into my head at the sweet fullness, the slight sting from the stretching. It's pain and pleasure and the most addictive sensation all rolled into one. It's perfect.

"Look at me, Sydney. I want you to watch me as I fuck you."

I really, really like bossy Drew.

Mesmerized, I watch his gorgeous face, twisted in ecstasy as he plunges into me over and over again. He pulls out almost all the way, slamming back in with each hard, raw stroke. I revel in his masculine beauty. The sweat beading on his brow just under his messy dark hair makes me want to catch each drop on my tongue. That perfectly angular jaw he has clenched tight, straining from the effort of holding back his release.

I find his pulse throbbing under the flushed, stubble-covered skin of his neck and want to bite down on the spot, then lick it to soothe his flesh. My eyes catch the narrow obliques that ripple and stretch with each and every thrust. Lastly, I take in his swollen, pink lips parted in pleasure as his breath comes fast and hard the closer he gets to his climax. Everything about Drew's body is perfectly suited to me, as if I ordered him up special and had him delivered to my front door.

Drew reaches down to put his thumb on my clit, encouraging me to let go. I cry, shuddering beneath his body, shattering to pieces as I fly apart again. A few more agonizingly deep strokes and Drew joins me, calling my name loudly as he thrusts one final time then falls to his knees on the floor, laying his head on my chest.

My strength sapped, I weakly reach down to push his sweaty hair off of his forehead, gently scraping my nails down his back.

"Mmmmmm. That feels good." Drew moans. Lifting his head he rests his chin between my breasts, still kneeling on the floor with my legs hanging off the mattress on either side of him. "You're amazing." I continue scratching his back until he climbs onto the bed with me. He snuggles up and pulls me close.

"Thanks for letting me in enough to come here with me, Sydney." His voice is soft and kind as he strokes my skin and kisses my ear.

"I wouldn't want to be anywhere else right now."

I manage to shock myself when I realize that I'm telling the truth.

CHAPTER 9

"So, snorkeling, hiking, jet skiing, sailing, what would you like to do today, Sydney?"

I twist around to look at Drew from the lounge chair where I'm enjoying my morning coffee, listening to the tropical birds sing to one another.

"Those all sound wonderful. Anything would be great." I have to shade my eyes with my hand so I can block out the bright sunlight and see his relaxed face.

"Well, how about we take out a sailboat, and if we want to, we can snorkel. Otherwise we'll just relax onboard and enjoy the day?" Drew smiles at me from under his gross *lucky* hat, which he decided he needed to wear every day so we would have good weather all weekend.

"Sounds great, I'll just go shower off so we can go." I stand up to make my way into the house.

Drew grabs my hand as I pass by his chair. "I just have to make a few calls to arrange the boat and I'll join you in a minute. Don't finish too quickly." His mischievous grin makes my brain stall and my heart stutter in my chest.

I blink hard to clear my head, then smirk. "Don't worry, I'll let you wash my back." I wink and leave Drew to go into the bedroom.

I ditch the tank top and panties that I put on after rolling out of bed and gather my bath supplies. I've just stepped outside into the natural stone shower when I hear snippets of an irritated Drew on the phone with someone.

"I mean it, not a word."

"Yeah...they bettah"

"Oh, I'm very serious."

"Bettah not heah or see a thing."

"Yes...an hour."

"Okay."

Drew must hang up because I hear him enter the master suite. Moments later, he joins me under the warm spray.

"Everything okay with the boat?" I don't want Drew to think I was eavesdropping, but his accent was pretty pronounced on the phone, so I know he was getting worked up. I haven't known him long, but it doesn't take a genius to figure out that he only goes full-Boston if he's pissed or excited, and he didn't sound excited. At all.

Drew pauses before slipping his arms around me, pressing his heavy erection against my stomach. "Everything's great babe. Philippe will be here in less than an hour."

"Well then. Let's hurry, shall we?"

After our quickie in the shower, I pack a few things in my tote and throw on a deep green maxi-dress with my casual flip flops. I gather my hair into a high pony tail, slather my face in sunscreen and I'm ready to go.

Philippe drives us down the hill in the same little Mini Moke that we rode in yesterday. Drew has on his ridiculous hat and sunglasses, and his face has a few days of growth on it so his appearance is strikingly similar to the day we bumped into each other in the café. He catches me staring and smiles broadly.

"I'm excited for a day on the water, how about you?"

I'm so thrilled I feel like my grin is going to split my face in half. "Very excited, Drew. It's so beautiful here. Thank you again for this wonderful trip." He laces his fingers through mine and I wonder if life could get any better.

"Here we are," Philippe exclaims as he pulls up and parks in the sand alongside an empty beach. Drew helps me out of the car and I see a man standing by a small inflatable boat at the shoreline and a sleek blue sailboat moored just offshore, bobbing in the calm turquoise waters of the bay.

"It's beautiful. Whose boat is it?" I wonder out loud.

"It's Chad's. He has a crew on call, so I had them prep the boat and they'll sail it for us since I know nothing about sailing and this boat is too big for one person anyway."

This Chad guy really loves the finer things in life. It makes me feel a little guilty for using all of his things. "You have a great friend to let us use all of his expensive toys. I hope I get to thank him in person someday."

A disconcerting look flashes across Drew's face and is gone just as fast. "Yes, hopefully. Let's get aboard, ready Sydney?"

He holds out his hand and helps me into the dingy. Once Drew gets me settled on one of the round inflated sides of the boat that doubles as a seat, he places our bag with our bathing suits and other gear in the boat. Drew stops to tug his hat down over his brow and hops in across from me.

"Philippe, around 4pm?"

"I'll be here, Mr. Forrester. Miss Allen, enjoy your day."

Philippe pushes the inflatable out into the water and the man driving fires up the engine. The young man says nothing, and the trip to the boat is so short that introductions seem pointless, so we sit in silence as we bounce over the waves.

I take in the tropical greenery as it curves around the small rocky harbor that surrounds us. There are about a dozen other boats moored off shore, but most beachgoers are all the way on the other side of the bay, so they're just little dots on the sand. Since it's barely 10am, the beach is empty, most vacationers still sound asleep.

Our pilot steers the small craft up next to the sailboat and a middle-aged man dressed in a white polo shirt and white shorts and a similarly dressed younger man grab the ropes that are tossed to them and tie us up.

"Welcome to the *Magic Hour*," the man announces as he helps us onto the sailboat.

"Thank you, I'm Drew, this is Sydney." We all exchange handshakes.

"I'm Frederick, your Captain, and this is Robert, one of the crew. I'll give you a quick tour and we'll head out. Winds are perfect today. The water isn't too choppy so it's going to be a great sail." We follow Captain Frederick into the cabin as he describes the sailboat, "This is a 200ft Perini Navi sloop. She has five cabins and can sleep twelve. With her sails up she can reach 15.5 knots, which is about 20 miles per hour if you were wondering."

The captain continues talking about the technical aspects of the boat which has Drew fascinated, but I'm more interested in the lavish interior. Everything is honey colored hardwoods and white duck cloth. The main cabin has a huge L-shaped couch and matching oversized ottoman. Windows arc uninterrupted to span three sides of the room, offering panoramic views of the sea. A full galley and massive dining table are further back in the space as is the door to the office. Stairs lead down to the two levels of sleeping areas, each room well-appointed in the same white fabrics and blonde wood.

We go back up and outside to the main deck where there is a semi-circular padded bench that could seat twenty people. Drew leads me over and he throws his arm around me as we sit.

"So, sail around the island? Maybe a stop at a nearby reef for some swimming and snorkeling? What do you think, Sydney?" Drew asks as Frederick waits patiently for orders. From the corner of my eye I see Robert and another young man making preparations to leave.

"Sounds great." I spin his cap around backwards so I can plant a kiss on his beautiful lips. "Let's go."

Smiling, Drew turns to the captain. "You heard the lady, let's do it!" He grabs me playfully and nuzzles my neck, sending goose bumps down my spine, causing me to squeal in delight.

I've never been sailing, and the *Magic Hour* is spectacular. Once her massive sails are up, I can't see the top of them as they tower above us. We skim effortlessly across the sparkling Caribbean Sea, so clear in places that it seems as if we can see down hundreds of feet to the sandy bottom.

A nice young woman in the same white polo shirt and shorts brings us something to drink and asks us what we'd like to have her prepare for lunch. We ask her to make something light and tropical.

After making a wide circle around St. Bart's the crew moors the boat in a quiet spot by a small, rocky c-shaped island that juts out of the water as if reaching for the sun.

Drew and I sit at an outdoor dining table to enjoy a lunch of grilled snapper with coconut rice and mango salsa. It's exactly what I imagined a meal on a huge sailboat in the Caribbean would taste like, simple, fresh and slightly sweet.

"I can't believe you are drinking a panty ripper!" I laugh so hard that I have to wipe a tear away.

Drew gives me a belligerent look. "It's just pineapple juice and coconut rum, Syd. Besides, you're drinking one."

He frowns as I watch him attempt to sip his drink, a wedge of pineapple on the glass and a tiny umbrella stuck in it and hysterically laugh all over again.

He glares at me and I try to stop giggling, but I can't. When a smile cracks his attempt to be mad at me, I know he's only pretending to be upset.

After lunch we decide to sunbathe on deck, waiting to snorkel around the reefs that surround the boat. The high point for me is getting to slather sunblock all over Drew's back and shoulders.

I cheat a little, feeling him up longer than necessary, but I can't help it. His body is just so touchable. His skin feels hot and hard under my hands as I smooth the creamy lotion on. Suddenly, I'm dizzy with desire. The alcohol from lunch, the smell of coconut lotion, and the rubbing of Drew's half naked body have given my libido a swift kick start.

Frustrated, I fling myself down on my chair to avoid making a spectacle. It's hard to remember that we aren't alone, even though the crew does a great job of becoming almost invisible. In fact, the only people who've said anything to us directly are the captain and the nameless girl who brings us food and drinks.

Drew grins and leans over toward my chair. "Did you enjoy molesting me, Miss Allen?"

I huff and turn back to my book. "No, not at all."

He laughs and resumes reading whatever it is that he has on his iPad, not saying another word.

A few hours later, we're floating around in the warm water, watching the schools of colorful fish dart around the anemones that live amongst the coral. It's so peaceful, except for when Drew swims in front of me and makes weird faces behind his mask. I nearly choke when I laugh too hard into my snorkel.

Drew points out a huge green turtle paddling along the bottom of the ocean, nibbling the sea grass that sways in the current. The turtle must be almost five feet long from head to tail. I remember from my research that it's illegal to harm or even touch one of these graceful creatures, so I keep my distance, even swimming back some when he gets a little too close.

After a while, Drew indicates that it's time to go by gesturing at his wrist like he's checking the time. Grabbing my hand we swim back to the boat.

For the return trip to the harbor we decide to sit on the huge couch in the main cabin. Being a red-head and all, I felt like I might be getting too much sun, and Drew was particularly concerned about getting burned on his face and shoulders even though he's barely gotten any color. He stretches out on the couch and I lay on top of him, loving the feel of his body beneath me, the scent of the sea mingling with the scent of Drew.

I think we both must fall asleep because Robert comes in to let us know that we're back at the harbor. Even with the nap, I'm exhausted by the time we get out of the rubber dingy and trudge up onto the sand where Philippe waits for us, but I still can't seem to wipe the smile from my face.

When I wake up I feel the warm ocean breeze caress my naked skin. I reach over for Drew and realize I'm alone. Another night without a single bad dream or memory from my childhood.

I stretch and think about how perfect yesterday was. After the day of sailing, we had a light dinner and made love outside by a crackling fire that Drew started in the fire pit by the pool. How have I gone so long without regular sex? Grinning, I get out of bed and go looking for Drew.

I find him sitting on one of the double chaises, staring out at the sea. He looks uncharacteristically sad, so I tuck myself in next to him.

"Hey," he says, putting his arm around me.

"Hey, are you okay? You seem so unhappy sitting here. Did you sleep okay?" I put my hand on his arm and rub my thumb back and forth over his smooth skin, tracing the sinewy tendons.

"Yeah, I'm great. I've been checking emails, prepping for work. Just thinking about going back tomorrow and having to leave for California later in the week. About how little we know about each other. About how much I'll miss you." He turns to stare right into the depths of my eyes as he says the last part.

I swallow uneasily. He knows I hate talking about myself, but it clearly bothers him that we aren't closer. Drew wants to be closer, I can feel it. He wants to confirm that I feel the same way before he leaves for California. And I do, I *want* to know about him. I just need more time to trust him with that part of me. To escape the heavy chains of denial that I've used to hide from my pain.

These feelings are still too new for me. I'm in uncharted territory, so used to putting up the wall and keeping everyone out. I can't just turn it off at will. He told me I don't have to answer anything that I don't want to, so I have to trust that he'll respect that.

"What do you want to know?" I ask quietly, watching the trees move in the gentle wind.

Drew sits up straight and out of the corner of my eye, I can see that he has twisted his upper body towards me. I can't look at him directly. I know he wants me to face him so he can stare me down with those all-seeing eyes of his, but I'm too uncomfortable. He's way too observant.

"Why don't you watch TV or read magazines or go to the movies?"

Straight for the jugular, in true Drew style.

I inhale a shaky breath. "I….it's just…I mean." My hands are trembling in my lap. Fear knots in my throat, almost choking me.

Drew reaches out and pulls my chin up so I have no choice but to look at him. "Sydney, you can trust me. I care about you."

His gaze captures me and I freeze, green to blue, his eyes pleading with me to say something. I see an emotion there, behind his concern, but I can't make it out clearly.

It feels as though my voice is coming from under water when I speak. "It has to do with my parents. Their divorce, it was ugly. It was public." I screw my eyes shut. "That's really all I can give you right now, I'm sorry."

He shifts me so my legs drape sideways over his and holds my face with his big, gentle hands. I open my eyes to see his face directly in front of mine, a mere inch away. "Thank you, Sydney. For what it's worth, I'm happy that you trust me, even if it's only part of the story."

Drew tilts his head and slides his mouth over my lips. His scent invades my nostrils and his taste permeates my tongue. I open my mouth to let him in. We move together in a sensual dance that sends a rush of desire through my body, gathering in a hot rush between my thighs. I turn on his lap so I can grind against his shorts, running my hands up and down his broad chest as I writhe. Drew leans away and I groan in displeasure, pouting.

"So, what do you want to do on our last day here?"

"I thought I was showing you what I want to do today." I tip my head back toward his and lick across his lips, nipping them as I wriggle against the prominent bulge in his shorts. Drew grunts as I shift back and forth shamelessly. I quickly unbutton his shorts and open his zipper before he can protest, reaching in to grasp his cock firmly.

"Sydney," he warns, "what are you doing to me?"

And somehow I know he doesn't mean in just this moment physically, but what are we doing to each other's minds and souls? He is changing me irrevocably. I know that now. Drew is letting me know that he feels the same.

Since I can't talk about it, about me, I lift myself off his lap and push him down on the lounger, ripping down his shorts to unleash his thick, painfully erect shaft. I want this control-freak to give himself up to me just this one time.

I kneel down and lean in to taste that impressive length. "Fuck!" he cries and nearly bucks off of the chair when my tongue makes contact. I smile and mentally high-five myself then take him into my mouth as deep as he'll go, swirling my tongue around the head. Drew grabs my hair in his fists and hisses out a barely restrained breath.

The control-freak is slowly losing control.

I love that I can undo him like this. This big, confident, bossy man will do whatever I want when I take him this way. I slowly pleasure him with my mouth, letting him hit the back of my throat and then sucking hard as I pull back. He's panting, trying to increase the pace by pressing his hands on my head, but I won't let him. It's my turn to torture him, and I love every second of it.

Drew grunts in a combination of frustration and pleasure as I take him deep over and over again, at a leisurely pace, laving my tongue over the head every time I pull back. I glance up and see Drew unraveling. His head is thrown back, eyes rolled up in his head. His beautiful mouth is hanging slack and his breath is coming fast and uneven.

It's one of the hottest things I've ever seen in my life.

I speed up the pace and feel his muscles tighten. As I'm sucking him harder and forcing him against my throat he suddenly comes, yelling out a random jumble of words as I swallow him down. My scalp burns from his fists that are tangled in my hair.

I drop back next to him on the chair. Trying to catch his breath, Drew and rakes his hand through his hair to push it off of his sweaty brow. He grabs my face, kissing me passionately before lying back again, his chest still heaving.

"That was without a doubt, the most intense orgasm of my entire life. You own me, Sydney."

Right back at you Forrester.

"Merci, bonne journée. Thank you, have a nice day," the saleswoman says to me as she hands me my bag.

"You too, thanks so much." I put my sunglasses on and head back out into the Caribbean sun. I've been shopping for several hours, avoiding stores like Hermes and Gucci and instead spending time discovering all of the little boutiques that dot the streets of Gustavia. I found a great pair of woven sling backs, a new dress for myself, and gorgeous handmade black coral bracelets for both my mom and Leah.

Philippe waits for me in a small lot nearby, sitting in the Mini Moke with his feet up on the dash and his eyes closed.

Is he asleep?

Well, it doesn't matter since I still have to find something for Drew. He declined coming shopping downtown with me, begging off to stay behind and check his email. His phone buzzes a lot. He eventually turned the notifications off, but I can tell he has tons to do for work if the stress lines on his face are any indication

I smile as I think about this morning's activities. After the incident on the lounge chair, Drew scooped me up and made love to me slowly and sweetly in the bedroom, his green eyes gazing into mine as we joined together perfectly.

I'm unfamiliar with the new feelings zipping through my mind and body. All of my thoughts and senses are consumed with Drew, drawn to him in ways I never knew possible. I'm twenty-four years old and I've never even had a boyfriend, let alone fallen in love. Is that what this is?

Love?

The ringing of my phone snaps me from my contemplation. I hurriedly dig through my bag for it. My service has been sketchy at the villa so I'm surprised that it works in town. Sitting at a little bistro table outside the stores, I look at the screen. It's Jeff Talley from the Warren Hotel. Interesting.

"Hello Mr. Talley, how are you?" I chirp, my good mood evident as I rummage for a pen and pad ready to take notes for my client.

"Sydney! I'm great, just great. Call me Jeff!"

He's unusually happy today.

"That's wonderful, Jeff. Is everything okay with the remodel? I'll be there Tuesday to start the install as we discussed and—"

"No, no Sydney, everything's going great with the club. I didn't call because of a problem." Jeff chuckles and continues, "I called because I have news to share with you."

"News for me? Alright, Jeff, let's have it. You sound pretty excited."

And he does sound excited. If I could see him I'd bet that he was jumping from one foot to the other. The man seems positively giddy. I roll my eyes as I imagine the uptight executive in his expensive suits with his perfectly styled gray hair and trimmed beard dancing around his office.

"As you know, the Warren Hotel chain has a certain reputation in the industry for catering to young jet-setters. The launch of Verve is going to set the tone for our nightclub redesigns worldwide. There's been quite a lot of buzz over the opening of Verve, and due to extraordinary interest, we've scheduled our opening night party."

My heart jumps into my throat. How can he schedule the party when I haven't even laid eyes on the pieces to be sure everything is correct? Mistakes can happen, furniture might not fit to spec, glassware can ship late…the possibilities are endless!

"But… I haven't even been on site yet to see that everything will go as planned." My mouth suddenly feels as if it's filled with sawdust. "I appreciate the confidence in me and my firm, but things can happen—"

Jeff cuts me off again, too excited to let me finish. "I have every faith in you Sydney. In fact, it's because of you that Verve has attracted so much fascination."

What is he talking about?

"I'm not sure I understand—"

"No worries, Sydney. I just called to give you the date of the opening. It's March 8th. I have a meeting to rush off to. We can talk more when I see you on Tuesday. Bye Sydney."

My phone goes dead. I stare at it in my hand. That was bizarre. No one schedules a huge opening night bash until the designer has a chance to inventory the pieces and at the very least, lay eyes on how the space is coming out. And March 8th is less than six weeks away.

Great. My vacation lasts until tomorrow morning and I refuse to let this consume my last day here. I press my lips together and toss the phone back into my bag. I still have to find something for Drew, so I force smile on my face and head for another shop.

Drew is on the phone when Philippe drops me back off at the villa. As I cross the great room, I can see him sitting shirtless on a lounger by the pool. The wall of windows is open and I don't want to accidentally eavesdrop again, so I head into the master bedroom with my bags and stuff them in my suitcase.

I'm pretty excited by the purchase I made for Drew. It's more of a joke than a serious gift, but I hope he'll like the black baseball cap I found in a little tourist trap that says *Good Luck Charm* across the front in green script. I know it will never replace that nasty Red Sox hat of his, but like they say it's the thought that counts, right?

CHAPTER 10

"Sydney, we're almost home." Drew is softly running his hands through my hair. I open my eyes and realize that at some point must have fallen asleep on the plane. I'm curled up on the couch with my head in Drew's lap.

"You need to put your seatbelt on, babe."

I reach over to buckle the belt but Drew beats me to it, wrapping it seductively around my waist and grinning as it snaps shut. "Thanks."

"You're welcome," he whispers and gives me a quick kiss.

"I can't believe I fell asleep. How long was I out?"

"I can believe it. We didn't exactly do a lot of sleeping these past few days."

My mouth drops open from his statement. I close it quickly and try to look affronted, but start giggling when he winks at me and makes a hilarious face, wagging his eyebrows in a fake suggestive way.

"You've been out about an hour."

Gail breezes into the cabin and makes sure we're prepared for landing. She lets us know we'll be on the ground in about fifteen minutes then leaves just as quickly as she came.

Looking out the windows, I see New York City below us twinkling in the fading light as the sun sets. I love my home. Usually it's massive size gives me comfort. Today it doesn't.

I'm sad to be leaving my isolation with Drew. I can be myself with him, with no pressure or worry that he's using me. He's fascinating and beautiful and makes me feel so safe and protected that my anxieties melt away when we're together. I feel actual physical pain when I think about him leaving for California in a few days.

Drew promised that he'll be back several times during the six weeks he's gone, but I'm already so used to having him around that my life will seem empty. He filled a void that I didn't even acknowledge I had until I met him.

After living my life alone for so long, I can't just go back to how it was before Drew. Now that I know what I've been missing all this time, the loss of having him near me every day is crushing. I'm afraid that my anxiety will come rushing back with a vengeance without him there to comfort me. Once again, since my usual method is denial, I am at a total loss as to how to cope.

The pilots land the jet smoothly. I'm so distracted with my impending freak out, I barely feel the wheels make contact.

Gail comes in to hold out our coats for us. "You're not in the Caribbean anymore. The captain says it's only forty degrees out."

Drew thanks her as I slip into my jacket, pulling it up to hide my face so Drew won't see the panic that my wayward thoughts have induced. He's so good at reading my expressions, there's no way he'll miss it if I can't control my negative feelings.

The cabin door opens and Bruce comes up the stairs and grabs our luggage, bringing a gust of cold wind with him.

Oddly enough, the pilots are standing by the door with huge grins on their faces as we exit the plane. We stop and shake their hands. "Mr. Forrester, it's a pleasure to meet you." They both clasp Drew's hand so enthusiastically and fawn all over him that I wonder if they're trying to suck up for a tip.

I see Drew give them a dark, threatening look out of the corner of my eye and the gushing stops immediately. Bizarre.

"Miss." They shake my hand with more restraint. I thank them for their hard work.

Drew insists on bringing my suitcase upstairs when he drops me off at my place. I don't bother to argue. He won't listen. I've gotten used to his need to take care of me all of the time. To me, it's charming and sweet even though I know Leah would find it horribly oppressive.

It was dark in the car, so Drew couldn't see the panic in my eyes on the ride from the airport. Now that we're inside, it's brightly lit and I have nowhere to hide. I look directly ahead at the elevator doors so he can't get a good read on me.

Drew stares pointedly as if his eyes were burning holes into my cheek, but I ignore him. I know he's getting either pissed off or worried. All I want is to get away without suffering the third degree about my feelings. I don't want Drew to think I'm some clingy girl who gets all possessive and weepy after two weeks of dating.

The elevator doors open and I rush off, shoving my key into the lock. Once I get it open, I dart inside and wait for Drew to set my bags down so I can hustle him back out.

Drew being Drew, not willing to leave without an explanation, walks down the hallway to bring my things to the bedroom. He's refusing to acknowledge my need to be alone.

Drew leaves me no choice but to follow. I'm surprised to find him sitting on one of the chairs I have next to the windows, his gorgeous face lined with stress. I sink down into the other chair, waiting for him to say something. He stays silent, watching me, reading my face with those intelligent eyes. Looking through me, digging out my secrets.

After what seems like an eternity, Drew finally speaks. "Sydney, are you upset with me?" He leans forward and places his elbows on his knees, catching my gaze and holding it, willing me to open up. I see a hint of fear on his face, hiding behind the confident facade.

"No, Drew. I'm not upset with you. I've had the best weekend. Really, it was wonderful. I'm…I guess I'm just nervous about work tomorrow."

I press my hands against my thighs, hoping he'll accept my terrible lie. I can't let him know that I'm falling apart at the thought of being away from him. That would cause my anxiety to come roaring back.

Drew leans back and sighs, pausing before speaking again. "One of these days Sydney, I'll get you to trust me. If you say it's not me, then I believe you. But I don't like leaving here knowing that you're upset and won't tell me why."

Drew reaches over and takes my hands, clutching them in his. He brings our joined hands to his mouth, kissing my knuckles, holding them in place.

After a moment, Drew drops my hands and stands up. I follow suit, looking up at him through wet eyes, blinking back the tears.

"Drew. I'm sorry I can't tell you. Please, be patient with me. I have…issues that I'm dealing with. And I *am* dealing with them. I don't want you to feel like any of it is your fault. You're perfect. This weekend was perfect."

I stand on my toes and tentatively kiss him. He's unsure what's happening between us so he stands there like a statue. When I slip out my tongue and run it over his lips, he puts his arms around me and kisses me desperately, as if he's afraid this will be the last time.

When we stop to catch our breath Drew leans down and presses his forehead to mine. "Whatever it is Sydney, it can't be that bad. It won't change how I feel about you. And hopefully, if you ever find out something about me that is unexpected or surprising, you won't let it change your feelings for me. Call me tomorrow after you leave work."

He looks at me and instead of that open, sincere look I love, his face is a mask of sadness. It cuts me deep to know that I've taken away his confidence. I look away, ashamed by my actions.

"Yes, I'll call you tomorrow." He kisses me one last time and leaves.

I wait to hear the door to my loft close before I change my clothes and get into bed, crying myself to sleep at my screwed-up inability to be a normal human being.

****

"Hey, you need to leave." I pull on my pants and turn to face the naked man on my couch. "Seriously."

"What's the hurry, gorgeous?" The handsome guy in my living room is still not moving to put his clothes on and leave my loft. "I'm getting ready for round two." He smiles, his good-looking frat boy face fully confident that he's staying. He probably never gets told no.

"I told you when we met at the club earlier that you couldn't stay. I meant it. Start getting dressed." I throw his shirt at him and he looks stunned.

"You really want me to leave?" He sits up and puts on his shirt, covering his ripped twenty-one year old body. It's a shame to cover up those abs, but I need him to go— now.

"Yes. We had sex, that's it. I don't do anything else. No overnights, no conversations, no relationships. No strings, remember? And I have class early in the morning. Finals week." I finish getting the rest of my clothes on and stand rigid, waiting for him to follow suit.

He shrugs. "Okay, whatever you want, beautiful." That's the good thing about young guys in New York. They don't expect much and don't care if you treat them like crap. He ties his boots and stands up.

"Hey, isn't that Evangeline Allen?" He's standing in front of my fireplace, looking at my photos.

Fear races up my spine, sending chills over my skin.

I never bring guys here. We always go to their place so I can leave immediately after. But he lives in Brooklyn and I live two blocks from Optic, the club where I met… whoever this guy is. His place was geographically undesirable. He was hot, we had a couple of drinks, and I wanted some sort of human contact. Stupid mistake.

I snatch the photo from his hand, placing it facedown on the mantle. "No, it's not. That's my friend, she's a celebrity impersonator. Please leave." I put my hands on my hips and stare him down.

"What did you say your name was again?" He leans forward, narrowing his eyes.

"I didn't, now go." I open the front door to my loft and wait.

"Whatever, thanks for the awesome fuck, gorgeous." He turns and walks out as I slam the door behind him.

Just damn.

****

I tap my foot as I wait in the third floor conference room of the Warren Hotel. Jeff Talley was supposed to be here thirty minutes ago and I'm becoming impatient. I woke up this morning with a blinding headache after dredging up yet another repressed memory I wish I could forget. Two cups of coffee and four ibuprofen have done nothing to stop the pounding in my temples.

That's what I get for crying half the night. I chastise myself as I rub my forehead. Not only did I wake with a migraine, but the crying erased any positive effects that the last few days of relaxation have had. The dark circles under my eyes are back with a vengeance.

I check my phone again for some sort of contact from the Warren, no texts, no emails, no missed calls. Jeff hasn't even sent anyone to make sure I'm not dead.

I wonder if I should just go up to the 53rd floor to Verve. Was I supposed to meet him there and not in this conference room? I double check the last email from him. Nope, it clearly says 9am in conference room three. I'm about to get up and start pacing the room when the door opens and Jeff comes striding into the room throwing apologies at me as he shakes my hand.

"Sydney, I'm so sorry. I couldn't get off the phone. It was a very important call from the U.K. In fact, it has to do with the nightclub opening so I needed to take it so I could discuss it with you afterwards. Would you like anything?"

"I would love some water, Jeff. Thank you." I straighten my clothes and wait for him to begin.

Jeff presses a button on the phone and asks for a pitcher of ice water and a carafe of coffee to be brought to us. He looks at me with a satisfied grin on his face. He's normally very polished and professional, but today he's chatting with me like we're best friends.

"Sydney, when we last spoke I gave you the date for the launch party for Verve."

"Yes, Jeff, but—"

Too excited to wait, he interrupts. "Well, I mentioned that the buzz around the opening has increased which is why we wanted to go ahead and schedule the party even though construction isn't finished yet."

Isn't finished? It's barely even started. I haven't even set foot in the space in almost a month!

Jeff holds up a finger to keep me from jumping in. "We have *you* to thank for that attention, Sydney." Leaning forward he lowers his voice and speaks as if we're sharing a secret. "Why didn't you ever mention that you were friends with Adam Reynolds?"

Oh my god, the article!

I've been so wrapped up in Drew that I completely forgot about Adam's *GQ* interview.

Freaking out, I hold up my hand to stop him. "Jeff, I know it seemed as though Adam and I are great friends, but really, he's just an acquaintance."

Jeff smirks like he doesn't believe me and my mouth drops open.

His secretary breezes in with the drinks and leaves. Jeff pours me an ice water and I gulp it down gratefully, my mouth parched.

"You don't have to be modest that you have famous friends, Sydney. Adam Reynolds had his PR guy call the other day and ask for an invite to the party. I just hung up with him to finalize the details.

He specifically wants to go as *your* date. I think he was disappointed that you didn't invite him personally." Jeff sits back smugly, convinced that he caught me lying about my relationship with Adam.

"Th-th-that's ridiculous!" I jump to my feet to stand behind my chair. "I'm not going to the launch party with Adam!" I use my fingers to count out my reasons. "First, I don't attend functions that include lots of celebrities and paparazzi, ever. Second, I'm seeing someone and he certainly isn't Adam Reynolds! And third, I don't have Adam's phone number so how would I even invite him?"

I'm trying to contain my shock and anger. This scenario is exactly what I was talking about when I told Leah I would never date someone like Adam. Jeff is trying to use me to get publicity for his club via Adam. And, if I showed up with him, I'd have to walk the red carpet and do interviews and pose for photos, which I refuse to do. These club openings always have in-house photographers mingling inside, snapping pictures of all of the famous people drinking and dancing and enjoying the new venue. It's everything I've spent years avoiding rolled up into one giant disastrous event.

"Sydney, Adam Reynolds gave us publicity that we could never buy. He's young, attractive, and an A-list celebrity. All he's asking is that you go to the opening of a club that *you're* redesigning, and hang out with him. We can't refuse such a simple request. Just from him hinting that he wants to come to the party in that interview we have had an explosion of requests for invites from Hollywood's hottest and most popular young stars.

"This launch is going to rival some of the openings of the biggest clubs in Las Vegas, and let me tell you, parties like that don't happen here in New York. This is going to be epic, and we have Adam Reynolds to thank for that."

I hang my pounding head and rub my temples. I can't think. I definitely can't come to terms with a middle-aged suit like Jeff Talley using the word *epic*. I feel dizzy and nauseous. This cannot be happening.

"Jeff, I can't do what you're asking. I have a boyfriend, how would he feel if I went on a date with another man?"

I don't even know if Drew is my boyfriend. Especially after my behavior last night.

"Bring him! It's all appearances, Sydney. You don't actually have to date Adam Reynolds. Why you don't want to, I can't figure out. According to my wife he's the *hottest thing she's ever laid eyes on*." He makes little quote signs with his fingers to emphasize his wife's words. "You just have to hang out with him."

I'm not getting through to this guy. I have to be professional. I can't wreck the firm's reputation by slapping this arrogant ass.

I cross my arms over my chest. "I won't walk the red carpet, Jeff. And I won't allow any photos of me to be published."

Jeff looks dumbfounded. "Wait— you don't want to go to a club opening with superstar Adam Reynolds. You don't want your picture taken with him. You don't want to be interviewed with him for TV….Are you actually a living breathing female?" He chuckles.

"You're probably the only woman in New York that would turn that down." Jeff rubs his buffed and manicured fingers across his neatly bearded chin. "Okay Sydney, I accept your conditions. The hotel's PR team controls all photos taken inside the club, you don't have to walk the carpet and we won't release any pictures of you or put them on the website. Just show up, make Adam Reynolds happy and I'll be happy and my boss will be happy. You can even bring your boyfriend, deal?" He stretches his arm out across the table.

Defeated, I lift my hand and shake his firmly. "Deal."

With all of the Hollywood party nonsense behind us, we head up to see the club. I'm pleasantly surprised to see that the entire space has been ripped down to the studs, electricians are setting the wiring for the new light fixtures, and a group of men is drilling holes in the subfloor to support the new bar.

More comfortable with this aspect of the job than the part that took place in the conference room, I meet up with the on-site project manager from Allen Deconstruction and we start to take inventory of the shipments. One nagging thought keeps popping up as my day goes on.

What am I supposed to tell Drew about Adam?

I call Drew from the back seat of the Warren Hotel's private car service as the driver maneuvers down Lexington. It'll be a good hour until I get home at this rate and I right now, I really need to relax in a nice hot bath.

"Hey babe." Drew answers with his sexy voice. My mood lifts instantly.

"Hey."

"Are you headed home?"

"Yeah, stuck on Lexington. Traffic is pretty bad."

"Sydney? You sound weird, are you ok?"

Protective Drew is coming out to play. "Ummm, I had a bad day at work, that's all."

Oh, and I have to go on a date with Adam Reynolds, who may or may not want in my pants. You don't mind, right?

"I don't like this. I need to see you. Can I come over?"

He sounds genuinely worried. Do I sound that bad?

I have to tell Drew about the party at some point. Do I tell him now, or do I chicken out and tell him over the phone once he's three-thousand miles away? My need to be physically close to him wins. "Yes please. I'd like to see you."

"I'm at home packing for California. Have your driver swing by and get me and I'll ride to your loft with you."

Bossy Drew taking control. At this point, I don't mind. I'm more than happy to have him carry some of my load right now.

"Okay, I'll see you in thirty to forty-five minutes depending on traffic." I give the driver Drew's address and attempt to relax against the plush leather of the Mercedes.

I text Drew as we pull down his street and he jumps into the car the second it stops in front of his brownstone. I notice he has a small duffel with him and he's wearing his new *Good Luck* hat.

"Wishful thinking, Mr. Forrester?" I nod my head towards his bag and his hat.

"A man can hope, Sydney." He smiles and kisses me. "We can talk later, just relax babe." I inhale his intoxicating scent and burrow under his arm for the short ride to my place.

Drew drops his bag by the door and hugs me close. "Are you hungry? I can order something."

"Actually, I just want to soak in the tub. Care to join me?"

He ducks his head and I can feel him smile against my ear. "A guy would have to be crazy to turn down an invitation like that."

You may not like me as much after I tell you about the meeting I had today.

I start the water for the giant jetted tub. Opening a drawer by the sink, I grab an elastic and knot my hair up into a messy bun on my head.

Drew comes into the bathroom with two bottles of beer and sets them on the far side of the tub.

"Let me undress you." He deftly takes my suit jacket, slides it down my shoulders, and sets it neatly on the countertop. Untucking the ivory silk camisole underneath, Drew pulls it over my head and places it with the jacket.

"Turn around."

I comply and he lowers the zipper on my skirt, letting it drop to the floor. I kick it aside as he guides me to sit on the edge of the tub. Drew puts his hands on my left thigh, sliding them down to my foot. Kneeling, he unbuckles my heel and removes it while staring directly into my eyes. Letting the shoe clatter to the tile floor, Drew reaches up and repeats his movements with my other shoe.

Still kneeling between my legs Drew takes off his hat, wraps his arms around my waist and plants soft, hot kisses on my belly. My skin tingles from his wet mouth and his hot breath skating over my body.

Drew stands up and begins to shed his own clothes. In one swift motion he grabs the back collar of his T-shirt and pulls it over his head, dropping it behind him. He kicks off his Chucks and removes his jeans, boxer briefs and socks all at once.

He's so beautiful that I can't breathe. I take in his gorgeous face, his seductive mouth, his flawlessly toned physique and can't decide which part is my favorite. I lower my gaze over his six-pack abs and that 'v' his obliques make at his waist and continue down to his waiting erection and shiver in anticipation.

"Stand up, Sydney."

I do as he says without thinking. Drew steps forward, reaching around to unclasp my bra, his hardness pressing against my stomach. He slides the lace down my arms and lets it fall. Hooking his fingers into my panties, he quickly disposes of those as well.

Drew holds out a hand. I take it and sink into the hot water. He carefully slips in behind me and hands me one of the cold bottles.

"Mmmmm, the water feels so good." I take a sip of my beer and lean against Drew, letting the jets ease my tense muscles.

"*You* feel so good." Drew rubs my shoulders. I groan and drop my head back against his chest. "Talk now or later?"

"Later," I sigh. He takes my beer and puts it on the edge of the tub. Squirting a large amount of body wash into his hands he starts washing me. Large, strong fingers glide over my arms and up to my collarbone, then down to knead my breasts. I luxuriate in the sensation, pushing back on the rock hard length that rests against my back.

Drew's hands freeze for a second on my breasts, then continue to massage me. He rolls my sensitive nipples in his fingers, quickly bringing them to hard peaks under the bubbles of the jets.

He gets more soap and thoroughly washes my back, snaking his arms around me when he reaches my waist. Drew drops one hand between my legs to draw circles on the sensitized bundle of nerves, sending a jolt of electricity through me. Gasping, I gyrate against his body, unable to control myself as the scorching heat quickly builds inside.

I'm desperate to feel close to Drew before I tell him about the party. What if this is the last time he wants to see me?

My mind wiped clear of everything except getting him inside me, I lift slightly and push back. Reaching underwater between my legs, I grasp his cock tightly and direct the swollen head into my slick opening, sliding down as far as I can.

"Ahhhh, Sydney." His warm breath caresses the back of my neck.

I start gliding up and down, sitting on his lap with my back to his front. The full sensation consumes me, the stretching, the rub of his cock on that perfect spot deep inside.

Drew moans. "Fuck, I can't believe how good you feel." He starts biting my neck and shoulder roughly, uncharacteristically out of control. Both of us are, our needs are primal and animalistic in this moment.

My breath comes faster. "Yes Drew, oh God."

I slam down on his lap and frantically raise and lower my hips, needing it fast and hard. He wraps his big hands around my waist and jerks me down as he slams his hips up into me faster, over and over, bringing us both to the precipice.

I grip the sides of the tub to ground myself, my knuckles turning white from the pressure. Drew continues meeting each of my downward movements with an upward thrust. The noises we're both making fill the bathroom. They're uninhibited, hedonistic—the sound of two people fulfilling a need.

We come together, water sloshing all around as we both fall over the edge into a blissful spiral of pleasure. Drew grunts loudly as I grip him tight, convulsing around his cock as he comes.

Blissed out, I lean back on his heaving chest, breathing rapidly as heavenly tingling sensations fire through every nerve ending in my body. Shifting slightly, I peek over my shoulder to see Drew's head thrown back against the edge of the tub, his eyes closed as he recovers.

Smiling, I turn around, straddling his lap so I can look at his beautiful face. He lifts his head and brings his hands to my cheeks, pressing soft kisses to my lips.

Filled with contentment, I wrap my arms around Drew's neck and kiss him back tenderly. This is the closest I've ever felt to another person and I never want this moment to end.

But it does end, and as usual, it ends spectacularly. The alarmed look on Drew's face says it all.

"Sydney, I didn't wear a condom."

That was the sound of my final nerve snapping.

Drew is freaking out, pacing in front of my fireplace like a caged animal.

"I can't believe I was so careless! I've never done that, never!" He's shouting as he walks back and forth, stressing me out more with each step.

"Drew, calm down." I'm curled up on the couch, watching the confident, controlled man I know unravel.

His head snaps up. "Calm? Sydney, I'm pissed at myself. I can't believe I did that to you. I'm so sorry. I just don't even know what to say."

Whoa! He's mad because he thinks he wronged me somehow not because he didn't use a condom?

"Wait, I was just as caught up in the moment as you were, Drew. It's not your fault. You didn't do anything to me that I didn't want you to do."

He drops to the floor in front of me and puts his head in my lap. "I'm so sorry, Sydney. It's the first time I've ever forgotten to use protection." *Oh my god, he really is blaming himself!* "I'm supposed to take care of you and look out for you, not put you into more stressful situations for my own selfish pleasure."

"I'm sure it's fine. Look at me." I run my fingers through his damp hair. This man I care about so much, lifts his head and I capture his gaze with mine. "It's okay, Drew. I exercise so much I don't even get regular periods, so I'm sure nothing will happen. You don't owe me an apology. I won't allow you to feel like this. It was consensual, and we're both adults, we'll deal with whatever happens."

I wish I felt as confident as I sound.

I'm not lying about my cycles. Whenever I stress out and over exercise, I lose weight and my period all but stops. It's pretty common in female athletes.

Drew relents, but I can see that it's not by choice. "Alright, but I don't like this at all Syd. But I trust you. If you say you're not upset, then I'll let it go, for now. Just understand that I won't let anything or anyone hurt you, not even me."

So he's upset because he thinks he hurt me and he's blaming himself? God he's such a caveman sometimes. A hot, sexy, bossy, well-meaning caveman. I don't want to discuss this anymore.

"Let's order some food."

I kiss him on the lips to end the conversation. I can't even wrap my brain around the possibility of being pregnant, so I do what I always do— deny, deny, deny and pretend it isn't happening.

We eat in relative silence, containers of Thai food scattered on the kitchen counter. We awkwardly discuss unimportant stuff. Drew tells me how he wasn't sure what to pack for California, since it would be unlikely that he'd get out much. I mention how the club is already stripped to the studs and work is progressing nicely.

Drew lets me know that he passed along my sincere thanks to Chad, his friend who owns the St. Bart's villa and the sailboat, *Magic Hour.* Apparently Chad was more than happy to have someone using both, since he hardly ever gets to go there himself. Drew describes Chad, and how he's known him for more than ten years.

When he tells me how long he's known his friend, I jolt at a realization. "Drew, how old are you?" I'm embarrassed that I never bothered to ask him.

He smiles, probably ecstatic that I'm asking him such a personal question. "Twenty-nine. I'll be thirty on March 8th."

My breath leaves my lungs as if I were punched. It's the same day as the launch party for Verve. Of course, Drew being Drew, observant as usual, sees my face fall.

"What, am I too old for you or something?" He looks nervous, like I'm going to dump him because of his age.

"No, that's not it," I reassure him, "it just reminded me that I have something to ask you, related to my work." I wipe my mouth with a napkin and stand up from the table. "Are you done? Let's go into the living room."

Without a word, Drew stands up, puts his dish in the sink, and follows me down the hall.

We curl up on one of the couches and I decide how to begin. Clearing my throat nervously, I pray I can get through this.

"Okay, you know that I'm redesigning the new nightclub at the Warren." He nods. "Well, when one of these clubs launches, they have a huge party. They invite people who will bring the most exposure to their business, like…you know…celebrities and what not."

I feel Drew tense up next to me. He sits up a little straighter and waits. I clear my throat again. This is harder than I thought.

"Ummmm, the bigwigs that run the Warren Hotel chain saw the interview in *GQ*."

Drew's head whips around and he glares at me, his eyes narrowed. "The interview with Adam Reynolds?"

My eyes widen at his hostility. The hairs on my arms stand on end. "Yes, that interview. Adam mentioned Verve and that he knew about it through me, and called the Warren to get an invite."

"Okay. Is that why you were so unhappy when you left work? You already knew about the article."

I cannot for the life of me read his expression. His face has morphed from irate to totally neutral in the span of a few seconds. It reminds me of the mask that my mom would wear to hide something from either me or the public.

"Well, ummmm…"

The hot burn of embarrassment floods my face. I'm mortified to have to ask the guy I'm seeing to be okay with me going on a fake date with a hot celebrity, and I'm more than humiliated to have to admit that the hot celebrity wants to go on a date with me more than I want to go with him.

"So, the, uhhh, mention in the article set off a firestorm of A-listers calling to get on the invite list. Management at the Warren feel it's only right to repay Adam by granting his request to be at the party…and…ummm, his request to be my date." I cringe, my hands balled at my sides as I wait for his reaction.

Drew sits there, processing what I've said.

"And you said yes?" I glance down to see his fists clench in his lap.

And there's the problem, right there. I said yes.

I didn't actually say yes, not really, but somehow that's how it ended up and that's what's going to matter to Drew.

"No. Not at first."

"Not at first," he repeats slowly, still showing no emotion whatsoever except for those tight fists.

"Drew, I said no! I told them I was seeing someone, and I wouldn't go on a date with anyone but you."

His careful composure breaks and his eyes grow large and I swear— they almost bulge right out of his head.

"You mentioned *me*?"

"Well, I told them I was seeing someone. I didn't mention *you* specifically." It's my turn to narrow my eyes. "Why, do I embarrass you or something?" Now *I'm* getting pissed, but I can't wear the neutral mask like Drew can. No doubt he can see how angry I'm becoming.

"Of course you don't embarrass me Sydney!" Drew bellows. "You're the one who doesn't want to talk about anything, or know anything! I'm just shocked as hell that you would even tell anyone that I exist!"

My breath leaves my body as though I've been sucker punched. "That's how you think I feel about you? That I want to pretend you don't exist?" I choke out breathlessly.

"No, that's not what I meant, shit. I don't know Sydney, I'm still stuck on the whole date with Adam Reynolds bomb you dropped on me. I. Don't. Share."

He runs his hands through his thick hair, tugging on it until it sticks out every which way on his head. He looks even hotter when he's pissed and bewildered and that kind of makes me angrier.

"It's not a date!" I yell, standing up and facing him. "I told them I would only go if I could bring you and that Adam understood that we," I motion between the two of us, "would hang out with him and talk to him but that's it!"

Drew gets to his feet and towers in front of me, a good seven inches taller, roaring back. "But you can't stand celebrities, Sydney! That's what you said! There will be cameras and famous people everywhere! I just don't get it!"

I refuse to back down, he doesn't understand that this isn't my decision. "I don't like any of that shit, Drew! I hate it! It fucking ruined my life, okay? I'm still screwed up from it. I don't want to go to the party at all, but when the boss of a multi-billion dollar hotel chain tells you to show up at his party, you have to show up! I have no choice!"

I fall back on the couch and fold my arms across my chest, a sullen scowl on my face.

Drew sighs, hanging his head. He takes a deep breath and sits down next to me. I can feel him trying to rein in the anger that is radiating off of his body.

"I'm sorry Sydney. I won't ask you about your past, since you aren't ready to tell me, but I won't know if I can go with you until I get to California and see how my schedule is and how the project is going. I understand that you have to be there, but I'm not going to pretend to like it. In fact, it makes me want to punch Adam Reynolds right in the head."

He's jealous! I can't believe it. Drew is a thousand times hotter than Adam and he's jealous of him.

"I'm sorry. I'm sorry for dumping this on you. It's on your birthday and it's probably not your idea of a good time." I feel so horrible for doing this to Drew, possibly ruining our fledgling relationship. "If you can't make it, I get it."

He leans in and touches his nose to mine. "I'll try my best to be there, if for no other reason than to keep him from hitting on my girl. Let's go to bed."

I don't deserve him. Most men wouldn't be this understanding.

Now I have to wait and see how this plays out. It has everything I hate and fear rolled into one awful night—celebrities, paparazzi, attention on me, and a pissed off Drew looking to punch an international rock star.

What could go wrong?

CHAPTER II

I have the Warren Hotel's driver drop me off at Leah's place after work the next day. Drew got a call and had to leave a day earlier than he thought, so he's somewhere over the Rocky Mountains right now. I hate that we fought right before he left. Even though we made up, it was still a little tense this morning.

Stupid Jeff Talley and Adam Reynolds!

I haven't seen Leah since I got back from the Caribbean with Drew, and she's dying for details. Plus, she had a couple more dates with the Media Mogul's son and wants to dish. So we're having a *girl's night in*, complete with margaritas and veggie pizza from our favorite place.

I'm not telling her about the bathtub incident yet. She'll lose her mind and never let up on me about my stupidity. Instead, I decide to fake drinking the alcohol to avoid explaining.

"Sydney!" Leah's squeal just about shatters my eardrums as she lets me into her East Village condo.

"Hey Leah." I return her enthusiastic hug and throw my bag and coat on the big gray chair near the door. I kick my shoes off and throw myself down on her enormous white couch curling my legs up underneath my body.

"Grab a drink. I put one on the end table for you. Pizza will be here soon." Leah comes out from the kitchen with her margarita and sits on other end of the couch. She's adorable all dressed down with no makeup, in her yoga pants and oversized T-shirt with her dad's latest Broadway play emblazed on the front. Her blonde hair is swept up into a messy bun.

"So…" she looks at me expectantly. "Drew? Caribbean? Got anything to say about it?"

She giggles and scoops up her margarita, popping the lime off of the edge of the glass and sucking on it playfully, then dropping it into her drink and downing a big gulp. At least one of us gets to act like they're in their early twenties.

I smile coyly and pretend to sip my margarita. "We had fun."

Leah straightens up, her smile vanishing. "Oh no, no way. I want details. *Lots* of them. You can't stay single all this time, leave my coffee shop with one of the most gorgeous men I've ever seen, go away with him to a super-exclusive island in the Caribbean, and just tell me you had fun!" Her blonde hair is bobbing around on the top of her head as she chastises me.

Laughing at her mini tantrum, I tell Leah about the private jet, the extravagant villa on the hill, the sailboat with a full crew. I show her pictures that I took of the garden at the house, on the sailboat, of Drew asleep by the pool. *He has no idea I took that one.*

Leah just about loses it whenever I show her a photo of Drew shirtless. She squeals again when I give her the black coral bracelet I bought for her on St. Bart's.

"Syd, it looks like it was so fantastic. I'm really, really happy for you. So, what's the plan from here?"

Obviously, my best friend wants to know where my relationship is going. She's been waiting to have this conversation since we were sixteen and I should have had my first boyfriend. If I were normal—which I'm clearly not.

"Well, you know he's working out of town for the next six weeks or so," she nods and makes a hurry up and continue motion with her hand. "So, he's going to fly back several times while he's gone and I guess we're not seeing other people." I shrug. "That's it."

The pizza chooses that moment to arrive and I manage to escape any more of her questioning. We move to the dining table that's up against the wall of windows. I look out at the city as we eat and urge Leah to tell me all about her dates with Carter.

He sounds pretty nice. He took her to an impossible to get into restaurant last week, and she cooked dinner for him this past weekend. He actually calls when he says he will and isn't a complete bastard like most of Leah's previous boyfriends. So in my eyes, that makes him great.

I mention that she could double-date with me and Drew when he gets back from California. She chokes on her pizza and deflects the question. Okaaay, no double dates then.

When we're done eating, we move back to the living room and I tell her about the launch party and how Drew reacted when I told him about Adam.

She's speechless, which is a rare event as far as Leah is concerned. Her mouth is hanging open in shock. After a few moments recovery time, she's able to communicate.

"Wait, let me get this right. You have two smoking hot guys that want you, one of whom is willing to fight the other for you, and that's a problem? I think I might hate you right now." She pouts, throwing a napkin at me as she says that last part.

I swat it away and laugh. "This is serious, Leah!" I know I sound whiney, but it's not as cool or fun as she's trying to make it sound. "I don't know what to do. Drew said he'll try to make it to the party, but—"

"Wait!" She throws up her hands. "Drew said he'd take you to the opening of Verve?"

"He said he'd try to come back for it, but he's not sure yet. It's the same night as his 30ᵗʰ birthday, actually."

"Whoa. I can't believe he said he'd go with you." She takes a big gulp of her margarita, shaking her head in disbelief.

"What the heck, Leah? Why wouldn't he want to go with me? Am I embarrassing or something?" I give her my best glare.

This is exactly what Drew said, am I that bad?

"Oh, no. Sydney, it's not like that. God, you're gorgeous and sweet and you know it. I just, I guess—" she's fumbling to explain, just like Drew was.

What the heck?

"I mean, I'm surprised he'd want to go if you're supposed to pretend to be with Adam, that's all."

I huff. "Well, Drew knows that I want him there. Actually, he knows I don't want to go at all, but since I have to go I want him to be my date. He's pretty pissed off at Adam too, which I admit is kind of hot."

I smile at the thought of my MMA-loving boyfriend challenging some big shot celebrity to a fight over me. His words replay in my head, *"I don't share,"* and I grin, shivering in response to his territorial statement.

"What about all of the cameras and celebrities and stuff, Syd? How are you going to avoid all of that? These club openings are crazy and get a lot of press."

I explain the agreement that I made with Jeff to skip the red carpet and that they won't release or print any photos of me. Leah seems to think it over for minute before responding. "Then… it sounds great. I mean, I'd love to go if Drew can't make it. I'll be your date, Sydney!"

"It's a deal!" We laugh and for a few hours, I'm able to forget that Drew is gone, that I might be pregnant, that my boss is an ass, and manage to simply be happy.

Over the next week, I spend most of my time at the hotel, making sure that the club comes together in time for the launch.

I try to squeeze in a long run every day, even when I'm so exhausted that all I want to do is go straight home to bed. The running helps with my anxiety, and it keeps me from missing Drew.

I don't want to sit around my empty loft, feeling sorry for myself. Keeping busy is my best defense against doing irrational things and giving myself the chance to overthink or dredge up the past.

Today, everything at work went smoothly for once. No messed up orders or problems with deliveries or wiring. I even left while it was still light outside, a rarity in New York in the winter.

Since I ran early this morning before going to the hotel, I have an entire evening free. Drew is supposed to Skype me around 11p.m. because of the time difference.

I decide it's time for an errand that's been hanging over me since he left a little over a week ago. I have the car service drop me off at the Duane Reade a few blocks my building and walk out ten minutes later with my purchase in a plastic sac.

I walk home as fast as I can without flat out sprinting down the sidewalk in my heels. I'm too nervous to even enjoy the unseasonably warm early February afternoon, my stomach doing summersaults until I feel sick.

When Richard smiles as he opens the door for me, I rush past head straight upstairs. Dropping my stuff on the hardwood floors of my foyer, I snatch up the plastic bag and beeline for my room. The brightly colored box that I dump on my bed is an almost comical contrast to the dark, paralyzing fear that grips me.

You can do this. You need to do this. Give Drew good news tonight.

I exhale, closing my eyes for a second. Not allowing myself time to change my mind, my shaking hands rip open the package and I run into the bathroom.

Seconds later, I march out empty-handed and stand in front of my bedroom windows. Leaning my forehead against the cool glass, I watch the tiny cars and taxis weave through traffic in their endless rat race around the city.

Okay. *Breathe Sydney.* I swallow down my panic and walk back into the bathroom, dragging my feet as though I'm headed to my own execution. Trembling, I peek over at the pregnancy test balanced precariously on the edge of my sink.

Not Pregnant

Thank God.

Feeling as if a giant weight has been lifted from my shoulders, I smile and toss the stick into the trash. One anxiety down, only about fifty-seven more to go.

Happier than I've been since Drew left, I change into a tank top and yoga capris and heat up my dinner. I haven't eaten much this week from all of the stress, so it'll be good to have a full meal in my stomach.

I head into the office to answer some emails while I scarf down my food, and then call my mom.

Her phone rings so many times that I'm about to give up when she answers. "Hello dear," she says sweetly. "Sorry I couldn't find my phone, you know how it is," she giggles.

I frown at the phone. Why is my mom giggling?

"It's okay mom. What did you think of the pics I forwarded to you earlier?"

"Sydney, it's coming along perfectly. You're doing excellent work for your first project of this size."

Until now, I've only designed private homes and small offices. She knows that this nightclub is a huge step for me in my career. Mom assigned it to me instead of one of the more experienced designers to give me a chance to prove my talent.

"Thanks, it means a lot to me that you like it. You should see the space, mom, it's extraordinary. Next time you're in the city we can go there for a drink. We could sit in the VIP room or something."

No way would Evangeline Allen be seen out in the common area where people could approach her or take photos.

"Oh honey, I fully intend to see your biggest success up close and personal. I'm sure it will be even better than I imagine." She laughs and I can practically feel her smile coming through the phone. "I have to go Sydney. Keep sending me photos, and don't forget I'm sending Bridget Williams from the office over to the hotel tomorrow to help out with the workload."

"I won't forget, talk to you later." I disconnect and put the phone on the desk. Mom sounded particularly happy tonight, with an almost mischievous attitude, as though she knows something that I don't.

I hate that.

I'm glad she's doing well, though. I don't see her for the six months she spends in Belize each year, something she's done since I finished high school. I find myself missing her immensely, and it's only the first week of February.

I sigh. She'll be back in a few months. She doesn't know about Drew yet. I don't want to mention him until we're in a more permanent situation. No sense getting her all excited if things don't go well. The thought of things not going well with Drew makes my dinner sit in my stomach like a rock.

I still have an hour until Drew is supposed to Skype. I boot up my MacBook and log in so I'll be online when he calls. The photo that Captain Frederick took of me and Drew on the deck of the *Magic Hour* is my home screen wallpaper.

I notice how fantastically happy we both look. Drew has his arm around my shoulders, clutching me to his side and staring down at me, gorgeous as usual and smiling like a fool. I'm laughing and staring right back at him adoringly and grinning just as big as my hair whips around in the wind. We look like a real couple, something I've never been a part of before.

Right now, I'm riding an emotional high. The negative pregnancy test, the good day at work, my mom's praise for Verve—I shouldn't ruin my evening this way, but I have some time to kill, I've already had a glass of wine, and I'm not an anxiety-ridden ball of nerves for once, so this is as good of a time as any.

Quickly, so I can't come to my senses and stop myself, I bring up Google on the browser and type.

Reid Tannen Barbara Walters

Enter

The results fill the screen. I scroll down before I can change my mind.

Reid Tannen admits in Walters interview that he screwed up with Evangeline Allen

abcnews.com- The notoriously tight-lipped Tannen sat down with Barbara Walters for her "Most Fascinating Person of the Year" interview and shed a little bit of light on his relationship with his ex-wife, Evangeline Allen, and his estranged daughter Sydney. What small bits of information he...

Reid Tannen named Barbara Walters' "Most Fascinating Person of the Year" for 2013

AP- Hollywood A-lister Reid Tannen was revealed to be one of Walters' interviews for her annual "Most Fascinating People of the Year" special that airs next week. Along with Tannen, philanthropist Chelsea Baker and music phenomenon Archer Ford are on the list for......

<u>Walters dishes on behind the scenes with Reid Tannen</u>

abcnews- Barbara Walters discusses her upcoming special featuring movie heartthrob Reid Tannen. Tannen, one of Hollywood's highest paid leading men has had a tumultuous private life…

I hover the cursor over the interview link, and pause just a moment before clicking. I'm directed to a page on the ABC News website where I can either read a transcript of the interview, or watch the video.

Thank god. I have no idea if I can watch the video without freaking out, so I scroll down to read the transcript. Surprised at how well I'm holding myself together so far, I start skimming.

BW: So Reid, you've had quite a year. A hit movie, Oscar buzz for your performance as Vincent Van Gogh and quite a few photos of you shirtless in Hawaii filming Anti-Hero with co-star Maxon Sundry. How's life treating you?
RT: (Laughs) Yes, it's been an interesting year for me Barbara. Very busy, but great.

I move past the intro and search for my mom's name or my name. About halfway down, I find it. I suck in a breath as a sharp pain pierces my heart.

I have to do this. It's therapy, right? Or maybe I'll see something that messes me up even more.

No, I need to see it so I can heal. That's what four different therapists have told me—accept your dad for who he is and you can move on and rebuild your life.

BW: It's been over a decade since you were caught on video in a compromising position with a woman who wasn't your wife. Is it true that you haven't seen Evangeline Allen or your daughter, Sydney, since that incident?

RT: Barbara, first, let me say that what happened with my wife, and how everything played out in front of the media was entirely my fault. That moment remains the biggest regret of my life. I wronged my wife, but we were adults, we could move past it. Hurting Sydney, I'll never forgive myself for that. I'd do anything to get that time back. I miss her terribly.

BW: So you haven't spoken to your daughter in twelve years?

RT: No, I haven't. But I have to say, that if the paparazzi would have just left her alone, I would still have her in my life. Eva and I wanted to protect Sydney from all of the crap. I mean, a paparazzo almost killed my daughter when I was driving her to a tennis lesson. A lunatic broke into our house to get to her! Her mother wanted her as far removed from the people who were following everything we did as she could get her. I take responsibility for my actions, but the tabloids need to take responsibility for what they did and continue to do to innocent children like Sydney.

I agreed to let Sydney go to keep her from the intense media scrutiny. It was never going to stop, Barbara. She was always going to be hounded by reporters. It wasn't fair for her to live that way, and it was clearly dangerous. When the story about me came out, we knew it was only going to get worse for her, so her mother took her out of the situation. It was the only thing that we could figure out to make it right for her. Eva gave up her career and I gave up my daughter. It killed me, but was worth it if she's happy today.

BW: I remember that incident with the paparazzi smashing up your car.

RT: They smashed up my daughter; I could have cared less about the car.

BW: I actually applauded you for protecting her.

RT: Thanks, Barbara. (chuckling) I got into a lot of trouble for that.

BW: But what about Sydney needing her father? Was it right for you both to make that decision for her?

RT: We made the best decision we felt we could under the circumstances we were faced with. Was it what I wanted or her mother wanted for that matter? No. But video or no video, the paparazzi were slowly eroding any kind of life Sydney was having in California. It was something we never anticipated. Like I said, if she's happy, then I'm content to live with the decision we made.

I stop reading and close the browser, feeling a little dizzy, as if all of the blood in my body has left my head and traveled to my sputtering heart. I'm trying to let this sink in. My mom and dad decided *together* to take me away from California. Dad didn't abandon me. He let me go because he loves me and wanted me safe.

I choke back tears as I process this information. Strangely, I'm not freaking out as much as I expected. Yes, I'm freaking out, but not in the extreme panic attack, press my head on the window, run ten miles classic Sydney kind of freak out. I'm either getting better at handling extreme stress, or reading my dad's words is helping to push me toward accepting what happened.

I need to discuss this with my mom, but it's something I don't want to do over the phone. That means waiting two or three months, which will feel like forever, but I've waited twelve years so I guess I can wait a little longer.

My Skype starts ringing, keeping me from thinking about my dad right now. Like everything else in my life that I can't face, I shove it into the back of my mind for later.

I click the button to answer and Drew's handsome face fills my computer screen.

"Hey beautiful, I miss you."

God he's so sweet. "I miss you too," I whisper.

Drew bolts upright at the sight of me. "Sydney? What's wrong? Why are you so thin?"

I forgot how unbelievably perceptive he is. I shouldn't have looked up my dad right before talking to Drew on a webcam where he can see my facial expressions. Especially since this is our first Skype in a few days, so my weight loss is likely more noticeable.

"Are you okay? Do I need to send over a doctor?"

My sweet, caring boyfriend is freaking out over my freak out. "Nothing's wrong, Drew. I'm just tired that's all."

He huffs in exasperation, pulling his hair though his fingers.

"One day, Sydney, you'll let me in so I can protect you from whatever it is that haunts you. Between the shit you're going through personally, the extra workload, and that ass Adam Reynolds trying to steal you from me—I should have just cancelled this project and stayed with you!"

Drew can't control my situation from California and it's getting to him. But honestly, he wouldn't be able to control it from here either. His face is flushed with anger and he keeps raking his hands through his hair, which is a sign of his frustration.

I feel bad that he knows I'm hiding something from him. It's in his nature to take care of me, protect me, and when I won't let him he gets upset. I look down at my hands, ashamed that I won't allow Drew to help.

"I know, I'm sorry. And Adam Reynolds isn't trying to steal me, Drew." Changing subjects, I get more animated. "Oh! I forgot, I have news."

He perks up at the sudden uptick in my mood. "What news?" Drew still looks nervous, as though afraid he isn't going to like whatever I say.

"Not pregnant." I smile as I say it.

One less thing to put stress on our relationship. The distance between us is hard enough without Drew blaming himself for the whole no condom incident. He finally stopped apologizing when I wouldn't Skype with him the past three days. I had to put my foot down to get him to let it go.

I'm a grown woman and it was just as much my fault as his. I don't even think he was upset because I could've been pregnant. It's more like Drew feels that a pregnancy would have sent me over the edge and it's his job to shelter me from anything that could upset me or cause pain.

I expect him to be more excited at the news. Instead he gives me a small smile.

"That's great, Syd. Really great. The timing would have been awful."

Timing? There is no good time to get knocked up by a guy you've been dating less than a month.

"I know. It's a relief to have a little less to worry about."

"If you're less stressed, then it's great, Sydney. So, I also have news." He smirks and I see a hint of dimple.

Playful Drew is back, thank god. I really need him right now.

Drew reaches down and taps on his phone. After a moment, he puts the phone up to the camera so it fills my screen. I see an email with the confirmation for his flight to New York dated for tomorrow.

"You're coming home tomorrow?" I screech and practically jump from my chair. He laughs and lowers his phone so I can see his face. He's so excited, and I love that I can make him happy. His sexy dimple makes an appearance. I think about all of the ways I'll get to have his naked body on top of me. I'm so thrilled. Tomorrow, I get to lick that dimple.

"Yep. I got Chad to rearrange a few things with the schedule so I can see my girl!" I melt when I hear him call me *his girl*. Could I be any luckier?

"I cannot wait to have you here. Should I get you from the airport? I can use the hotel car service—"

"No!" He shouts at me. I jerk back in surprise at his tone. He smiles, softening his voice. "I don't want you to have to go all the way to JFK. I have Bruce to drive me. I'll swing by my place to grab a few things then can I stay with you?"

"Of course I want you to stay with me, just call me when you land. You get in at seven, right?"

"Yes, and since I won't be bringing any luggage I can just go straight from the plane to the car. So I'll probably be over around 8 or 8:30, sound good?" We're both grinning like idiots.

"Sounds amazing!" I feel myself relaxing knowing he'll be with me tomorrow.

Even though we speak every day, we never have awkward silences. It sounds so cheesy, but it feels as if I've known him forever. Like Drew is a puzzle piece that I hadn't realized was missing until I found him. Now he fits so perfectly in my life that there would be a Drew-sized hole if I lost him.

Our conversations had been somewhat tense with the possibility of an unintended pregnancy hanging over our heads. Well—I was worried about the pregnancy. Drew was worried about hurting me. Now we just have to get past my freakish secrecy, his need to protect me from everything, and his extreme jealousy over Adam and we'll be great.

I think.

CHAPTER 12

I'm so depressed. Drew left a few hours ago to go back to the airport after spending Thursday, Friday and Saturday night here with me. We acted like a couple of shut-ins, and didn't leave my loft for almost the entire weekend. Drew did go back to his place to change out some clothes and do a few things for work, but otherwise it was heaven, living in our perfect little bubble. Food was delivered when we were hungry so we could spend every possible minute wrapped around each other in bed, and on the couch, and the floor, and against the windows.

Leah stopped by Saturday morning with croissants and coffee. It was nice to see my best friend get along so well with my boyfriend. She told us a hilarious story about a couple that made a huge scene at an upscale restaurant she was at with Carter. Food was thrown, wine was dumped, and someone stomped out in the middle of dinner. We all got a kick out of that one.

I got the impression that Leah didn't seem to think dating Drew was such a great idea at first, but after spending time with him she's become a member of Team Sydney & Drew.

Drew was miserable this afternoon as he packed his overnight bag to head out. In all honesty, he was in a pretty bad mood all morning as well. I asked if I did anything to upset him, but he assured me that we were fine. It felt like he wanted to get something off of his chest but whenever he looked as if he were about to say something, he pressed his lips together and stayed silent.

Of course, I'm too much of a screwed up mess to beg him to tell me. And why should he open up? I won't open up to him, and it hurts him deeply, I can tell. I'm sure he thinks I would shut down if he tried to have a serious discussion with me.

If it were about the *date* with Adam. I would probably scream.

About an hour after Drew left I made the decision to tell him about my parents. He deserves the truth, not an anxious, nerve-wracked girlfriend with a bunch of secrets.

Plus, I think I'm in love with him.

I'm jumping in head first without making sure the pool has water in it. Drew will catch me, right?

The next week threatens to break me. Both Drew and I have been so consumed by work that we haven't had time to speak more than a few minutes here and there. I had to work through the entire weekend to fix a problem with the carpet in the main lounge area in order to stay on schedule for the launch party, which is now only three weeks away.

Drew is always working late too. With the three hour time difference and my long hours, I'm asleep by the time he's able to call. Drew still hasn't been able to confirm if he can come with me to the Warren, so I put Leah on notice that she may end up being my date.

Well, my other date if you don't count Adam, which I definitely don't.

Another week flies by before I know it. It's been two weeks since I've seen Drew, and it's becoming unbearable. He was supposed to fly out this past weekend, but because of hotel management insisting on scheduling a massive party an unreasonably short amount of time after beginning the remodel, I had to spend all weekend at the site again. I only leave the hotel to eat and sleep, and I barely do either of those these days. I didn't even get my run in for three days straight.

Without Drew and without exercise, I haven't been able to sleep much at all. I'm feeling run down and tired from the grueling schedule and lack of sleep. Of course, I'm at work late again when Jeff Talley walks into the club where I'm supervising the setup of the piece behind the main bar.

"Hello, Jeff."

I manage to keep my tone polite, barely. I'm still pissed at him for causing problems in my relationship with Drew by making me go with Adam to the launch.

"Hello, Sydney."

Jeff strides across the room to where I'm leaning on the bar watching the crew assemble the taps and the shelves that will hold all of the liquor bottles. "The shelves are coming together nicely."

The shelves are a focal design element. Instead of long parallel lines, there are hundreds of different sizes of boxes that line the entire wall. Each one is under lit by a small bulb hidden in the wood of the box. Liquor bottles of various sizes and shapes will fit perfectly into each specific cubby and glow when the room is dark. I hired a local artist to design it and it's going to be stunning once it's complete.

I glance over at Jeff as he watches the workers carefully. Some people would think Jeff is handsome, and technically, I guess he is. He's not as tall as Drew, but somewhere just under six feet. Slender and fit for a man in his late forties or early fifties, he keeps everything about himself neat and orderly, from his short graying hair and beard to his expensive custom suits.

Jeff has rubbed me the wrong way with pushing the club opening and the whole Adam thing. That seriously detracts from his looks for me.

"Yes, I agree. It's going to be the main element for the room. Jeff, as long as you're here, I was hoping we could go over the details for the night of the party." I pack up my files and my MacBook, both of which are currently spread along a three-foot length of the highly polished brown ebony and chrome bar.

"Okay, let's go to my office." He gestures that I should go first toward the elevators and follows behind me.

We enter Jeff's large office on the third floor business wing of the hotel. I sit in one of the leather chairs across from his desk and dump my bag on the floor.

Jeff takes his seat behind his obscenely huge modern desk, a gorgeous view of Central Park laid out behind him. He moves a few folders stacked on his worktop off to the side and leans back so he can put one of his ankles up on his knee.

"So Sydney, the project is going well. Everything looks flawless, I expect that you believe Verve will be ready for the launch as planned in two weeks? I've personally spoken to many very important celebrities that will be here for our grand opening. So far Delilah Fornier, Benson Hale and Kiera Radcliff have all confirmed."

Ugh! I cringe.

Jeff has that arrogant attitude people get when they think rubbing shoulders with famous people makes them special or better. Who knew that Jeff Talley was a name-dropping suck-up? He's already acting different, and he hasn't even met these people yet. I hate it.

"Yes, the club should be ready by the 8th. And I'm sorry; I have no idea who any of those people are." I try hard not to look disgusted, but I think Jeff can tell I'm unimpressed. I can't keep my feelings from showing on my face.

He leans over the desk. "You know Adam Reynolds, the man whose band currently holds the record for the highest-grossing concert tour of all time, and you don't know who three of the top actors in Hollywood are? Pfffttt, I don't believe that for a second. You can't tell me you don't want to go on this date with him." He waves me off with a hand gesture that pretty much says *no way*.

Now I'm beyond irritated. Who the heck is he to tell me who I want to date? "Well Jeff, Believe it. I don't care about celebrities and I don't go to the movies. I'm also involved with someone whom

I care about very much, so no, I don't want to date Adam. That's not why I wanted to discuss the party though." I speak through clenched teeth, trying hard not to scream in his face that he should date Adam since he loves him so much.

"What can I do for you then, Sydney? Obviously, you won't be asking me for an introduction to any famous people that night." He laughs like he's the funniest guy on earth. I can't believe I used to think this guy was nice.

"I just wanted to make sure that our deal still stands and neither photos of me, nor my name will be printed or released to anyone for any use. Also, I still don't know if I'm bringing my boyfriend Drew, or my friend Leah, so I'd like to have them both put on the VIP list just in case."

I look Jeff directly in the eyes so he knows I'm dead serious. He doesn't think that anyone would ask to *not* be associated with fame, since he thinks so highly of it himself.

Jeff taps his index finger against his lips, trying to decide if I truly don't want any public link to the opening and the guests or if I'm just feigning modesty. After a tense moment, he finally concedes.

"Okay, no problem Sydney. Just give my secretary Donna your friends' names and she'll make sure they're on the list. Bring them both if you want. She's handling the entire guest list anyway."

"Thank you, Jeff." I stand up to leave, and he hops to his feet to see me out. I guess even self-absorbed jerks can be gentlemen every once in a while. "I'm heading home now, but I'll be here at seven again tomorrow."

He shakes my hand and says goodbye. "Oh and Sydney, I wanted to tell you, the CEO and CFO of the Warren Hotel worldwide chain will be here next week for a final walk through before the opening. I'll let you know which day as soon as they narrow it down for me. So be prepared to be available for any questions that they might have."

I turn and look back at him from the hallway and give him my biggest, fakest smile. "Sure thing Jeff. Looking forward to it."

I head down the hall and scribble Drew Forrester and Leah Quinn-Slade on a piece of hotel stationary with a note stating they are to be added to the VIP list as my guests and leave it on his secretary's desk. *She* gets to leave at a reasonable hour, so of course, she's already gone.

CHAPTER 13

I feel awful after leaving Verve again today. I think I've been working way too hard. The long hours, coupled with my run, that I had to shorten to just three miles since I'm not at one-hundred percent, have made me an exhausted wreck.

Maybe I need another vacation. My mind wanders and I think about St. Bart's and Drew and now I'm not only tired, but sexually frustrated and lonely too.

There's only ten days left until the opening night, and Drew still hasn't been able to find out if his schedule will allow him to attend the party with me. I can't even tell if he *wants* to go or not. If anything, he only wants to be there so he can keep Adam in line. I smile.

Such a Caveman.

Leah is looking for a dress. She doesn't want to leave it hanging until the last minute just because Drew can't give me an answer.

There's also only ten days left until Drew's 30th birthday and I'm fairly certain that he won't be spending it with me. That makes me sad. I don't even have a California address to send him a gift.

I'm going to tell him about my parents the next time I see him. Unfortunately, I had to cancel the last weekend visit he was supposed to make and his schedule doesn't allow any more cross country trips until his project is complete in two and a half weeks.

The only exception is if he can persuade Chad to let him come to the party.

Drew isn't begging for an invite to the party or asking me what celebrities will be there, so I'm satisfied he won't speed dial TMZ when I tell him about my famous parents. And his only response to finding out Adam Reynolds, international superstar, would be attending was to describe his desire to connect his fist to Adam's face.

Too tired and weak to do anything else tonight, I shed my clothes and drop into my bed. I can't even keep my eyes open long enough to wait for Drew to Skype.

****

"Isn't this great Heartbreaker?" Daddy grins as he drives his little black sports car through the winding roads of the Hollywood Hills.

"It's amazing Daddy. I love this car, it's so cool."

I run my hands over the soft black and red leather seat of the Bugatti and look at my dad. He's so awesome. I'm glad he's been home for a few weeks this summer. I get to spend time with him and today he's taking me to my tennis lesson. Usually my mom's driver and my bodyguard take me. It's summer break and I don't start school for two months and Daddy is filming a movie here in L.A. so I get to see him almost every day.

"So Heartbreaker, how's your backhand coming? Your teacher said it's—God damn parasites!" My dad is suddenly yelling and cursing at the rearview mirror. "Hold tight Sydney." He starts driving faster, the engine roaring as he weaves in and out of cars.

"Daddy, you're scaring me!" I clutch the smooth red dashboard and close my eyes.

"Heartbreaker, sit back and make sure your seatbelt is tight, baby."

Daddy is speaking gently but his jaw is clenched tight and his teeth are bared. It's the face he makes when he's really really mad. Like the time I threw one of his scripts into the pool. He turns a corner on a green light so fast I swear I feel my heart leap out of my chest.

"This isn't the way to my tennis lesson, Daddy. Why are you driving like this?"

"Shhhh, Sydney, it's okay."

My dad reaches over and gives my hand a squeeze. I feel better just from Daddy telling me it's okay, but I'm still scared. I look out my window to see where we are and scream. A tan car is next to us and a man with an enormous telephoto lens is hanging out of the front seat snapping pictures and driving at the same time.

"Daddy! Daddy! There's a man, he's scaring me!"

Tears are running down my face and I'm near hysterical at this point. I don't think I've ever been this afraid in my life, not even when a strange woman tried to snatch me at my elementary school several years ago.

"God damn son of a bitch!"

My dad downshifts and tries to get past the tan car but there's another car in front of us. He slams on the brakes just in time.

The tan car, however, doesn't notice the stopped traffic and swerves into us to avoid rear-ending a pickup truck. The front of the car hits us on my door. My head snaps to the side and then whips back to smash against the window. I feel a sharp pain in my arm and we're spinning. The world goes by so fast I can't see anything. All I can do is hold on and scream.

I'm going to die.

Our car comes to a stop when it jumps a curb and crashes into a utility pole that lines the street. I can hear someone screaming and they won't stop. Daddy is grabbing me, unsnapping my seatbelt and clutching me to his chest.

"Hush baby, it's okay. We're okay. Shhhh." That's when I realize that the screaming is coming from me.

I burst into tears and my entire body shudders violently. Daddy is still holding me and kissing the top of my head when I hear the clicking. We both look up at the same time and see the photographer that crashed into us standing outside our car on Daddy's side, taking pictures.

"Sit here Sydney, don't get out of the car, and don't move."

He looks into my eyes and I nod that I understand. My arm hurts, bad. Then I notice that my dad has a big gash over his eyebrow and blood is running down his cheek. He glances down at my arm and a dark shadow crosses his face.

I want to tell Daddy that he's bleeding, but he's gone.

My dad jumps out of the car and directly onto the man with the big camera. He punches the guy in the face, rips the camera from his neck and shoves him to the ground. Daddy slams the camera ferociously into the ground. I wince when it shatters into a thousand pieces across the pavement. He turns back to the man and jumps on him, pinning him down, slamming his fists into him over and over again, yelling and swearing the entire time.

Two men come running up and grab Daddy's arms, pulling him off of the photographer. I see blood all over my Daddy and I cry even harder. Half of his face is covered in cuts and sticky red liquid, and his right hand is swollen and bloody.

Daddy is yelling so loud a huge crowd has gathered to watch. People are taking pictures with their own cameras. I don't even look at the man on the ground. I don't care if he's okay or not, I just want my dad.

By the time a police car pulls up the crowd has swelled around the car. People are trying to get to me, but my door won't open. Strangers are talking to me through the broken window. Scared, I start screaming for Daddy.

Two officers get out of their car and they put handcuffs on my dad. Daddy didn't do anything wrong! I know Daddy said to stay put, but I can't let them take him. Who will bring me home? They can't just leave me here alone with strangers.

"Don't touch my Daddy!" I yell, but when I try to open the car door, my arm won't work and it hurts so badly I think I might pass out. I feel something wet and sticky running down my head behind my ear, and I see black spots in front of my eyes. My last thought is that I love my Daddy so much, then the awful scene around me disappears as I slip away.

****

Waking up just as dawn arrives, my stomach churns violently and I feel terrible. I reach over and rub the faint scar on the underside of my right arm. A permanent reminder of that horrifying day.

I'm covered in sweat and shivering. From the memory? Or am I sick? I briefly wonder if I should go to the doctor. This is exactly how I felt when I had the flu last year.

I should have gotten the flu shot that I swore I would get when I was suffering with a 104 fever and was stuck in my bed for four days last winter. Great, I cannot be sick right now. I try to go back to sleep, but it's no use, I can't shake the horrific memory.

It was my dad's worst nightmare. He couldn't protect me from his life and it almost killed us both. Dad had a terrible concussion and I had a fractured skull and a shattered arm. I throw back the covers and force myself from bed. There's a text from Leah time stamped from last night after I had fallen asleep.

Leah —Come to café in am, broke up with Carter

What a self-absorbed friend I am. I feel awful that I've been too fixated on my own problems to even call Leah over the last week. I get dressed and head out as quickly as I can manage without throwing up. Hopefully I'm not contagious. I don't want Leah to be sick too.

Richard hails a cab for me since I'm too weak to walk. Minutes later, I get out at the Village Coffee Bar. I order my Kona and a croissant from Ben, even though the thought of eating makes my stomach feel even worse.

Leah is flat-out shocked when she sees me. "You look terrible, Syd. You really need to get more sleep and stop working so hard."

"Leah, don't worry about me, how are you? What happened with Carter? Do you have a minute to chat?" I nod toward my usual table. She looks better than I would after a break up. Well—I've never had a break up since I've never dated anyone until now, so how do I know what I'd look like after a break up?

"Give me five and I'll be there."

She watches me warily from the corner of her eye as I take a seat in the corner. A small bite of gingerbread croissant does wonders for my nausea. Waiting to make sure my tender stomach doesn't reject the food, I slowly sip my coffee as Leah joins me at the small table.

"What the heck Syd? This job is going to kill you! I haven't seen you in weeks. You're obviously working yourself to death!"

She's furious. I knew I looked bad, but not as bad as she's making it sound.

"Don't be so dramatic, Leah. I think I may be coming down with something. Either that or you're right. I've been pulling twelve hour days for I don't even know how long. Running every morning, not eating all day, I haven't exactly been the picture of health."

"Well, you should take a day off if you're sick. You'll just make it worse by putting in another long day." My friend is so good to me.

"What happened with Carter?" I dodge her question and try my best to look concerned and not queasy.

"Eh, it's not a big deal. We've only been dating a few weeks. He's great, don't get me wrong, but he's boring as hell." She looks at me and smiles. "He's all work and work related events. I got sick of competing with his daddy issues and Carter needing to prove that he can take over the empire." She makes a grossed out face, twisting her pretty features into a grimace.

I laugh. "That's terrible! You can't compete with the Media Mogul, that's for sure."

"I don't want to compete with anyone, Syd. I want someone who puts me as high up on their list of priorities as they are on mine. I'm not going to be number three after a job and dad." Leah looks me up and down again. "So, are you going to take a day off or what?"

"I didn't come here to have you beat me up for my failure to take care of myself. I came here thinking you were wallowing in misery, but you seem like you could care less about Carter."

"Stop avoiding my question, Sydney." Leah's glaring at me with her intense blue eyes.

"You know I have to finish the club for the opening night. There's not time to take a day off." I pause, waiting for her to stop scowling before continuing, "I have something to tell you too. I wanted to let you know. The next time I see Drew I'm going to tell him who I am." I watch carefully so I can gauge her reaction.

Leah doesn't disappoint. Her eyes widen in shock. "You're going to tell him? Are you sure? You haven't known him all that long, Syd. I think it's great, but I want you to one-hundred percent feel good about doing this."

I let out a huge breath. "I know I haven't known him long, but this secret is driving a wedge between us, and I trust him Leah. I think I'm in love with him. Is that crazy?" Tears burn behind my eyes. I blink to force them back.

"What! Are you sure?" Her big blue eyes pop and her mouth falls open. I can't tell if she's happy or horrified.

"Yes, I'm sure." And I am, without a shadow of a doubt, I'm in love with Drew.

"Then I'm happy for you," she says simply, but cautiously. "You guys have a lot to talk about then. When will you see him?"

"If he comes to the party, then I'll see him that weekend. If he can't make it, then about two weeks from now." I shrug. I have no idea when he'll be back.

"If he's going to the party with you, then you need to have that talk beforehand," she says firmly.

"Why, what does it matter?"

Leah looks flustered. "Oh, ummm, well, you don't want to, you know, have that hanging over you all night." She stumbles over her words, but she makes a good point.

"Yeah, it probably would make him happy to finally know my secrets. It drives him nuts that I hide so much and it's his birthday so I thought it would make a good gift. Plus, he'll be way less jealous of Adam if he knows why I would never date him."

"Uhhh, sure, yeah, good idea Syd. Well, he probably has his own secrets too." She says it so matter of fact. It's easy to believe that I'm not that strange after all.

Maybe there's hope for me yet.

Three days later, I feel a whole lot better. I find that if I eat a little in the morning with my coffee, that my stomach stops roiling almost immediately. I'm still more tired than usual, but interestingly, I must be sleeping deep because I haven't had any more flashbacks to my childhood.

I keep my run short this morning, not wanting to push myself too hard, but I'm afraid that if I give up my exercise then the bug I caught might take over.

I drag my sorry butt to the club, and spend the morning directing the placement of tables and booths for the main room. Happy to snag one of the long leather booths to sit on, I rest my weary body.

I'm about to take a big sip from my water bottle when I hear my phone ringing from my bag. Frustrated, my hand finds it just as it stops chirping. Missed call from Drew. I dial him back as I get up to find some privacy.

"Hey sexy girl, how are you? Feeling any better? Need me to call that Jeff guy and tell him what an ass he is?"

The other night I told Drew how I hadn't been feeling well, and that it was a good thing he hadn't been in town or he would have caught whatever I have. Drew blames it on the stress from Jeff forcing the launch party to happen a month sooner than it should. He's probably right, but I don't tell him that. He'd kill Jeff if he knew I felt that way.

"Yeah, still tired, but much better. My stomach seems to have calmed some. And no, please don't call Jeff. I need him mad at me like I need a hole in my head. I miss you so much." My heart speeds up and my skin grows warm just from talking to him.

"I miss you too baby." His seductive voice makes me ache to have him inside me. Even this sickness hasn't dampened my sex drive, and it's been much too long since I've seen Drew. "So, I finally got Chad to give me a definite for next Saturday."

"And—" Silence. "Drew! Stop keeping me waiting." I can't believe I'm actually stomping my foot in frustration like a petulant teenager.

"And he managed to alter the schedule so I'll be finished out here by that morning. I have a flight that lands in New York at 5p.m. on the 8th and I won't have to come back out here the following week either." I can hear his excitement mixed with apprehension through the phone.

"So that's great! Right? The party doesn't start until nine, the celebrities don't start arriving until ten or so. You should be here in plenty of time to make it. I'm just sorry that you'll be on a plane on your birthday.

"Actually, I'm hoping we could meet at your place and go together. I wanted to see you before we go."

Good, I can tell him about my parents in private at the same time.

"That's perfect. Just so you know, Leah made me promise that I wouldn't revoke her invite just because you're coming, so we'll see her there. She doesn't want to ride with us. She'll feel too much like a third-wheel. Her words, not mine." I laugh.

He chuckles. "Yes, that's fine. As long as we're alone before we go to the party."

I hope Drew isn't thinking we're going to have time to fool around. Not that I won't want to, but I'm sure I'll already have my hair and makeup done, and I need time to talk to him without him distracting me with his sinful body and skilled hands.

"We will be, don't worry. I'm so excited, Drew. You being there is going to make this potentially awful night so much better, so long as you don't actually throat punch Adam."

"I can't make any promises about that, Sydney. He needs to keep his hands and disgusting thoughts to himself. I just hope you're glad that I'm there with you at the party." He sounds sad.

Why wouldn't I want him there?

"Sydney! We need you over here!" The booming voice of my foreman, Greg, is echoing across the entire club. I see Bethany Williams, an assistant from the firm, gesturing for me to come over.

"Drew, I'm sorry, I have to go. They're calling for me. Thank you so much for agreeing to go with me. Tell Chad thanks too."

"I will baby, you're welcome. I'll talk to you tomorrow. I have a late night of work today."

"Okay, bye." I end the call and stuff my phone in my pocket, a huge smile on my face. Finally, things are getting a little less gloom and doom.

I don't know how I found time to leave the club, but here I am on the 4th floor of Bergdorf's, shopping for dresses with Leah again. This time, I told her I wouldn't go unless she agreed to use a personal shopper because I refuse to stomp all over the store to find dresses for the opening of Verve.

The shopper put several dresses in our sizes in a room for us to try on. I insisted on us sharing a fitting room, otherwise Leah would try to sneak out and roam the department for dresses on her own.

"Syd, this party is going to be the biggest club opening in over a decade. Several entertainment magazines plus the Post and the Times said so." Leah unzips another dress and puts it back on a hanger. "Apparently it's the hottest party in town if you can get on the list, which is next to impossible."

"Leah!" I shoot daggers at her. "Stop telling me this stuff! You know I don't want to hear anything printed about any of that. All you're doing is making me more nervous."

"Okay, okay!" She tries on a black lace Dolce & Gabbana mini-dress and I zip it up for her. "So you know, Adam has done several more interviews and he mentions the club every time. He has the hots for you, girl."

"Jesus, Leah! I asked you to stop! And he doesn't have the hots for me. He never even suggested that he was interested in me that way. Not once. All he's doing is bringing very unwelcome attention to me with all of these interviews."

"Okay, sorry! He doesn't know your last name so chill out. It's not like anyone's going to figure out who you are."

"Leah, you and I both know that the press is nothing if not persistent and could find out who I was in a heartbeat if they had even just a teeny tiny bit of information."

"Yeah, I know." She twirls in front of me in the D&G. "Well? What do you think?"

"Wow! That's the one. It's perfect."

Leah is so gorgeous in the dress that the celebrities will pale in comparison.

"I need to be hot so I can find a new man, Syd."

I shake my head. Leah's always on the lookout for a new guy. I hope she chooses better this time.

"Every guy there will be worshipping at your feet if you wear that, Leah."

And they will. I mean, in just her regular jeans and T-shirt, she has dozens of admirers at the café. They come in every day under the guise of wanting a coffee, then they either ask her out or sit around and stare at her. She always says no to their requests for a date. Apparently it's bad business to date customers.

I fall in love with a black and white belted A-line. The fluted hemline shows off my toned legs and the back dips down to my tailbone. It's the sexiest little dress I've ever worn.

We let the shopper bring us dozens of shoes to wear with our dresses. Leah tells me that comfort is not a priority for Saturday, so I somehow end up with silver 4" sandals with a thick silver chain for an ankle strap. Leah goes all out and ends up with a 5" black calfskin sandal, with gold metal leaves that wrap around the top of her foot and ankle.

She tried on so many I was about to stab her with a stiletto. I have so much other stuff to do besides shoe shopping that I nearly cry with relief when she picks out the Zanottis. When Leah suggests accessory shopping, I give her a look so venomous that she shrinks back in fear.

We get in the car with only our shoes in tow. The dresses will be tailored and sent to our homes in two days.

"Do you think Drew knows how to dress for one of these things? Should I call him and let him know—" I stop when I notice that Leah is giving me an incredulous look. "What? Why are you looking at me like that?"

She rolls her eyes. "Sydney, I think he knows *exactly* how to dress for the party. That's one thing I'm sure you don't have to worry about."

Her dry tone makes me feel kind of stupid, but I'm not sure why.

"Yeah, he has money and obviously knows people. He's probably been to a lot of high class functions, rubbing elbows with *celebrities*." I make those annoying little air quotes around the word celebrities.

Leah and I laugh our asses off the rest of the way home. Somehow, I get the feeling we are laughing at two totally different things.

CHAPTER 14

Even though last five and a half weeks dragged on endlessly, it seems as though I blinked and it's already March 8th. How did it get here so fast, when every day seemed to never end?

I spend the morning pacing my bedroom which makes me so anxious and edgy that I decide to go for a long run to relax. I've been feeling much better physically, so I want to get back into my exercise routine. I pop in my ear buds, crank up Radiohead and put in some miles.

I devote my run to thinking about the conversation I'm going to have with Drew. A conversation I've never had with anyone. Ever. I'm nervous, but I've also accepted that this has to happen.

Drew is so protective and concerned for my welfare, that I know he'll understand why my parents took me from L.A. and why I avoid everything Hollywood. He would want me safe from that too. That's why I trust him completely with my secret. I've been dreading it for years, but now that the moment is here, I can't wait to tear down the wall that I've kept up for so long and let Drew know all of me.

As I run past the piers, I smile so wide that people who see me can't help but smile back. So this is what it feels like to be in love. You act ridiculously happy out in public and it rubs off on everyone around you. I'm okay with that.

I get back to my loft and take a quick shower. The Warren hired a hairdresser and makeup artist to come over and they're due to be here in an hour. My dress arrived two days ago and it fits perfectly. Drew should be calling me soon to let me know that his flight landed safely. I spoke to him before I went running and he was on his way to the airport. Everything seems to be falling into place.

The concierge rings as I'm grabbing a quick snack to stop my nervous stomach from rumbling. I tell him to let my guests come up.

Minutes later, there's a loud knock on my door.

"Hi! I'm Sasha," says a spunky girl with lots of piercings and pink tips in her hair as she hauls a massive makeup case into my foyer. She jabs a finger back toward the door. "That's Michael."

A tall man with perfectly styled blonde hair walks in behind her. "Hi, you must be Sydney. I'm Michael, hairdresser extraordinaire."

"Hi, Sasha, Michael, come in please." I usher them into my loft and show them where to set up their supplies.

As they're getting ready I realize that it's six o'clock and still no call from Drew. I grab my phone and notice he left a message several hours ago. Probably while I was out running. I hit replay and listen to his seductive voice.

"Hey babe, I'm still at the airport in LA, my flight is delayed. They think we'll be in around 7 or so. Try to wait for me before you leave. I know you have to be there, but I really want to talk to you before we go. Miss you."

I hang up and stand in the hallway freaking out. He has to be here for this. I *need* Drew to keep me sane.

I dial him back. Of course it goes straight to voicemail. He called hours ago. He's sure to be on the plane right now. Crud, I can only hope he gets here in time for me to tell him about my past and go over to Verve together. I guess I can tell him tomorrow morning. I sigh. It's not ideal but it can wait.

I wonder what he wanted to talk about?

Squeezing my eyes shut, I count to ten and head toward my room to let Sasha and Michael work their magic on my too skinny, too tired face and my overgrown, messy head of hair.

By seven, I'm slicked down, styled, made-up, and have slipped into my gorgeous dress. Michael gave my long auburn hair big shiny waves that he pinned to cascade over one shoulder so my exposed back would be a focal point.

Sasha gave me dark smoky eyes highlighted with a tiny bit of silver. My lashes are thick and long and make my blue eyes look huge. She went for subtle blush and lipstick with just a hint of pink so I don't look washed out.

I look young. I look exactly how a normal twenty-four year old going to a nightclub should look. I put in my diamond teardrop earrings and am ready to go.

Checking myself out in the full-length mirror, I suck in a sharp breath. I look almost exactly like my mother did when she was younger; except her hair is a rich, dark brown and I have my dad's fuller lips and blue eyes.

Are people going to see her in me and figure it out? I have to sit in front of my bedroom window to stop panicking. I don't want to ruin my makeup by nervously sweating all night.

It's now 8 p.m. and four more calls to Drew have all gone straight to voicemail, indicating that his phone is still off. I groan in frustration. I have no choice but to leave and hope he meets me there. Jeff wants me to be there no later than 9p.m. so I can greet people as they start to arrive. The tour for the CEO and CFO went off without a hitch, they loved everything they saw.

They're both going to be there tonight. It's important that I'm not late for the big unveiling of their flagship nightclub. Plus, I have to show Adam around personally, one of the sticking points of my deal to be his *date*.

I haven't seen him since I found out that he's super-famous or since Drew told me he thinks Adam's an ass who he wants to pound into a small stain on the sidewalk, so… that won't be awkward or anything.

Richard helps me into the sleek black Mercedes that has been waiting patiently out front for the last hour and a half. "You look gorgeous, Miss Allen. I hope your party is a big success. You deserve it after all of those weekends you put in at work." Richard smiles kindly. I give him a hug and peck on the cheek for his thoughtfulness, careful not to mess up Sasha's meticulous makeup.

"I hope so too, Richard. Thank you so much." I slide across the luxurious gray leather seat and apologize to the driver for my tardiness. He smiles and tells me it's no problem and smoothly pulls the car out into the Saturday night traffic, heading uptown.

We get within a half a block of the Warren and I see the giant crowd that swells out from the sidewalk and onto the busy street.

Traffic out front is snarled up from the throng of people. Spotlights have been installed to light up the front of the hotel brighter than the Vegas strip.

I'm too far away to see individual faces, but I can see a lot of cameras. Reporters with microphones and people waving pens and paper to get autographs of their favorite celebrities when they start arriving are crowding the red carpet, pressing against the ropes that were set up to allow guests to pass safely.

Suppressing the panic that I feel rising up, I instruct my driver to go around to the back entrance of the hotel where the deliveries arrive. I sent Jeff a text when we left my place and he said he would have someone at the service entrance to let me in.

I wait in the car and try Drew one last time. Straight to voicemail, crud. Then I hear his sexy voice and sparks of heat shoot through me in anticipation of seeing him tonight after weeks apart.

"It's Drew, now you say something—"

"Ummm, hey babe, I guess your flight is much later than we thought it would be. I have to go over to the hotel, so when you get in, just head on over. I won't be able to carry my phone since I don't want to lug a purse around all night. So ummm, find me when you get to the club or just ask an employee to get me, you're on the list. Okay, bye."

I tuck my phone back into my bag. I brought my work files in case anyone had any questions about products and I brought business cards. A few other necessities like lipstick and breath mints are tucked into the inner pocket with my wallet. I plan on stowing my messenger bag behind the bar so I can pull it out if I need anything. I can't exactly wear my beat up leather portfolio across my cocktail dress and I certainly can't fit everything I need into a dainty little clutch.

A hyperactive hotel employee with an earpiece and a clipboard eagerly greets me at the back door.

"Hi Miss Allen! I'm Stephanie and I'm going to escort you up to Verve. Isn't this exciting? I can't believe some of the people who are coming tonight!"

She is babbling incessantly about the party, and how awesome it's going to be and how great this celebrity is and that television personality is and she can't wait to meet them. I eventually have to tune her out and throw out a "*Wow*" or "*Uh huh*" whenever there's a pause in conversation, which isn't very often. Mostly, I just follow behind her and try not to break an ankle in my Jimmy Choos as she speed walks through the hotel loading dock.

Security greets us at the elevators and Stephanie starts right in on the burly man. "Hi Alec. This is Sydney Allen, she's on the list. She designed the club, can you believe it?"

Alec rolls his eyes at her enthusiasm and checks his list. I have to squelch a giggle at his reaction to Stephanie. Satisfied, he allows us to get into the private elevator that goes straight to the club level at the top of the hotel. None of the other elevators will go up to the nightclub tonight, and the stairwell doors to the top floor have been locked from the outside so no one can sneak in, but people can still get out if there's an emergency.

Nervous sweat starts to make my palms slippery. I wish Drew were here to calm me down. I clench my hands into fists and stare holes into the digital sign that shows the floor numbers fly by as I'm whisked up to meet all of my fears and anxieties face-to-face. I take a few cleansing breaths and the elevator doors slide open.

Stepping out, I'm greeted by another assistant with an earpiece and a clipboard. My overexcited friend has stayed in the elevator to go back down to the lobby to greet more guests.

"Hi, Miss Allen. Jeff and the other managers are doing a final walkthrough. You should be able to meet up with them at the main bar."

"Thanks." I prepare to face my worst nightmare.

I give myself a little pep talk in my head as I stow my bag behind the bar.

"Sydney my dear! You look gorgeous!" Ben Walton's booming voice grabs my attention from across the room.

I see the gray-haired CFO of the Warren Hotel Group walking toward me confidently. Behind him, Jeff Talley, Natasha Lin and the CEO, Sander Yates are following slowly, chatting with each other and smiling. All of them are impeccably dressed and ready to kiss up to all of the important people that will be here tonight.

"Mr. Walton, aren't you dashing tonight." He leans in and kisses my cheek, then stands back to appreciate my dress. Sixty-two year-old Ben Walton has been running the Warren Hotel Group's financial matters for the last fifteen years. Distinguished and handsome in his dark suit, he's a very charming man. I like him a lot.

"Beautiful dress, Sydney. Just beautiful. The club looks remarkable. The work you have done here is no less than the best I've seen. Sander and I have been talking business. We can discuss it another time with you, but let's just say we hope to see more of your work in Warren Hotels in the future." He moves his hands in a sweeping gesture of the room to indicate how much he loves the space.

"Thank you so much Mr. Walton, your satisfaction means the world to me."

"Let's have a toast. This is a celebration isn't it?" Sander Yates says as he motions to a bartender. Within minutes we are each holding a glass flute of expensive champagne. "I'd like to thank everyone for their hard work making the initial rebranding of the Warren Hotel nightclubs an astounding success. And special thanks to this young lady here for her brilliant designs, and her special connections that have made this the most important party of the year." He winks at me when he says special connections.

I curb the urge to roll my eyes.

"To Verve!" We all join in and clink glasses and sip our champagne.

When an assistant runs over to breathlessly let us know that people are beginning to arrive, I turn my back and down my entire glass in two quick gulps.

I'll take all the courage I can get, liquid or otherwise.

Smoothing my hands down the front of my dress one last time, I paste on my best fake smile. It's time to face my fears.

An hour later, I'm shocked to find myself having an enjoyable time. Leah is here, helping me navigate the who's who since I don't recognize ninety percent of the faces in the club. There are several older actors that I remember from my childhood. I think I've even met some of them way back when, but most of the guests are around my age so I wouldn't have a clue who they are, which keeps my anxiety about celebrities in check.

Leah gets giddy over a few of the young men, which surprises me since she's not one to be easily impressed by fame.

"Oh my God Sydney, that's Ryker Bancroft!" she shrieks in my ear.

"Jesus Leah, don't break my eardrum." I look in the direction she's indicated and see a guy that I don't recognize. "I have no idea who that is."

"Ugh! It's impossible to talk to you about some stuff. He's the star of the *Quantum Stranger Trilogy*, Syd." I give her a blank look and she puts her hands on her hips, glaring at me. "Come on! Haven't you read those books? They're unbelievable! And he plays the hero of the story."

"I'm sorry Leah. I haven't read them." The exasperated look on her face tells me that she's not happy with my severely lacking knowledge of modern pop-culture.

"Well, you're coming with me to meet him. I'm not going by myself." She grabs my arm and drags me behind her, making a beeline for the attractive guy on the other side of the room.

"Hi," Leah says nervously. "I'm Leah and this is my friend Sydney. She designed the club, do you like it?"

I glare at her. Jeez! Way to put the focus on me Leah.

"Hi, I'm Ryker. Nice to meet you ladies." He politely shakes our hands and shoves his unruly hair out of his eyes.

Leah is super nervous around this guy, which is very rare for her. She keeps her excitement toned down, but I can tell she's freaking out. I try hard to push away the memories of people acting like that around my dad, all giddy and foaming at the mouth. It was so uncomfortable. Especially when women would openly proposition him right in front of me.

"Nice work on the design," Ryker says to me. "It's really cool here."

Leah is dead silent, so I nod and smile at him, grateful to have a glass of champagne to keep my hands busy or else I'd tear my hair out or slap Leah for acting like such a fangirl.

As I sip, I take a good look at Ryker. He's cute in a bad boy kind of way, and he's very friendly with us, especially Leah. She finally snaps out of her stupor and the two of them discuss living in New York and other things. I tune them out, too anxious worrying about Drew to pay attention.

"So Sydney," Ryker takes a break from flirting with Leah to turn back to me, pulling me back to the present. "Has anyone ever told you that you look a lot like Evangeline Allen?"

Leah's mouth drops open. In a panic, I mumble out an excuse to go get a refill on my drink. Ryker can think I'm rude for all

I care. I'm not having *that* conversation. Leah can talk to him by herself.

By eleven I'm starting to get very concerned that Drew hasn't shown up. I pray that everything is okay with his flight. He's late. Very, very late. I'm about to go check my phone when I feel a warm, rough hand on my bare shoulder.

"Hello Sydney." I know that accent. Freezing, I twist around to see Adam standing behind me, smiling like the cat that ate the canary.

I have to admit, Adam looks unbelievable tonight. Gone is the hat, winter coat, and scarf that usually hide his gorgeous face and body. His fitted white dress shirt clings wonderfully to his lean torso and his masculine jaw is covered with the appropriate amount of sexy scruff.

"Well, if it isn't Mr. *GQ*?" I tease even though inside I'm completely falling apart, worried about Drew and about Adam's reasons for wanting to be here with me.

I have to convince myself not to go off on Adam for being famous and calling me out in those articles. It's thanks to him that my bosses are ecstatic about tonight and everything is such a huge success.

It's not Adam's fault I have massive issues. I take a deep breath and smile, pretending everything is just great.

Adam grins, looking me up and down appreciatively. He leans in for the cheek kiss that everyone in Hollywood loves so much. "You look a vision tonight, Sydney. I see you went with the leather and chrome bar stools. Great choice, Sweetheart."

He runs his hand across the distressed leather seat and accepts a drink from a circulating hostess, taking a hearty sip. I look to Leah for help and see she's still all wrapped up in Ryker something or other the actor-guy.

Great friend and wingman she turned out to be.

"Yes, thank you. They do look perfect don't they? Good work Mr. Reynolds. You could have a future in interior design if being a world famous singer doesn't work out."

I bat my eyelashes and pretend to be a gushing fan. I sigh, it's time to give Adam the attention he wanted. "Just kidding, would you like a tour?" I smile playfully, nodding in the direction of the main area of the club.

"Why yes I would like that very much. Who wouldn't want a personal tour from the woman behind the vision?" He reaches down and grasps my hand in his. When his fingers wrap around mine I can feel the calluses that certainly come from his guitar playing as he tows me through the crowd.

I'm initially uncomfortable with the personal contact, but Adam has always been nothing but gracious so I allow him to pull me around from one area of the club to another. We stop frequently to speak with people who either know him or want to meet him. Adam introduces me to each one but never lets go of my hand.

It's a little possessive, but without Drew here, Adam will at the very least keep any handsy men away.

It takes forever to get through each space because of Adam's celebrity status. I don't see how my parents dealt with it, strangers constantly interrupting you, making small talk, acting like they know you as they're kissing up. It's nauseating to watch, and very annoying. If this were a real date, I'd be furious that it kept getting disrupted by random fans and other celebrities.

Adam is in the middle of introducing me to a rap star that he collaborated with on his last song, when I see a tall, stunning blonde in a dark blue dress stalking toward us from across the room.

She stops directly next to me and scowls at our intertwined fingers. I drop Adam's hand like I've been burned, blood rushing up to my neck and face. Adam's rap star friend is smarter than me and excuses himself, vanishing before I can blink. I find myself alternately admiring and hating him, wishing I could do the same and disappear.

"Adam," she purrs, "introduce me to your little friend."

My embarrassment turns to anger as she belittles me at my own event. It makes me want to slap her silly.

"Sydney Allen, this is my *ex*-girlfriend, Kiera Radcliff. Kiera, Sydney is the genius who did the interior design for Verve. She's quite the talented one, isn't she?" He looks at me proudly and smiles, putting his hand around my waist in a way too intimate gesture. My eyebrows shoot into my hairline.

What the heck, Reynolds!

Kiera is obviously annoyed to be referred to as his ex and she's clearly jealous that Adam is here with me, even though he isn't here with me on an actual date. She doesn't seem to know that, especially when it seems as though Adam is deliberately trying to make her jealous by holding me close.

"Nice to meet you, Sydney." She doesn't offer to shake hands and there is no way I'm air kissing her.

"You too, Kiera. So, what do you do that earned you a spot on the list tonight?" I don't really care what she does, but diverting her attention away from me would be a good thing. And she seems like the type that loves to talk about herself.

She's as beautiful as any supermodel on the pages of *Sports Illustrated*. Her flawless skin is radiant and her blonde hair hangs in perfect beach worthy waves down her back. She's wearing a dress that I had seen at Bergdorf's but passed on. A double layer, one shoulder, indigo silk gown with an asymmetrical hemline. She had it tailored from its original floor length style to above the knee. It looks stunning on her tan skin whereas it washed me out completely.

Kiera gasps at my question. "Don't you know who I am?" I cringe as if she dragged her nails down a chalkboard. That sentence is one of the things I hate the most about some famous people. They are so used to adoration that their ego can't take it when someone doesn't drop to their knees and worship them.

Adam's fingers dig into my hip as he interrupts. "I don't think Sydney is much into the scene, Kiera." Hmmm, so Adam knows that I didn't recognize him at the café.

Adam is the complete opposite of this woman, modest, shunning attention, and trying to be himself without all of the celebrity garbage. I get the feeling he loved the fact that I treated him normally, just two people hanging out and having coffee.

Why the heck was he ever with her?

Besides her obvious jaw-dropping beauty, because frankly, her personality sucks.

"Well," she huffs, "I'm an actress, obviously. I've been in some of the biggest movies of the last few years." She glares at me with her hawk-like blue eyes. If looks could kill, I'd be dead right now. I want to sarcastically clap my hands for her but I manage to hold it inside.

Yay for you, you're an actress!

"I'm so sorry, Kiera. I don't go to the movies. I'm sure your films are wonderful."

She narrows her gaze, trying to figure out if I'm being sincere. I'm not sure if I am or not, maybe her films are wonderful and maybe they're total crap. What the heck do I know?

"Yes, well, they are." She turns her angry glare on Adam's arm, still wrapped around me, then up to his face. "I didn't realize you had moved on already, Adam. I thought you still loved me."

What? I'm so not getting involved in this.

I try to shuffle out of his arm, but Adam tightens his hold. I see a hint of a smirk on the corner of his mouth. He is totally doing this on purpose!

"Oh, Kiera. We aren't involved like that. I'm just showing Adam around the club because he asked me for a tour. We have coffee every once in a while, that's all."

I finally manage to take a step away from him and she stares at me, irritated that she should even have to stoop to asking about our relationship. Clearly, Kiera didn't get the memo that she and Adam are no longer a couple.

"In fact, I'm waiting on my boyfriend. I haven't seen him yet." I continue babbling like an idiot because of my nerves.

Twisting my head, I look around the packed club, as if I'd actually be able to see Drew in this crowd. Maybe the mention of my being involved with someone will make both of them stop acting so annoying.

Adam looks surprised to hear that I have a boyfriend. Probably because I've never mentioned one, but then, he didn't ask before he forced me into this date.

"Sydney," she says in a syrupy sweet voice. "What's his name, I know almost everyone here." Yuck, she sounds so full of herself.

I'm sure you do know everyone here, honey, probably half of the men intimately. Oops, that was really catty of me.

I look at Kiera skeptically. "I doubt you know him."

She doesn't like that I challenge her, because she lobs it right back at me. "Try me. Unless you're trying to hide the fact that you're here on a date with Adam."

"Kiera—" Adam's voice is clearly telling her to back off as he moves to step between us.

I put my hand around Adam's surprisingly muscled arm to hold him back. "No, it's okay Adam. I'll play." I turn to face her. "My boyfriend is Drew Forrester. His flight from L.A. was delayed. He should be here soon." I'm confident, knowing that there's no way Kiera has ever met Drew before.

Kiera starts laughing at me in a patronizing tone. "You mean *Andrew* Forrester? Yeah right. That's funny."

Now I'm fuming. This person mocks me at my own club opening, then accuses me of making up a relationship?

"It's not funny. I don't see what your problem is. And his name is Drew. How would you even know him?"

I blanch. Oh my god, what if they used to have sex? I don't think I could stand it if they did. The hairs on the back of my neck stand up and I start to feel the nausea that's been plaguing me rush back with a vengeance. Suddenly, I feel as if I might be sick.

"Andrew Forrester… Hollywood's highest paid actor for the last three years?" She takes in my queasy expression and smirks. "*People* magazine's Sexiest Man Alive… twice. The notorious bachelor who hasn't been photographed romantically with a woman in years? The co-star of my next film. *He's* your boyfriend?" Kiera says patronizingly.

I swallow nervously and look to Adam for help. He rolls his eyes and shrugs, completely confused and unsure of what to say.

"No, he's not an actor. You must be thinking of a different Forrester. It's a common last name." My skin feels clammy and the temperature in the club seems to rise as my panic ratchets up a notch.

Leah comes up behind me and greets Adam. When he doesn't take his eyes off of Kiera and me to respond, she knows something is wrong and freezes.

"Here, we can solve this quickly enough." Kiera whips out her phone and taps on it with a perfectly manicured nail.

"What's going on Sydney?" Leah steps forward to talk to me, but I can't make any words come out. "Syd?"

Kiera turns and holds the phone up so I can see the screen. On it, there's photo of a man standing on a red carpet, smiling at the camera, with his hands tucked into the pockets of his perfectly fitted suit pants, I see the gorgeous face that I know so well. Drew.

My mouth gapes open and closed like a guppy and I feel the blood in my head rushing to my aching stiletto-clad feet. I'm no longer worried about throwing up. I'm worried about passing out.

The caption reads *"Actor Andrew Forrester arrives at the L.A. premiere of his new film"*.

Leah takes in my expression and grabs Kiera's hand to tilt the phone so she can look. She shoves it away in disgust and puts her arm around my back, hugging me to her.

"Sydney, it's okay," Leah says calmly.

I can't do this. I can't be here. I'm suffocating. Drew, actor, celebrity, highest paid—no. No! Kiera and Adam are gawking at us, puzzled by my bizarre reaction.

I twist out of Leah's grip. "I...I have to go. Nice to see you again Adam, nice meeting you Kiera." I turn and bolt for the elevator.

The crowded club closes in around me, my hard work twists and spins in my blurry vision as I struggle to breathe. I get to the elevator and stab the button furiously, willing it to show up before people notice that I'm absolutely freaking out.

"Syd!" Leah grabs my hand and tries to pull me around to look at her. "Don't you dare run, Sydney. It doesn't change who he is. You *love* him. I'm positive he loves you too. Don't do this."

I shake her off. "I can't do this right now, Leah. Not here. Please. I need to process this. Alone." The elevator doors open and I can't get in fast enough.

The last thing I see as the doors shut is Leah's disappointed look.

CHAPTER 15

Oh my god, oh my god, oh my god!

I slide into one of the hotel cars and come straight back to my loft. Once there, I realize I left my bag behind the bar at Verve. I have the concierge use his copy of my key so I can get inside. No way am I going back to the club to get my stuff and chance running into Drew or Kiera or Adam.

I no sooner open my door when the nausea comes rushing back with a vengeance. I barely make it to the bathroom before losing everything in my stomach in a spectacular fashion.

Gasping, I furiously brush my teeth, yank all of the pins out of my hair, and rip the designer dress from my body, tossing it in the garbage. I hurl the silver Jimmy Choos across the room, wanting everything from this evening as far from me as possible. Standing in just my panties I collapse in my closet and let the tears come.

I'm able to stop crying enough to function, but barely. I pile stuff in the open suitcase on my bed as fast as I can, a plan all figured out. It's not a great plan, but it's the only thing I can manage to piece together in my frenetic state of mind. I zip the bag shut and haul it over to the front door.

Thank god I have my passport, my back up credit card, and my checkbook since I left my wallet at the club with the rest of my stuff. Dragging my suitcase out the front door, I lock it behind me and do what I've been taught to do my whole life—I run.

The bright sun and warm weather is a welcome contrast to the cold New York winter. I feel a stab of pain when it reminds me of my Caribbean vacation with Drew. I shove the memory down, trying to keep it together. I'm physically and mentally exhausted.

After leaving my loft I spent the night at the LaGuardia Plaza hotel and hopped the first flight I could in the morning. Eight miserable hours of travel, including a layover in Atlanta, and I'm finally here.

I wasn't in the right frame of mind to think of booking a private jet and there's no direct flight from New York. Needless to say it's been a long day. Especially since whenever I fly commercial, the titanium pins in my arm set off the metal detectors, causing a nightmare for me at security.

Taking a deep breath, I roll my suitcase across the sunny tarmac and into the tiny airport to go through customs.

By late afternoon, the water taxi pulls up to my final destination. Stepping off the boat, I take in the tropical vegetation, the brilliant greens and yellow and reds. I forgot how beautiful it is here. I stumble down the paved stone path, the flip-flops I bought at the airport clicking against my feet, and stop in front of the massive front door. I ring the bell and wait…then it swings open slowly.

"Sydney?"

"Hi Mom."

I let out the tears that I had been holding in all day and sink into the comfort of my mother's arms.

Blessedly, my mom doesn't ask a single question. She lets me cry myself out on the couch then leads me to a guest room and puts me to bed.

****

I can hear my mom and dad in the kitchen, yelling at each other and another man. They think I'm in my room, but I snuck out to sleep in the back living room on the sofa. They don't know that I do this sometimes. If they do, they never say anything. This house is too big. I hate being in the upstairs wing all by myself, especially after what happened last week.

"Scott, how did this happen again?" I hear my mom ask.

"Ms. Allen, I assure you, we are rechecking the entire perimeter wall for the breach."

That must be Scott.

My dad's voice reverberates throughout the house. "I don't want to hear your bullshit! That goddamn freak was in my daughter's room! Now he's trying to get to her again! Last time they found a knife on him! I will not have it!"

Daddy sounds really mad. He wasn't here when I went to sleep. He must have come over. He hasn't been staying here much since the accident.

I shudder uncontrollably. Someone was trying to get in my room again. Last week a crazy man showed up at our house and slept in my bed. I was out late with my mom and when we came home I went into my room to change and he tried to hurt me. I screamed until my mom and our housekeeper, Anna, came running in.

The scary guy was trying to hold me down and hug me, saying how much he loved me. Mommy started hitting him and Anna ran for Robbie, Mom's bodyguard. Robbie punched him and held him down until the police took him away.

He had touched a bunch of my stuff that Mommy said we had to throw away and buy all new. I hated that. She threw out all of my pillows and my comforter and some of my clothes because he did bad things to them.

It sounds like he came back tonight to hurt me. I'm so scared that I'm shaking. I'll never forget the look on his face. It was like he wanted to kill me, even though he kept saying that he loved me.

"I'm sorry, Mr. Tannen— "

"I don't want to hear any of your excuses, Scott. Find the fucking problem in our security system and fucking fix it, now!"

"Reid, what are we going to do? This sick man keeps trying to get to Sydney." Mommy sounds like she's crying. "I thought he was supposed to be in jail?"

"Ms. Allen, the police said that this time, he won't get bail. It's a repeat of the same crime, and he broke the protective order." Scott says.

"Scott, I told you to get the fuck outside and find out what happened! Get out there, meet with the cops that are in *my* yard, and the other security that I pay to keep *my* family safe, and don't come back in here without a goddamn answer for me!" Daddy has that low scary voice he uses, right before he's going to punch someone.

"Yes sir." I hear the front door close behind Scott.

"Reid, it's time. The accident, this crazy psycho—we're not going to be able to stop it. It's getting worse the older she gets."

I reach over and touch the faded pink cast on my arm when my mom mentions the accident. One more week and I can get this itchy thing off.

"I know, Eva. You don't know how it makes me feel that I can't keep her safe. I make it worse, *we* make it worse, Eva." Daddy sounds like he might cry, and my dad never ever cries. He's always the hero, the one who makes everything better. If he can't fix this, who can?

"One month, Reid. Then it's done."

Done? I wonder what my mom is talking about.

****

"What happened, Sydney? Why are you here?" My mom is sitting next to me on an outdoor couch under a huge pergola. "You don't look well, dear."

It's a beautiful morning on my mother's tiny island off the coast of Belize. I never understood before, but now I can see why she loves it so much. Peace. Isolation.

I glance up. She looks terrified for me. And sad. "I don't feel well, Mom. I haven't been eating or sleeping much. Stress from work, the club, I've been sick all the time. Drew."

Her brows scrunch together. "Who's Drew honey?" She puts her hand on my leg and waits patiently for me to speak.

I steel myself and tell my mom about my very first boyfriend. How we met, how much fun we have. She lights up when I explain how thoughtful and sweet he is. Mom is impressed by the vacation to St. Bart's.

When I give her details about the trip, she looks at me strangely. "The villa, did it have a name?"

"What Mom?" I'm puzzled by her question.

"You know, was the estate named? Just like this home is called Silent Escape. Did the villa have a name?"

"Yes, Villa Sur la Colline, why?" Mom looks troubled.

"And the boat was called *Magic Hour,* you're sure?"

"Yes, do you know something Mom?"

She totally knows something. Something I'm not going to like.

"Well, I know who owns that villa, I've been there." *Of course she has.* "The boat must be new, but the name makes sense. It's owned by Thomas C. Sullivan, the director. The magic hour is the time of day near sunrise and sunset that directors love because it gives them perfect lighting. I've worked with him before and he's one of the few people I've remained friends with since I left the business. So, how did you end up at his villa? I know you wouldn't have gone there if you knew who owned it."

"No, Mom. It's owned by Drew's friend Chad, not a Thomas."

My mom gives me a look filled with pity.

"Honey, Thomas C. Sullivan is Chad. He goes by his middle name with friends and family."

I press my hand to my forehead. This is so not happening. I would stand up and pace or throw something if I had any energy.

"So Sydney, the question is, who is Drew and why are you here?" She leans over and takes my hands in hers.

"He…I didn't know. I-I don't like to answer questions about me, you know that." She nods, urging me to continue. "He was willing to be with me and not push me for information. He told me …" I sob. "He told me that he was an investor. That he financed projects and helped direct and market them, I think he even used the words *playing a role*. I'm so stupid, I should have seen it! Drew knows I don't like the whole celebrity scene, so he explained his job in a way that wasn't a lie, but not the whole truth. I never asked questions because I don't like to answer any in response. So I just accepted what he told me even though it didn't make sense."

I'm getting more and more anxious as I speak, my voice breaking over the words.

"At the club opening the other night, I met someone who asked about my boyfriend, and when I told her his name, she showed me a photo on her phone. He's Andrew Forrester, Mom! Some huge actor! And not just any actor, he's some huge heartthrob *Sexiest Man Alive* actor! I can't do it Mom. I can't be like you and Dad!"

My voice hitches and I burst into tears. My mom gathers me in her arms, lightly stroking my knotted hair.

"Shhhh, it doesn't have to be like this Sydney. You can't keep everyone out. You have to be who you are and let the chips fall where they may. Don't live your life based on what happened with me and your dad." She puts her hands on either side of my face and looks at me. "Do you love him?"

I can't lie to her. "Yes. I love him."

"Does he love you?"

"I...I don't know. Leah thinks he does." Tears start streaming down my cheeks again. I wouldn't have thought I had any more in me after crying all night.

"Then the rest doesn't matter. Follow your heart, sweetie." This advice is so unlike the mother I grew up with who told me to guard my identity like it was part of a redacted CIA file.

"I can't be out there like that, Mom. If I date him, I'll be right back where I was twelve years ago with the paparazzi and the fans and the stalkers. I don't think I'm strong enough for that. I like being nobody," I choke out.

"Sydney, you will *never* be a nobody. It's time to be Sydney Tannen again. You're not twelve honey, you're twenty-four. I've been waiting for you to grow up and not need to hide out anymore, but you're still trying to escape life. You *are* strong enough. I was going to tell you when I came to New York next week—"

My head snaps up as if she threw a glass of water in my face. "You were coming to New York next week?"

"Yes, I still am. I wanted to see your beautiful work at the Warren. It was going to be a surprise." That explains her sneaky attitude on the phone the other night. "But I'm going back for another reason, Sydney."

She takes a deep breath and I get the feeling that my mom, Evangeline Allen, a woman who accepted an Oscar on television broadcast live to tens of millions of people, is nervous to tell me something.

"You're old enough to deal with this now. I've decided to go back, Sydney. I'm meeting with the head of Black Spark Studios about my return to acting. He sent me a script and I love it. It was written specifically for me. It's perfect. I can't pass it up."

I'm gripping the cushion of the outdoor sofa so hard that my knuckles turn white. "You're going to start acting again," I say flatly. "But, if *you* go back, then—" I can't say it, I just can't.

"Then they'll be looking for you."

Well, Mom had no problem saying it.

I spend five days in Belize with my mom, sleeping, crying and generally feeling miserable for myself. My mood isn't improved by Mom breezing around the house with a perma-grin on her face. She tries to give me the neutral Evangeline Allen mask whenever I'm around, but it's obvious that she's excited to be acting again. And I can't blame her. She gave that all up for me and now she deserves to be doing what she loves.

That's another thing hanging over my head. The revelation that my parents planned my escape from California and the lifestyle we were living solely to protect me. My mother and father gave up a lot to keep me safe. It was with the best intentions and done out of love, but now I'm so used to hiding that I don't know if I can change. It's who I am. Who I've been forced to become.

On my third day of moping around, barely eating a thing since the queasiness is still lingering, I tell my mom that I read the transcript from the Barbara Walters' interview with Dad. I'm ready to bring this out in the open.

"Did you read it because your dad won an Oscar?"

"What? He won?" I'm shocked, but happy for my dad. Especially since I know he gave me up to protect me, not to chuck me aside for a new life. "I didn't know. I read the interview before the awards aired, and you know I don't watch that stuff. So the interview, Mom, I'm guessing you've seen it." I look at her and wait for her to say something.

"Oh, honey. I wanted to tell you. But your father and I decided that your safety was a top priority. After the car crash, it was only a matter of time until someone really hurt you to get to us or to get a story. Then there were crazy fans that had broken into the house several times, another crazy woman who kept trying to get into your school by saying she was your mother, it was terrifying for us Sydney."

"So dad's affair?" I choke on the words as my mom sits across from me at the dining set by the pool.

"Sydney," my mom reaches over and places her hand over mine. She looks at me sadly, her gorgeous face troubled. "Your dad and I had been having problems for several years by the time that video came out. He wasn't even living in the house with us. You never noticed because he was always gone so much.

"I admit that it hurt me deeply that the entire world saw our relationship go under and he made me look like a fool, but we had already been talking about divorce by that time. I was just so angry that he would put us in that position with the tabloids. More specifically, that he put *you* in that situation with the media. The firestorm that was coming with that video, and the breakup of *Hollywood's It Couple,*" she makes a sour face, "was going to make what had happened to you so far look like nothing."

"So you let me think everything was Dad's fault?" Tears are threatening to fall.

"No honey. Dad *wanted* you to think everything was his fault. He wanted you to be able to leave with a clean break. He felt guilty and wanted to be punished for it. For driving the car when it crashed, for not able to keep you safe at home. It was killing him to be so helpless. Yes, my ego was shattered in front of the whole world, but I would have been fine eventually. We would have announced that we had split before the video was filmed, I could have stayed and kept acting.

"We wanted you to grow up normal and when we got the call that your dad was caught on tape with another woman and it was going to air nationally the next night, it was time to go. I was leaving with you anyway, the scandal just moved the date up."

She pats my hand comfortingly. "I know it's going to be a tough change, Sydney. For years you've been told to hide from the fame that comes with being our daughter. It was so you could become a young woman without the outside pressure of millions of eyes on you and to keep you safe from the things we couldn't control. Now that you're an adult, it's time to embrace who you are and accept it."

"But it's all I know, Mom. I don't know how to be any other way." I sound like a baby. I can't help it. It's just too much for me to handle at once.

"It's our fault that you're so afraid, Sydney. We didn't know what else to do. I was hoping when we moved, you could grow up like everyone else. Without people jumping out of the bushes and making you cry, or perverted stalkers lurking in your bedroom because they say they love you, or photographers crashing the car you're in and taking pictures of you crying and broken in the remnants of the accident. That environment would have damaged you more if we stayed."

My mom and I are both crying as we hold hands and mourn the loss of my childhood. A childhood that wouldn't have been normal no matter which option my parents chose, crazy in California or hidden in New York. There is no normal for the child of such scrutinized public figures. They took the only road that could keep me physically safe.

"I love you Mom." I stand up and hug my mom.

"I love you too, Sydney."

"Thanks for saving me when I was twelve, and for saving me again now, Mom"

And because she sacrificed everything for me when I was a kid, I think I can suck it up and make some sacrifices now to repay her. It scares the crap out of me, but it's time. I tell her my plan and she absolutely loves it.

CHAPTER 16

"Where the hell have you been?"

Leah's expression is alternating between wanting to hug me and wanting to punch me. It's been five days since the party at the Verve, and I haven't contacted anyone since I left. I flew back from Belize this morning and when I got home, the concierge had the messenger bag that I left at the club.

My phone was dead so I plugged it in to charge. It beeped about a million times when it came to life. I had so many voicemails, my mailbox was full. Most were from Drew and Leah. One was from Adam apologizing for Kiera, *(how did he get my number?)*, and three were from Jeff Talley, Sander Yates and Ben Walton at the Warren, all congratulating me for the design and the success of the opening.

At least they didn't notice my early departure.

I erase the ones from Drew without listening to them. I have too much going on to start crying again. And frankly, I'm not ready to talk to him just yet. There are also so many text messages from Drew and Leah that I couldn't possibly read them all. I delete those as well.

After calling Leah and telling her I'm home, she's standing over me less than ten minutes later, screeching like a banshee. Who knew that someone so small could be so intimidating?

"I went to Belize and stayed with my mom. I had to think. I couldn't do that here with the pressure from you and Drew."

"So you left and didn't tell me? Or Drew? He went absolutely nuts and caused a huge scene at the club when he found out what happened, Sydney." I wince at her words. "The man arrives from flying cross-country to see you and finds out that you've vanished! He was devastated, Syd. You should have stayed and talked to him!"

"You know how I feel about that, Leah. I—"

She cuts me off, angrier than I've ever seen her.

"I know that you love him! That's what I know! I know that he loves you too! Nothing else matters! You have got to let this crazy paranoia go or you're going to be miserable. I've known you a long time, Syd, and Drew has made you happier than I've ever seen you! And you're ruining it because of his job!" Leah is pacing my den, hostility radiating off of her small form.

"You can't know that he loves me, Leah. He hasn't even told me yet." I glare at her, trying to be angry so I won't cry. I *can't* cry anymore.

Leah spins around to face me. "Well he told *me* that he loves you." She puts her hands on her hips defiantly. My mouth gapes and I can't make any words come out.

"That's right, he knew I recognized him. He knew I did him a favor by not telling you he was an actor. He's not stupid, Sydney. He figured out enough from that crap with Adam to know that if he revealed who he is, you'd leave him.

"Drew came to see me at the café the last time he was in town to visit you. He wanted to know why you were so afraid of fame and celebrity. I let him know that I wasn't going to tell him. He was going to have to get that story from you. I also told him that he needed to explain to you what he does for a living, because you were going to find out eventually and hearing it from someone besides him would be really bad. He told me he was in love with you, Sydney. He was scared of you leaving him. I told him I thought you loved him enough to stick it out. Was I wrong?"

I sit paralyzed on the couch, knees pulled up to my chest, my arms clutched around my legs to hold myself together. I might fall to pieces any minute.

Leah continues her rant. "He was going to tell you before you left for the party. He couldn't walk into that club without you knowing. Shit, everyone there knows who he is. That bitch Kiera Radcliff is his co-star in his next movie for god's sake! But his flight was delayed in L.A. and then diverted to Denver due to a medical issue with one of the passengers. It was one big clusterfuck!

"He tried calling you to let you know where he was, but by the time he was able use his phone, yours must have been behind the bar at the club. He said that he planned on staying downstairs in one of the hotel's conference rooms when he arrived and he was going to have a staff member bring you to him to talk. But then Kiera told you who Drew was before he got there, and you left him!"

"He lied to me Leah. And you!" I stab my finger at her, "You knew who he was this entire time." I stare at my friend accusingly.

Her eyes narrow. "Yeah, I knew. It took me a minute to recognize him under that ugly-ass hat, but I knew. And you told me you were glad I never mentioned that Adam was a celebrity because you never would have given him the time of day and you found out he was actually a great person. So I did exactly what you said you wanted me to do. I let you get to know Drew as a person, Sydney, not Andrew Forrester, *Sexiest Man Alive*." Her words cut me to the quick.

I stare down at my toes, examining the bright red pedicure I had done for the club opening. "It sure does explain his fondness for that nasty baseball cap, doesn't it?"

I look up and can't help it when the corner of my mouth lifts in amusement. It actually explains a lot, like the pilots' reaction to him and the private dining rooms. God, and that homeless running outfit. I know I go to extremes with denial, but I'm completely oblivious even when it's staring me in the face.

She starts laughing, "Yeah, it does." My smile fades as quickly as it appeared when Leah keeps talking. "You have to talk to him Sydney. You didn't see how devastated he was. He got to the party and the staff told him you were gone. I swear it was only thirty minutes after you left. I found him in the club and told him what happened.

"He went nuclear on Kiera. I've never seen anyone so angry, Syd. I had to physically get between them. Kiera had this nasty smirk on her face and said something rude about you, and I swear I thought he was going to punch her. Then he turned on Adam and threatened to kick the crap out of him for trying to steal his girlfriend. Someone even got a picture of it and posted it to some online blog. It was a total shitstorm."

"Holy cow, Leah, Kiera was rude and all, but it's not her fault! He's the one who didn't tell me who he was."

"But he was going to tell you, just like you were going to tell him about your parents prior to the party. You both had secrets. You both wanted to make sure you were right for each other before sharing them. You're not exactly innocent, Sydney. After he made a scene, we left Verve and came here because we couldn't reach you on the phone."

I hang my head. "I left my phone in my bag at the club."

"I didn't know that at the time." Leah snaps. "An employee at the Warren found it behind the bar the next day and it had your business cards in it. They called the New York office listed on the card and a co-worker of yours brought it to your concierge on Monday.

"Anyway, we got here and you wouldn't answer your phone and the concierge wouldn't let us upstairs. Drew was going ballistic in your lobby, screaming at the concierge to open your door. When he refused, Drew threatened to call the police to let us in to make sure you weren't dead. I'm not kidding, Sydney, I've never seen a man have a complete breakdown, but I'm pretty sure I did that night."

I can't speak. My throat is swollen shut, and I have no response to Leah's accusatory stare.

"So, they finally let us in and we could tell that you had been here." Her eyes widen. "You threw away a four-thousand dollar Jason Wu? Are you nuts?"

"I don't ever want to look at that dress again."

"Real mature Sydney." Leah gives me an evil look. "Anyway, it's a good thing it was late, because only a couple of your neighbors came through the lobby while one of the world's biggest movie stars was having a meltdown at the front desk.

"Hours later we realized you weren't coming home. Drew only left when I shoved him out the door and promised him I'd let him know if I heard from you, even if you told me not to. You have got to call him Syd, otherwise I will. I gave him my word."

"I know Leah. I will. But first I need your help."

Leah is sitting on the edge of my bathtub, all of the color drained from her face. Leah, silenced by me again. I seem to be good at that lately.

"Leah! Leah!" I snap my fingers in front of her face. "Hey! I'm the one that needs to be comforted, okay?"

She looks at me, her trance broken. "This...this is..." she waves the positive pregnancy test in front of me. "This is huge, Syd. I can't believe it."

"I know." I'm so over-stressed that I've passed the point of reacting to anything and moved on to total numbness. "I already took one, it said I wasn't pregnant."

"What? You knew you could be pregnant?" She looks at me as if I sprouted a second head.

"It was one time a month and a half ago, Leah! A caught up in the moment thing. I took a test a week later and it was negative. I don't even get regular periods! But I've been sick for the last couple of weeks. I blamed it on stress and nerves." I sound whiney and I hate it.

"A week? You can't test for pregnancy until at the very least two weeks after you have unprotected sex, Sydney! How do you not know that? What about the morning after pill? Why didn't you just get that?" Leah jumps to her feet and is waving the test in front of me. She has an incredulous expression on her face, making me feel like I'm the stupidest person ever.

Which, I probably am right about now.

"I-I forgot about the morning after pill."

How could I have forgotten that? My face burns with shame.

"And I don't exactly use pregnancy tests every day, Leah! I just wanted to get the test over with so I wouldn't have to worry anymore!" I snatch the test out of her hand and throw it in the sink. "Leah, I have to call Drew."

"Yes, you do, for more than one reason. The time for excuses and denial has officially ended. Get over the fame thing, Syd. He's going to be the father of your child. You can't let potential tabloid shit come between you. Don't make the same decision your parents did. Don't let your kid grow up without a father."

Leah's face is sympathetic, but still distraught. Her dark blonde eyebrows are pulled together over her concerned blue eyes.

I've let her down. I let my mom down. I let Drew down. I was faced with my fears and ran away like the twelve year-old Sydney would. Now, it's time to stop running and fight.

I pull out my phone and dial.

CHAPTER 17

When the thunderous knocking starts, I hurry to open the door so my neighbors don't come out to see what's going on. A very disheveled and tired looking Drew comes rushing in, wrapping his arms around me. He kicks the door shut and pulls my head to his chest.

"Jesus, Sydney. You scared the shit out of me. I didn't think I'd ever see you again." I hear his voice crack a little.

Oh god. Don't cry Sydney.

I sink into his warm body and inhale his scent, that pure Drew—masculine and comforting. I relax into him and can't help it, the emotions catch up to me and I burst into tears.

"Shhhhh, it's okay babe. It's okay."

Drew scoops me up and brings me down the hall to my room, gently laying me on the bed. He uses his feet to remove his shoes and lays down with me, letting me cry into his shirt until I'm spent.

I wake up and see that Drew is still draped around me. He's awake. It appears I've caught him watching me sleep. I see the fear in his eyes behind the love that I know he feels for me. He doesn't trust that I won't run away again.

"Drew," I whisper, reaching up to run my fingers through his soft hair. "I'm not going anywhere."

Hesitantly, I lean in and press a gentle kiss on his mouth. We have so much to talk about, but right now, I need to be close to him. For him to make me his again.

"God, Sydney." He holds me and kisses me more aggressively, needing to prove to himself that we'll be okay. "I love you, Sydney," he whispers against my lips. "I can't be without you."

I grip his hair in my hands, my heart pounding from his declaration. "I love you too, Drew. I'm sorry I ran. I won't do it again."

He groans and rolls us until his hard body is pinning me down to the bed. Claiming me with his mouth, his slick tongue pushes in and tangles with mine. When I taste him on my lips, it feels like home.

"Sydney, I want you. I need to know that you're still mine," he breathes as he rubs his nose along my neck.

I nod and he grabs the bottom of my shirt and yanks it over my head then does the same to his. Drew lowers his head and grazes his teeth over my breasts, sending chills down my spine.

He groans against my skin. "I can't wait any longer." We shed our clothes and come back together, unwilling to be apart for even one more second. Drew rests his hard body back on top of mine and pulls my arms above my head, circling my wrists with hand. Reaching down he checks to see if I'm ready for him, sliding his finger several times across me. My hips arch up into his touch, craving more.

"Jesus, I missed you."

He produces a condom from somewhere and rolls it on. In the back of my brain I realize that he doesn't know that we don't need one anymore. I'm not going to stop him now. I wrap my legs around his waist and press my heels down on his backside, urging him to take me fast and hard.

Drew positions himself at my entrance and stares into my eyes as he sinks in slowly, letting me feel every inch as he fills me up.

"You feel so fucking good." Drew lets go of my hands and rests on his elbows, taking some of his weight off of me as he drives in and out in long, measured strokes. "I love you Sydney," he says, his voice cracking from the emotion.

His glistening green eyes are penetrating through my thick, protective wall. I can see the love he has for me reflected back. I can feel it with each slow thrust of his hips.

I lift my hips to counter his, moving faster as the need in us builds. My hands find his round ass and I hold on tight, gripping as if my life depends on it.

The delicious pleasure begins gathering in my core, starting as a trace of fire and building to a roaring inferno. Drew keeps up a punishing pace, plunging his tongue into my mouth then dragging his lips across my neck, whispering his declarations of love in my ear as he drives us both to an explosive climax.

"God, Drew, I love you so much." I fall over the edge into ecstasy, my pussy clenching around him as I go, pulling Drew over the brink with me. He snaps his hips deep twice more, his muscles tensing and flexing as he finds his own release.

"Fuck Sydney, don't ever leave me again," he says huskily as he shudders. Drew collapses, letting his full weight rest on top of me as he continues to press soft kisses on my lips and I drag my fingers lightly across his back.

When we finally part, we both fall asleep this time. Holding each other desperately, afraid to let go.

I wake up early, still too dark out to be anywhere near dawn. I look over at Drew sleeping next to me. His beautiful face is just inches from mine. He looks relaxed, but very tired, with dark circles under his eyes and bruises on his knuckles. His lips are slightly parted and his leg is thrown over my waist, keeping me from leaving even in his sleep.

I grin like an idiot, staring at him in the dark. I can't believe he loves me, even after what I put him through. I'm still scared to death of the future, but I know I can't live without him, regardless of his fame.

I untangle myself from Drew, careful not to wake him. He's been through so much because of me. I want to let him rest a little longer. I have a few more nuclear bombs to drop on him before the day is over.

I'm sitting on my couch, curled up with a hot cup of coffee, when Drew wanders in from the bedroom, dragging his hand over his unshaven face. He looks so adorable with his hair sticking up in the back, wearing just a t-shirt and his boxer briefs.

"Good morning gorgeous." He leans over and kisses the top of my head. "Is there more coffee?"

"Yes, there's a pot in the kitchen. I'll get it for you." I put my mug down and move to get up.

Drew gently pushes down on my shoulders. "No, sit. Relax Sydney. I'll be right back." He turns and heads for the kitchen. I watch his fine backside as he goes.

Drew comes back into the living room a few minutes later, sipping his own steaming mug of coffee. Putting his cup down on the table, he sits next to me and pulls my legs across his lap, his expression serious.

"You scared me, Sydney. I didn't know what happened to you. I couldn't get here. The damn flights kept getting fucked up."

He rakes a hand through his hair, making it even messier. "Then I find out I'm too late. That...well, you know, Kiera told you."

He spits the last part out and clamps his jaw down. I watch the muscles in his cheek twitch from the force.

"I came here with Leah. You wouldn't answer your phone, they wouldn't let us in. I thought...I thought..." Drew chokes on the words. "I don't understand why, Sydney."

I put my hand on his unshaven cheek. "I know babe, I know. I'm so sorry. I want to tell you everything. I was going to tell you before the party, as a kind of birthday present. I guess we both have secrets. Great birthday, huh?"

He leans in and puts his forehead against mine, holding my gaze. "I don't give a shit about my birthday and it doesn't matter what you tell me, Sydney. I'll still love you."

And I know he means what he says. He has that sincere, honest look on his face that is so totally Drew. Steeling myself, I begin.

"My childhood was... different."

I swallow nervously. This is the first time I've ever told anyone my story. Even the therapists I used to see already knew my family history.

"My parents, they weren't exactly normal."

Drew stiffens and leans back so he can see me better, the muscles in his neck flexing from stress. "What did they do to you?" He looks scary, the protector in him surfacing.

"Drew, it's not like that." I pause and continue, inhaling deeply to calm my fluttering heart. "My parents are Evangeline Allen and Reid Tannen. I'm Sydney Tannen." I haven't said that out loud in over a decade. I look at Drew, my hands shaking from nerves, and wait.

He sits there for a moment. I can almost see each different emotion cross his face as he processes this information. "So you...your parents are Evangeline Allen and Reid Tannen, the actors," he repeats, blinking rapidly to try and make sense of this.

"Yes. My mom took me away from California when I was twelve. My parents didn't feel that I was…that I was…safe anymore. The photographers, the lies, the stalkers, the crazy people…" I can barely make the words come out.

"I remember," he whispers after a moment, the pieces finally clicking into place. "The accident with your dad. *(click)* The photographer who caused it. *(click)* It was in the papers and on TV. *(click)* It was the summer before I started at Boston College…" He looks horrified as my life starts to make sense to him. His eyes widen in fear. "You were seriously hurt, Sydney. *(click)* Your dad was arrested." *(click)*

"Yes," I whisper as I watch his face become furious, then sad, then loving. All of the facts finally make sense.

A range of feelings—anger at the people who ruined my life, sad for me for having to live this way, and love for me in spite of it all.

I reflexively rub the scar on my arm that serves as a reminder of that painful time. Drew notices and grasps my arm, pulling it closer so he can see the mark that haunts me. His eyes grow wide as he gets his answer as to what the jagged pink line represents.

Drew's facial expression changes. Shock becomes anguish in the space of a heartbeat. He gasps as if in pain.

"I understand. My world scares you. It destroyed you. I'm so selfish Sydney. I had no idea. You don't need this in your life. You don't need me." He closes his eyes and shakes his head. Dropping my arm he moves my legs off of his lap and backs away.

"No Drew, I *do* need you. Whatever your life is, it's what I want as long as you're there with me." I grab his hands and desperately try to pull him back to me. Resisting, Drew opens his eyes. There are unshed tears welling up behind the brilliant green. "That's what I've been figuring out these past few days. I was at my mom's in Belize. She helped me realize that I can't keep hiding."

"Can you really live like that Sydney? The paparazzi? The fans? That's all part of the Andrew Forrester package. It's even worse now than it was back then, the internet and cell phone cameras and tabloid shows...it never stops.

"I mean shit, Sydney, there was even a blog the day after the party with a picture and an article that described how I argued with Kiera Radcliff and Adam Reynolds at Verve, fighting over an *unknown female!* One of the guests must have used their camera phone. If they find out who you are? It will go worldwide in about a half a second! I'm no good for you. I can't protect you from that."

He tries to shake my hands off but I grip him tighter and climb onto his lap, clinging to him, refusing to let go.

"Drew, I lost a lot when I was a child. I lost my home, my friends, my father..." Tears slide silently down my cheeks. I see my future in this man's eyes. "I refuse to let our child lose those things too, simply because I'm too afraid to stand up and live my life." I place my hands on either side of his beautiful, tired face, letting my words sink in.

"What?" He is stunned, his question so faint I can hardly hear it.

"Our child, Drew. I'm pregnant." He sits very still, the unmovable statue again, quietly processing the information.

"Child? But you said the test was negative. Are you sure?"

His voice is husky with emotion but the mask is back. The mask I now know is so easy for him because he's an actor. A very good one. The mask my mom used to slip on to hide her feelings.

I can't read him. Is he angry? Happy? Confused? All of the above?

I'm humiliated at my admission, prickly heat rushing to my cheeks. "I took the test a week too soon. I didn't know there was a time frame in which it wouldn't work." I drop my gaze, ashamed at my stupidity. "I've been sick for a few weeks, I can't eat much. I thought it was stress, but I realized that it all added up to one thing. Yes, I'm sure that I'm pregnant, Drew." I glance back up to see if I can figure out what he's thinking.

The mask cracks as he hugs me tight and crushes his mouth to mine. "I love you so much Sydney." He laughs. "I guess I shouldn't be this happy, but I am." His beautiful smile is back, all straight white teeth and sexy dimple.

I grin back. "I'm happy too, Drew. Scared, but happy." He brings his thumbs up and brushes away the remainder of my tears.

"We're actually going to do this?" He pushes my hair back from my face, skimming his hand down my back.

"Yes we are. We'll figure it out together. I have a doctor's appointment tomorrow if you want to go."

"Of course I want to go." Drew raises an eyebrow and smirks. "Do they have a back entrance?"

CHAPTER 18

Being with Andrew Forrester is already becoming a giant headache. I have a new appreciation for how hard this was for him to keep from me.

I had to call to arrange a special after-hours appointment with my OB-GYN so he can go with me and not be seen in the waiting room by any of the other patients. The office staff isn't allowed to say anything to anyone, but you can't stop the other patients that are seeing the doctor from taking cell phone videos and posting them online.

I turn to Drew in the back seat of the Town Car, on our way to the Upper East Side office of my doctor, a block from Mount Sinai Hospital.

"Drew, can I ask you something?"

"Of course, Sydney." He faces me and I see that honest and open look that's so totally Drew. I really, really love this guy.

"You'll tell me the truth, right?" I'm smiling as I say it, so he only looks slightly worried at what I'm going to ask.

"Yes, just ask and I'll tell you." He lifts one eyebrow in curiosity.

"Ok, well, when we were in St. Bart's, I accidentally overheard you on the phone. You were upset and yelling at someone. I could tell you were mad because I notice that your accent comes back when you get emotional and you were all Boston." I smile. "What was that?"

He thinks back for a minute, then seems embarrassed.

"Oh. I was making sure the crew on the boat didn't say anything if they recognized me. I didn't want any looks or weirdness that would freak you out." He stares at me, trying to figure out my reaction to his admission. "You're not mad are you?"

I laugh. "No, I'm not mad. It seems like so much trouble to go through just to date me though."

Drew scowls. "First, there's nothing I wouldn't have done to date you Sydney. Not knowing who I was when we met, that was a first for me and I loved it. I could date like a real person, no preconceived notions about Andrew Forrester the public figure already in your head. I could just be Drew, a guy from Boston.

"I regretted letting you leave the gym that day without a way to contact you, so when you sat with me in the café and told me how repellant I was, I knew I had to get to know you."

We laugh together as we remember that conversation. "Then you were so upset by that magazine, by a celebrity. I wanted to find out why, but I also didn't want you walking home alone after having been so shaken up."

I thread my fingers through his on the seat between us, "You do get a little protective sometimes." I smile, letting him know it's okay with me.

"I know, sometimes I go overboard a little, but I want to keep you from getting hurt, Sydney. You make me that way. I've never felt so protective of anyone else outside of my family. It's because I love you. I probably loved you from the moment you called me repellant."

He draws small circles on my hand and looks at me again. His expression is so reverent, so loving, I almost cry.

Then he smirks. "And you think the sailboat thing was difficult? I had to hide so much stuff, and I hated having to do it Sydney. It made me feel so crappy, but I wanted you desperately. I didn't want you to leave me without knowing the real me."

"What else did you have to hide?" Now I'm curious as to just how much effort he put into pursuing me.

"A lot," he huffs. "I had to hide all of my awards and photos at my house, all of my scripts that are usually lying around. My assistant, Jane, couldn't be around when you were. I had given her a weekend off since I was between projects anyway. You and I couldn't do any dates in public."

His beautiful eyes find mine, his lips pulled into a smile. "I was so glad that you were as happy staying in as I am. The pilots on the private jet almost blew it for me. I had to have Philippe clear Chad's awards and photos out of the villa and lock them in the office. I couldn't shop with you in St. Bart's. I had to wear my hat everywhere even though I knew you hated it…It was exhausting."

His eyes darken as he gives me a scorching hot look, "But totally worth it." That lopsided smirk of his has a suggestive innuendo to it. I have to bite my lip to contain my groan.

"Why go through all of that when you could have just dated someone you could be yourself around?" I stare out the window at the rows of brake lights on West 96th St.

"Sydney, look at me." I turn to find him staring intently at me again. Drew brings my hand up to his mouth and kisses the back of it gently. "I wanted to date you *because* I could be myself around you. Andrew Forrester isn't real. You know this. Your parents had to have done the same thing. Be one person for the public, and someone else in private."

I remember how I used to differentiate between my mom Eva Allen and the actress Evangeline Allen, and I nod. "I can't find anyone who doesn't already know Andrew Forrester, and therefore, they think they know me. *You* know me. They don't. They get the façade that I give them, and you get all of me." I swallow loudly. He's too good for me.

"When Bruce brought you into my gym, bleeding and hurt…" Drew closes his eyes as if it were his pain he's remembering. "I don't know why but I felt this overwhelming urge to protect you. When you didn't know who I was, I couldn't believe it. You have no idea how rare that is for me."

He brushes his hand across my cheek, tucking a wayward piece of hair behind my ear. "Then I let you leave without a way to find you, unless I wanted to stalk your building, which I seriously considered doing."

He grins. "Bruce had your address from dropping you off." I smile back. "But then Bruce gave me the napkin that he took from you, it said Village Coffee Bar. You must go there a lot because you showed up the first day I went there to find you."

So it wasn't a coincidence that Drew was in the café that day. He pursued me, quite actively. I can't help the grin that spreads across my face.

"Your smile is so beautiful. I hate when I can't put it there for you," he whispers.

The car slows to a stop in front of the green awning at the entrance to a tall, brownstone medical office building. Drew lowers the glass partition and tells Bruce to stay with the car and be back in about an hour to get us. Drew gets out and extends a hand for me to follow him inside.

"What floor?" he asks as we go into the lobby and over to the elevator bank.

"Tenth." He pushes it and we wait for the elevator to arrive.

"Excuse me, are you Andrew Forrester?" A woman on her way out of the building has stopped in front of us and is getting that nervous *ohmhgod I'm a huge fan* look on her face.

Drew smiles and speaks smoothly, "Yes. How are you?"

The woman practically collapses to the floor she's so excited. I realize that this is my first time out with Drew in public and I am freaking out. *He should have worn his hideous hat.* His voice sounds weird, stiff and rehearsed, with a smile that's too big. His body posture even changes slightly as he becomes the public version of himself.

If he's acting strange, this woman doesn't realize it. She's bought the Andrew Forrester act hook, line, and sinker. Now she's babbling on and on about how great Drew is.

Memories of my parents' fans start creeping in, making me dizzy with panic. The elevator pings and I almost jump out of my skin. Drew's mask slips for a minute and he throws me a concerned look. I'm sure he can tell that I'm falling apart, I can feel the anxiety flooding my body.

"I'm sorry, we have to go, it's nice to meet you." He gives the woman his perfect movie star smile and steers me into the elevator with his hand on my lower back. I stab the 10 as fast as I can to get away from the hyperventilating woman.

"Syd, are you okay? You don't look well." Drew has turned to me in the small space.

"I'm fine, I'll be okay. It's just weird. I remember that with my parents. I just can't reconcile you with this huge star that everyone knows. It's bizarre, that's all." I try to calm my breathing and wipe my hands on my jeans so he won't feel how sweaty they are.

The elevator stops and the doors slide open, saving me from an uncomfortable situation. I hurry out and head toward my doctor's suite, leaving Drew to catch up.

"There, see this tiny shaded area? That's the baby." Dr. Atiena Abasi is pointing at a blob on the small black and white ultrasound screen. Drew and I are squinting to see what the heck she's referring to because as far as I'm concerned, there's nothing there but a round black hole in a fuzzy gray field.

"The black hole?" I ask, confused by image on the blurry screen.

"The black area is the gestational sac around the fetus. The baby is the very small spot on the edge of the sac." Dr. Abasi types something and an arrow appears on the screen pointing at a small blob on the edge of the black hole. Then she types again and the word 'baby' appears above the arrow.

"Wow," I say, still not understanding what I'm looking at. Drew has moved even closer to the screen, studying the picture as the fuzz flutters.

He flinches back in surprise. "It moved, is that normal?"

Dr. Abasi laughs. "Perfectly normal, it's the baby's heartbeat. I'd guess you're about eight weeks pregnant with conception about six weeks ago?" I nod. She pushes a button and a paper curls out of the machine. "Here, take this picture with you." The doctor rips off the paper and hands it to me. It's a print out of the gray fuzz with the black hole and the arrow that says baby on it.

"Thanks." I take the printout and choke up. Our baby. Me and Drew. I can't wrap my mind around it.

The doctor removes the ultrasound wand and pushes the machine away. "You can get dressed and we'll talk in my office when you're ready." She smiles and leaves the room.

I sit up and hand the picture to Drew. He's been acting strange since we got here. I think the reality of this thing is sinking in and he's starting to lose it. Well, there's nothing I can say right now that will help. He'll have to do what I had to do and come to terms with this on his own. I hop down from the table and pull on my clothes.

We sit across a massive desk from my doctor. I've been seeing her since I was first sexually active at age seventeen and I like her a lot. She's pleasant and calming to talk to.

"So, I've calculated your due date to be October 1st, we can adjust that when the fetus is big enough to get more accurate measurements. But you seem pretty sure about the conception date, so it shouldn't change."

"I'm sure of the date." I look at Drew, he hasn't moved or said a word. The statue is back. He's going to need time to adjust.

"Then here are some prenatal vitamins, I'll give you samples so you won't have to be seen going into a pharmacy and picking them up. Gossip is easily started by coming out of any business related to medicine, believe me." She smiles. She's polite enough to ignore Drew's odd behavior.

"I'll see you in a month, Sydney. Just make an appointment with Jessie, she'll be at her desk as you leave. And don't worry, she's the only one left in the office besides me."

"Thank you so much Dr. Abasi and I'm sorry for keeping you late."

"It's no problem, you're not my first high profile pregnancy." The doctor glances over at Drew. No reaction, again. She's going to either think he's the rudest person she's ever met or she's seen men go catatonic from fear before and she'll recognize it. "Jessie will be sure to give you another evening appointment. Everyone here is very discreet so don't worry. Sydney, good to see you again and Drew, it's nice to meet you."

She stands and extends her slender hand across the desk, I shake it gratefully. "Thanks again, Doctor."

Drew snaps out of his stupor and shakes her hand. "Thanks Doctor. We appreciate your time." He gestures for me to go first and follows me out of her office.

Jessie is a small, freckle-covered red head about the same age as me. She checked us in when we arrived and had a very hard time keeping her professional demeanor when she looked up and saw Drew. Her eyes were bulging out of her head and she could barely speak as she handed me some paperwork to fill out. Jessie doesn't seem to have gotten over it yet, because her hands are shaking as she writes out my appointment card and places it on the counter.

Drew is leaning against the wall behind me, still quiet and removed, not even noticing Jessie's excitement at existing so close to him. I want to tell her to calm the heck down, but there's no point. Besides, he's so gorgeous she'd probably freak out even if he weren't *Andrew Forrester.*

I snatch up the card and grab Drew's hand, towing him out of the office. Once we get to the elevators, I turn to him. "Hey. Are you okay with all of this?"

Drew finally snaps out of it and notices me next to him. His distant expression becomes laser-focused on me. "I can't believe that my child is actually inside you."

"Yes, it is." It's not much but it's all I can think of to say.

His mouth twitches up at the corner. "I guess it just didn't seem real until now. I'm so happy, thank you for giving this to me." Drew pulls me into a crushing hug just as the elevator pings and the doors open.

He breaks the embrace and takes my hand, leading me into the elevator. Drew pushes G and turns back to me.

"I thought you were in there freaking out, you know, trying to find a way out of this situation."

Drew tugs on my hand, pulling me up against him. "No way would I ever want out, Sydney." He slants his mouth down over mine, skimming his tongue over my lips. I kiss him back, not holding back, as my heart pounds wildly in my chest.

The elevator pings again, and the doors open on the 4th floor. We break apart and a young man in a suit steps in. His head is down and he's reading something on his phone, so he doesn't notice us until he bumps into Drew.

"I'm so sorry," he says as he looks up. "I didn't expect anyone…" The man's face registers shock when he realizes whose foot he just stepped on. "I, I'm s-s-sorry." The poor guy's face is bright red and he turns to the front of the elevator.

Well, that's not awkward or anything.

I look at Drew and we both cover our mouths and silently laugh.

CHAPTER 19

I'm so nervous that I might throw up. I pace the tiny room, drawing stares from both my mom and Drew who are sitting calmly on the couch.

"Sydney, please stop. You're going to be a sweaty mess if you keep running around like that," my mom says in a soothing voice.

Drew stands up and puts his hands on my shoulders, forcing me to stop my pacing. I look up at his handsome, perfectly composed face.

"Syd, it's going to be okay. I'll be right off to the side where you can see me the entire time. They'll love you, but you can still back out if you want to."

He gives me a serious look and brushes his lips across mine. The contact is so soothing that I want him next to me when I do this. I know that's not going to happen. Today is not the day for that bomb to drop.

The door to the little room opens and a woman in a huge headset comes in. "Miss Allen, Ms. Allen, it's time." She gestures for us to follow.

"Actually, it's Miss Tannen now, not Allen," I say as I glance at my mom. She winks and walks out the door.

"Are you ready?" Drew asks, looking in my eyes for reassurance that I'm not going to fall apart. This was my idea for god's sake! I need to get it together.

"Like ripping off a Band-Aid, right?" I smile nervously. He smiles back and laughs uncomfortably. Drew thinks this is an absolutely awful idea, and is only going along with it at my insistence.

"Let's go." I take his hand, letting him lead me out behind my mom.

Soon, we're close enough to be able to hear the murmurings of a large crowd of people. The hallways get more and more crowded the further we walk. I start wondering what in the heck I was thinking when I suggested this to my mom. We made calls—well, Mom made a call to her agent who made the calls for us, but still—it was my idiotic idea.

I told her that the best way to stop the speculation about where I went twelve years ago and to reintroduce her to the public after her leave of absence was to go on the biggest nightly talk show in the country. In one hour we could both stop the media from digging to uncover me, and put my mom back into the spotlight for her return to acting.

When we told Drew, he vehemently opposed the idea, trying to tell me I couldn't do it. He'd rather have me stay hidden away. That's not realistic with stars as big as Drew and my mom in my life.

He's even more over-protective now that I'm pregnant and painstakingly went through each scenario point by point to see which option would be safest, coming to the conclusion that appearing on TV was the worst one as far as he was concerned.

In the end, I told him I was done hiding, done freaking out over exposure, and most importantly, I want to be able to be with him openly. Now, I'm thinking he was right and I may have made a huge mistake.

We reach the edge of the stage as the host of *Late Night Report*, Brandon Eastlake, starts his comedic monologue. Mom is paying close attention to the directions given to us by the assistant in the big earphones. I'm not listening. I figure I'll just follow my mom and do what she does. She's the celebrity after all. I'm just the curiosity from her past.

Drew has his hand on my lower back, keeping me close. I feel his other hand slide across my belly in a soft caress. He leans down close to my ear. "I love you Sydney, no matter what." His whisper sends chills down my spine.

I put my hand over his and look up at him. "I love you too, always." He gives me a kiss on the top of my head and it's time to go.

I follow my mom out from the backstage area and into the bright lights of the stage. Five million people watch this show every week. When they announced yesterday that Evangeline Allen and Sydney Tannen would be appearing tonight, they estimated that twenty million or more might watch just this one episode.

Even though I feel sick, I smile at the studio audience, or where I think they are, judging by the deafening roar. I can't see much due to the blinding spotlights. I manage to walk over to Brandon and get a hug and an air kiss, then sit down next to my mom on one of the plush blue chairs.

The crowd refuses to stop clapping and whistling, ecstatic to see my mom. I grin and look over at Drew, who's standing just beyond the view of the audience, applauding for her as well.

"Well well well!" says Brandon Eastlake, attempting to get the crowd to calm down. "That's gotta be the most enthusiastic reception we've ever had here on the show!" He smiles, clapping along with the audience.

After an eternity, the noise stops so he can begin the interview. "So…how've you both been?" The studio audience goes crazy again, and Brandon has to wave his hands to get them to stop. "No really, you both left California over ten years ago and there's been no mention of either of you since. What happened?"

"Hi Brandon," my mom says politely. She looks so beautiful here in her element. She's radiant, the epitome of a movie star. I, on the other hand, am shaking like a leaf, sitting on my hands to hide the twitching. "Where do I begin?" The crowd laughs, as entranced by her as they were twelve years ago.

"You did great, Sydney." Brandon Eastlake is congratulating me backstage after the show. He had been quite surprised to see that I was dating 'Sexiest Man Alive' Andrew Forrester, but understood why we didn't want to come out as a couple just yet. He said that our story about why we left Hollywood and how my parents sacrificed everything was so amazing, that even he was blown away.

When he had asked me onstage how it felt learning that the video seen round the world didn't break my parents up, I choked up on camera, earning sympathetic noises from the audience. I told him how grateful I was that my parents loved me enough to make such huge sacrifices for me.

Discussing the accident with the paparazzi became very emotional, my mom and I both on the verge of tears when describing what happened. Several times I glanced at Drew and saw him clenching his fists, completely stressed out. He looked like he was about one second from running on stage, scooping me up, and taking me away. Somehow, he managed to keep his promise and stay out of sight.

Brandon asked if I had any plans to reunite with my father now that I was out of hiding. I told him I would definitely reach out to my dad soon.

Mom discussed her future plans, and the movie she would begin filming next month in Georgia, a futuristic adaptation of *Gone With the Wind* called *Atlanta Burns*. The screenwriter remembered it was her favorite story and wrote the part just for her. I mean, my middle name is Scarlett, that pretty much says it all.

Then she recounted some of her most famous roles and Brandon asked about her favorite ones.

The audience, and Brandon for that matter, was floored when I said I didn't own a TV and had never seen his show. He made me promise that I would buy one just so I could see him every night before I went to bed. While the crowd laughed at his joke, Drew stood offstage and glared at the handsome host for flirting with me.

Drew seems to have gotten past his ridiculous jealousy over my lighthearted teasing onstage, and is having an animated conversation with Brandon Eastlake. He's met Brandon several times, *of course*, and they're discussing a football game from a few weeks ago where Drew's Patriots beat Brandon's Giants. Drew is more than happy to be an ungraceful winner, telling Brandon that his team will always be second to the Pats. That causes Brandon to start in on the Red Sox/Yankees rivalry and I have to excuse myself to get away from the testosterone.

"You did great, mom." I give my mom a big hug.

She smiles and hugs me back. "You are the one who did great, Syd. I'm so proud of you for getting out there and taking control of your future. Your dad is proud, I'm sure." Her eyes are a little teary when she mentions Dad. "You really think you'll call him? He would love that Sydney. I know he misses you terribly."

"I will Mom. I meant it. I just want to wait for this," I gesture around us, "mess to settle down first. Plus, Drew wants me to go to his movie premiere next week. Maybe I'll call him while we're in L.A. Although with tonight, then the premiere with Drew, the media is going to go nuts."

I stop myself from going down that road. "But you know, I'm doing things my way now, so who cares about the media? I'll call Dad when I'm in L.A. You don't happen to have his number, do you?"

She laughs and pulls out her phone.

Of course she does.

CHAPTER 20

I'm waiting for Leah to bring my packed suitcases over to Drew's brownstone. Ever since the *Late Night Report* interview aired two days ago, my loft has been under siege by reporters and paparazzi. I don't know why I thought that the show would satisfy everyone's curiosity about who Sydney Tannen is, but it didn't. I do think it will die down soon, they have to lose interest at some point. Maybe not after Drew and I walk the red carpet Saturday night, but eventually.

It has to, right?

Drew said a movie he wrapped last summer is going to be prepped for a limited release and asked if I would go with him to the Los Angeles premiere. I don't want to go, but I figured we're doing things the new way these days by 'going big or going home' so for some crazy reason I told him yes.

After the interview aired, I'm not surprised by the sheer number of blogs and gossip sites devoted to me and my mom and of course, the corresponding made up articles supposedly quoting my dad's reaction to everything.

What does surprise me is how little I care. Living through this as a kid is much different than as an adult. I know what is true and what isn't and that's pretty much all that matters. As a child, completely removed from the truth, but on the receiving end of the psychotic fans and teasing from classmates, it was impossible to understand.

"Thank god I'm out of there! Your neighbors must hate you, Sydney!" Leah bursts through Drew's front door. Bruce follows behind, hauling two giant suitcases and a hanging garment bag, straining under their weight.

"Leah! That is way too much stuff for one weekend!"

She huffs, putting her hands on her hips. "Well, you didn't have to run the gauntlet through those crazy people! I was under a lot of pressure! It's a good thing they don't know who I am. I was at least able to get inside without a camera getting stuck in my face. Poor Bruce was shoved by reporter who thought a girl with dark red hair delivering something to the concierge was you. He almost got trampled to death!"

On the inside, I'm laughing at Leah, because she insisted all these years that it wouldn't be a big deal for me to live normally and not hide my identity. Now she's on the receiving end of exactly how *not* normal my life is and it's pretty humorous.

"Thanks, Bruce." I pat Drew's driver on the arm. "I'm so sorry you almost got stepped on. Are you okay?"

He puts the suitcases down and smiles. "It's not nearly as dramatic as all that, Sydney. I was pushed and I stumbled a little. No big deal." His kind expression lets me know that he doesn't want to be fussed over.

Drew comes down the stairs and sees Leah, red-faced and dripping sweat, takes in my amused expression and chuckles. "They got you, huh Leah?"

"It's not funny, jerk. Bruce almost died!" She has a petulant look on her flushed face.

"Leah, stop it!" I laugh. "Bruce did not almost die!" Bruce turns an interesting shade of purple as we all stare at him.

Drew steps over and shakes his hand, clapping the older man's shoulder. "Bruce, man, thanks for the favor. We'll see you tomorrow morning."

"I'll just go then." The very relieved driver darts out the front door and sprints for the car.

Drew and I burst out laughing at the scene we just witnessed.

"You guys can just go get Sydney's stuff yourselves next time," Leah snaps and points a finger at us. She's all flustered and disheveled. Her blonde hair is falling out of her ponytail and her clothes are wrinkled and a little dirty.

"I'm sorry, Leah, we appreciate what you've done. There's no way either of us could go anywhere near my place right now. Maybe when we get back or something…" I stop talking when I notice the incredulous looks that Drew and Leah are giving me. "What?"

"Sydney, we're going public as a couple in a day and a half. We not only won't be able to go to your place, but they're going to be outside here as well," Drew says as he pulls me into his arms.

"Well," I push back from him and throw up my hands in frustration. "I guess we'll just live on the street then. I don't care." I stare them both down. "When we get back we're going to stay wherever we want to stay. I don't care if they're outside all day and night!"

"Syd, I love the new you." Drew grins and gives me a big kiss. "But I don't think I could kick that many asses if anything happened to you in that mob. So let's just play it by ear and stay in a hotel if we have to. I'd be willing to bet we could get a room at the Warren. I hear they just redid their nightclub and it's pretty impressive. All the cool celebrities want to go there."

I punch his arm lightly. "Smartass."

CHAPTER 21

Drew's agent, Quentin Adair, is checking us into the Sunset Marquis in West Hollywood while we wait in the car like children. I know it's better not to waltz into the lobby together and stand around at the front desk while guests stare at us, but I feel useless, forced into having someone else take care of me while I sit here. Plus it's late. Our flight from Teterboro got into Van Nuys over an hour ago and we just got to the hotel. I swear Los Angeles traffic could stand up to New York City traffic any day of the week.

While I'm sulking and irritated, Drew is in a great mood. He's frisky, continuously trying to feel me up in the back seat, saying that as long as we're sitting in the back of a car in the dark we might as well make out. Tired of fending him off, I allow him to slip his hand up my shirt, too fed up to protest anymore.

He takes advantage of my moment of weakness and pulls the cup of my bra down, rolling my nipple with his thumb and forefinger. I suck in a sharp breath, and he takes that as a green light. Drew yanks up my shirt and draws my breast into his hot mouth, sucking and nibbling until I'm writhing on the back seat.

"Drew, Quentin will be back soon."

He doesn't move his mouth away to answer me. "Don't think about him while I'm trying to seduce you, Sydney. I don't like it."

So jealous.

Drew continues torturing me, then tugs down the opposite side of my bra, releasing the other breast and begins laving that side.

He bites down causing me to gasp out loud, and vanishes, pulling my shirt back over my exposed breasts.

The front door of the car opens and Quentin hops in. He twists in the seat and hands Drew an envelope and two key cards. "Here's your info and your keys. You're in the Presidential Villa, so you'll have a little bit of a walk. Drew, you know the way, right?"

"Yes, thank you for doing this. Sydney wanted to walk right on in the front door," he says, ratting me out in front of someone I just met.

My mouth falls open and I smack his chest. "Don't be an ass, Drew."

Quentin throws his head back and laughs. "Man, I love to see someone who doesn't kiss your butt, pretty boy."

I like Drew's agent a lot. He's down to earth and about as un-Hollywood an agent you could find. He kind of reminds me of Drew, a man's man: honest, direct, and a little rough around the edges. Drew told me that Quentin signed him back in Boston, where they're both from.

Quentin was visiting family back home and went to see his nephew in a small playhouse production of Ibsen's *A Doll's House*. He was awestruck by nineteen year old Drew's performance as the complicated Krogstad. Shortly after, Quentin got Drew his first major role as Finn Connell in the Thomas C. Sullivan film *Greater Good*. Chad got an Oscar for directing, and Drew became a star overnight.

I had Drew tell me all of this on the flight from New Jersey, so between that and some help from a Google search I did on the plane, I hope I know enough about his work to officially be his girlfriend. I don't want to seem ignorant when it comes to Drew's acting.

I stopped short of watching any of his movies. The Google search was intimidating enough, similar to the search I did on my dad. Massive amounts of information about Drew are out there for anyone to read. I hate it. I looked at his IMBD page and his Wikipedia page. Both seemed accurate to my knowledge, which is zero.

I also broke down and read the blog about the night Drew confronted Adam and Kiera at Verve. I shouldn't have done that.

March 9

Written by Kate M.

Superhot superstar Andrew Forrester almost came to blows with sexy Brit rocker Adam Reynolds last night at the NYC launch party for Verve, the swank new nightclub at the top of the Warren Hotel. A partygoer tells us that Reynolds and an unknown smokin' hot redhead were getting cozy when Reynolds' ex Kiera Radcliff confronted the other woman. The redhead immediately left the hotel after exchanging words with Radcliff.

Forrester arrived thirty minutes later, looking incredibly agitated, and headed straight for Reynolds and Radcliff who were still arguing over the

departure of Reynolds' mystery date. Forrester reportedly got in Reynolds'
face and was yelling at him over the beautiful redhead. A female friend
intervened and convinced Forrester to leave the nightclub before any
punches were thrown.

Who's the redhead that has these two gorgeous hunks fighting over her?
What did Radcliff say to upset the unknown woman and cause Forrester
to come to her defense? Will it affect the chemistry between Forrester and
Radcliff in the movie they are supposed to start filming soon? We hope to
find this lucky girl soon and get some answers!

If that weren't bad enough, there was a picture of Drew
inches from Adam's face, his fists balled up at his side. Drew is
obviously shouting and Adam is holding his hands up in a gesture
meant to calm Drew down.

And the best part? There's one-hundred and five pound Leah
in her form-fitting little black dress, trying to push the towering Drew
away from Adam while Kiera Radcliff stands right behind her,
looking quite pleased with herself.

I turned my computer off after that, disgusted by the article.
After thinking about it for a while, I conclude that it actually didn't
say a single thing that wasn't true. Well, except for the *getting cozy* with
Adam part. I'm more mad at myself for putting Drew in the position
where he felt he had to defend me to Adam and Kiera. And now,
after meeting her? The thought of Drew working with her makes me
physically ill.

Quentin had a bellhop get our luggage out of the trunk when we got here, so Drew and I jump out of the car and head straight for our villa. We have to take an outdoor path to our room, but Drew knows exactly where to go.

He tugs my hand impatiently, hurrying me along. I smile, knowing he wants to continue what he started in the car. It's his own fault if he's feeling frustrated. I told him several times to stop.

When we get to our villa he hurriedly swipes the keycard, unlocking the door. Drew pulls me through and slams the door shut behind us. I turn to see him standing in front of the door, his eyes feral and intimidating but so hot that one look would make any female's panties combust on the spot.

Drew takes a step toward me, yanking his shirt over his head and throwing it aside as he advances, the muscles of his beautiful torso flexing with each graceful move.

Instinctively, I take a step back. He tilts his head and gives me a wicked smile. "Is that how it is, Sydney? Are you going to make me chase you?"

I attempt to answer, but nothing comes out. I have no idea why I stepped back. It's purely a visceral reaction to him stalking towards me. My heart is beating a million miles an hour from the devilish look on his face and the physical perfection of his abs. I take another step back, unable to stop myself.

"I see." Without breaking eye contact, he unbuckles his belt and unfastens his fly. Taking two slow steps, Drew kicks off each shoe and licks his lips. "I will catch you, and then I'm going to make you scream for teasing me."

Oh. My. God.

"I'm not teasing you," I whisper. The combination of excitement and nerves sends a streak of lightning through my body, rippling over my skin.

He takes another step toward me and strips off his pants and socks. I move back again, matching his forward movement by going back with each step. Drew is standing in front of me, clothed only in his low slung black boxer briefs. I realize I'm blatantly staring at the huge bulge in his briefs and flick my gaze back up.

"Eye fucking me again, Sydney?" He moves toward me again.

"No," I croak and step back into a wall.

Knowing that I'm trapped, Drew closes the final steps and puts his hands against the wall on either side of my head. The heat from his body is like a blowtorch on my skin.

"Why are you trying to get away from me?" He trails his lips up my neck and murmurs in my ear. "Don't you want me, Sydney?" He starts unbuttoning my jeans.

I like this version of Drew. He's intimidating but hot as hell. He dips his hand down the front of my pants and slides a finger down inside.

"Always so wet. I think you *do* want me, you just like to drive me crazy." He removes his hand and puts it inside my shirt, tracing wet circles on my breast with my own arousal.

"Drew." I throw my head back against the wall as he tortures me. Reaching out, I rake my nails down his hard chest, trailing them across his defined abs and stopping at the waistband of his briefs.

The sharp intake of his breath and the flinch of his skin when I touch him lets me know that he's hovering on the edge of losing control. I remove my hands and pull my shirt off, my breasts still exposed from when he freed them from my lingerie in the car.

"God you're so fucking hot, Syd. You have no idea what you do to me, to my self-control." Drew reaches around and unhooks the lace bra letting it fall to the floor.

He closes his eyes. I watch the muscles in his jaw working as he desperately tries to contain his lust. When he opens his eyes and looks into mine, I know that he's not going to be able to hold back much longer. I unzip my jeans and shimmy them down, then reach to him and slide my thumbs under the waistband of his briefs. Tugging hard, I yank his body against mine.

Drew groans when his hard shaft rubs against me. I hike one leg up around his hips and lock him tight against the lace of my panties.

"I want you." I tilt my head, dragging my wet tongue across his collarbone.

He steps back, breaking my grip. His eyes are wild with desire. Drew shoves down his boxer briefs and grabs the fabric of my panties at each hipbone. With one sharp tug, he tears them apart and flings the scraps aside.

Drew presses his hot length against me, reaches under my knee to lift up my leg, and thrusts into me roughly.

"Fuck, you feel so good," he grunts as he pulls up my other leg.

I use my thighs to clamp down around his narrow hips as Drew slides his hands under my backside, holding me against the wall. I wrap my arms around his neck and kiss him, probing with my tongue as he brands me as his. Drew drives up into my tight passage over and over at an unrelenting pace as I pant and whisper into his mouth.

"Don't hold back Sydney!"

I feel the building pressure of my climax rising as his strokes quicken. Drew rotates his hips, grinding into me roughly and I shatter, screaming his name as a powerful orgasm punches through me.

Drew bites down on my shoulder as I pulse around him, and comes in violent spurts. He holds me against the wall, letting us both return to earth from our high. I nuzzle his neck and inhale, loving the scent of him mixed with sex.

Not wanting to lose our intimate contact, Drew carries me over to the bedroom nearest to the door, keeping us locked together. He places me down on the bed and lies on top of me, gently kissing me as we catch our breath.

"I love you so much, Drew." I knead his strong arms and shoulders, reveling in the feel of his powerful body.

"I love you too, Syd." He presses one last kiss on my lips and rolls off of me, turning to pull me close to him. His hand spreads out over my belly, protective as always, and we fall asleep.

CHAPTER 22

A knock on the door of the villa alerts us that Drew's family has arrived. We're having brunch in our suite with the Forrester's, his parents Andy and Caroline, and his sister Allie, before we all go to the movie premiere later.

Drew's sister comes flying through the doorway, giving me one of the most enthusiastic hugs I've ever received. "I'm so glad my brother found you!" she exclaims as she releases me from her arms. "Is it true you've never seen a single one of his movies?" Allie flicks her wavy brown hair out of her familiar green eyes and the whole family turns to wait for my answer.

"Ummm, well yes. It's true. Tomorrow will be my first one." I can feel the prickly heat staining my cheeks. Drew has been talking about me behind my back.

"Oh my God! It's so great that you don't think he's some hot shot celebrity!" his sister squeals. "You realize that you, me, and my mom are the only three women on earth who aren't impressed by Drew's 'Sexiest Man' title?"

I glance over at Drew's mother, Caroline, who's nodding in agreement. Allie makes a face. "I can't even tell anyone who my brother is. If I did, people would be on my doorstep to meet him and the line would wrap around the earth three times, no joke!" Allie laughs, but I suspect there is some truth behind her statement.

The brunch has already been set up by the staff from the hotel, so everyone takes a seat at the dining room table and we pass around the dishes.

Drew's dad, Andy, looks at me smiling. "Sydney, we saw your interview on *Late Night Report*. You did well for someone not used to being on TV."

It's a little disconcerting looking at him. He's an older version of Drew but with brown eyes and gray in his hair.

"Yes, Sydney," Caroline says, turning her green eyes on me. "You were just charming dear. I'm so sorry about what happened to your family, though." She pats my hand sweetly.

I don't want to cry. I swallow the bite of fruit I was chewing before I answer. "It was tough, but I'm here now and that's what's important." I give her a shaky smile and sip some orange juice.

Mr. and Mrs. Forrester, or Andy and Caroline as they insist that I call them, are obviously ecstatic that Drew has found me. They are well aware that I'm with Drew for love and nothing more. I don't want the fame and I have my own fortune. According to them, they couldn't want anything better for their son.

We haven't told them about the pregnancy yet. We figure we can worry about that after we get through the media storm that tonight is going to create.

Drew's dad describes his job as an architect for the city of Boston school system, designing new schools and making improvements to older schools that are falling apart. I love any kind of design, so I listen intently as he tells me about his work.

Caroline Forrester is a tiny powerhouse. She's only about five foot three inches and one hundred pounds, maybe. She has shoulder length hair, the same rich brown color as Drew and Allie, along with those unusual green eyes. She used to teach elementary school, but retired when the fans and women coming to the school got to be too much to be safe for the children

"So you can't teach anymore?" The shock I feel must be evident in my voice.

Fame destroys a lot of things that people never think of.

"No, I still teach. I teach kids at the inpatient cancer ward for the Boston Children's Hospital. Through Drew's charity." Caroline takes a bite of her French toast.

I must look lost because she continues, turning her gaze on Drew. "Drew, you did tell Sydney about your wonderful charitable work, didn't you?"

He shifts uncomfortably in his chair, twisting his napkin. "No Mom, it never came up."

My gaze bounces from Drew to his mother and back. When I look over at Allie, she shrugs. "He doesn't want the attention. He's really modest that way. For a big-headed, super sexy, world famous celebrity that is." She smiles sweetly at her brother as she says the last part.

"You have a charity?" I ask softly, looking at Drew.

He's embarrassed to talk about it, an adorable blush spreading up his neck. He clears his throat. "Ummm, yes. It provides teachers and equipment to children who are hospitalized for long periods of time, mostly on the cancer units."

Caroline reaches out and pats my hand. "It's a wonderful organization. We have offices in six major cities in the U.S. now. We started with just me at one hospital in Boston." She beams as she talks about her son's accomplishments.

"Mom, you and the Grady's did all the work. I didn't do anything. Stop referring to it as *my* charity." Drew admonishes his mother.

"Stop it Drew," his dad says firmly, holding up a hand. "Without the money, there is no charity. You're just as important in keeping it afloat as the Grady's and your mother." Andy addresses me. "Sydney, Drew donated the startup money, does fund raisers to get more money every year, and continues to contribute personally. He thinks it's nothing, but it's not. It's everything."

"Who are the Grady's?" I ask Caroline, since it's obvious that Drew doesn't want to discuss this right now.

Allie obliges my curiosity. "Drew's best friend died of a brain tumor in high school. His surviving twin brother and their parents are the Grady's. They run the charity."

Could I possibly love him anymore than I already do?

"That's wonderful, Drew." My eyes burn with tears from the sheer strength of my love for him. I lean in and place a kiss on his jaw.

Drew glances over and gives me a small smile. Yep, I just fell in love with him a little more. We finish eating and his family heads back to their villa next door. Everyone wants to rest before getting ready for tonight.

"That one," Drew says, wandering in from the living room of our villa. I'm trying on one of the dozens of dresses that he had sent over to the hotel by various designers. Each designer hoping to be the one dressing the *mystery redhead* that the blogs have been wondering about since the incident at Verve.

They have no confirmation that Drew is bringing the *unknown female* to the premier. He's getting dresses for his sister for all they know. Which, technically, he is, since his sister is in the next villa and she has a rack of dresses of her own to try on.

Right now, I'm standing in the living room of the Presidential Villa at the Sunset Marquis, while a stylist and a seamstress whip off the dress that I chose to wear tonight to Drew's premier.

I went with the one he loved, a red floor length crepe gown with a top-stitched bustier and double shoulder straps that make the back different and visually interesting. It just needs minor adjustments so the seamstress is busy at work. There's only three hours until the red carpet, and it needs to fit perfectly.

Normally, this would have been done weeks ago but this is a special exception and Drew made it happen somehow. He made his poor assistant, Jane, fly out here the morning after I told Drew I would go with him to the premiere with instructions to call every major designer and get a dress in my size.

She was to tell them it was to be worn by Andrew Forrester's date at the red carpet debut for his new movie. The designers, knowing that Drew *never* brings a date to his events, and that the person wearing it might be the woman who caused the infamous blowup at Verve, jumped at the chance to dress me.

When I finally got to meet Jane, I liked her immensely. She brought the dresses by the hotel earlier today. Forty-five, short and slightly round, she's patient enough to put up with Drew's demands, but strong enough to deal with him when he acts like an ass. He told me that he couldn't possibly do his job without her.

I sit down and remove the 4" gold and bronze cutout patent leather sandals that I chose to go with the gown and set them on the floor. Drew comes over and sits next to me, sliding a finger up the open edge of my robe from my breast to my collarbone. I give him a reprimanding look. The seamstress is at the dining room table with only a thin wall separating us and he's getting frisky?

"Drew, stop it." I push his hand away. He laughs and kisses my cheek.

"How are you feeling?" I know he's asking about the pregnancy.

"Fine." I try not to twist my mouth into a scowl.

I've been a lot more nauseated today than normal. I'm not even nauseous really, it's more of an ache just below my stomach. I'm sure it's from the rich food we had this morning at brunch, but Drew gets way too worried about every little thing and if I told him I was unwell, he'd refuse to go to his own movie premiere. Besides, it's not nearly as bad as I felt a few weeks ago.

Drew arches an eyebrow at my sharp response and says nothing. He takes my hand and presses a kiss to my wrist. "I'm going to go check on my parents next door, I'll be right back okay?"

"Sure baby, go hang out with your parents. I'm going to lay down while my dress is finished."

I know he wants to have a beer with his father and watch SportsCenter. He's missed having guy time with people who don't treat him differently. He needs to loosen up before the premiere anyway.

He's very tense about my debut. I know it bothers him that he can't protect me from all of the attention that comes with his job. The scrutiny of the press, the rabid female fans, the men who will drool all over me—it drives him nuts that he can't control any of it.

It's interesting how little he cares about what people think or say about him, but he gets downright disturbed when he hears about anyone trying to get to close to me.

Drew read a few of the articles that were posted on some of the major tabloid websites the day after the interview with my mom. Bad idea. I found him breaking one of the laptops in his brownstone after reading a bunch of sexually explicit comments about me from men who, in Drew's words, needed to have "his foot put in their disgusting asses." I tried to keep him away from the computer after that.

The ache in my abdomen worsens, so I curl up on the huge bed in the master bedroom. I must have dozed off for a while because someone knocks on my door at some point and comes right on in.

"Here you go Miss Tannen." The tiny elderly seamstress enters the room with my gown.

I shake the sleep from my body, stand up and remove my robe, wearing only my strapless bra and thong panties. She helps me try it on again and I slip on my heels. It's perfect. I look tall and fit and almost exactly like my mom.

I must have been in major denial about blending in. How did no one ever figure this out? My last name was Allen for god's sake! The seamstress undoes the zipper and we hang it up until it's time to go.

I hear voices in the suite and glance at the clock. Hair and makeup must be here. I don't know if I'm ready for this, to walk the red carpet with Drew. Too late now. I take a deep breath, ignore the ache in my gut, and walk into the living room.

They're almost done caking a pound of foundation on my face when Drew returns to the villa. Allie is sitting next to me, getting the finishing touches on her makeup while the hairstylist is spraying a heavy coat on my *artfully tousled* hair.

Why spend two hours and a use an entire bottle of hairspray to look like you just rolled in from a day at the beach is beyond me, but it looks gorgeous. I guess that's what counts.

"Hey babe," I call out as Drew comes into the room. "I need help getting into my dress?"

"I'd rather keep you out of your dress if you don't mind," he jokes back suggestively.

"Ewwww, stop it!" Allie covers her ears so she doesn't have to hear her brother discuss getting me naked. "The whole shirtless, sexy thing is gross enough to have to deal with all the time. I can't be a part of listening to your sex talk!"

"Sorry Al. it's Sydney's fault for being so gorgeous." Drew grabs my hand and tows me toward the bedroom. I give Allie an apologetic look just as Drew yanks me in and shuts the door.

CHAPTER 23

We're both nervous wrecks in the back of the limo as we ride to the theater. Quentin is with us as is Jane and Drew's director of PR, Rhys Porter. Rhys has been yammering on the phone for the entire twenty minute drive, barking out instructions to whatever poor assistant is on the other end of the call. We're crawling along in a line of vehicles, inching up to the entrance of the theater.

I'm trying to hide my worsening stomach ache from Drew. I don't want to ruin today with some pregnancy ailment or stomach flu. That's all I need is to get to the theater and have diarrhea or something awful like that.

That would be just my luck. Especially since Drew won't be wearing his hideous lucky hat tonight. If he wore that gross thing on camera, a million fantasies would die on the spot. I mean, I love the hat, because I love Drew, but anyone who doesn't know him well enough to know how special that hat is, would run in the other direction as soon as he put it on.

Rhys disconnects the call and addresses me and Drew. "So, we're the last to arrive. Drew, you get out first, and help Sydney from the limo."

Drew looks at him sharply, annoyed that Rhys would assume he doesn't know to help me out of the car. Rhys ignores him and continues.

"Then Quentin and I will walk behind you, to make sure you have space and no one gets too close. Jane will walk in front of you to help get you to each reporter that we promised an interview to."

Jane nods so he turns his laser focus on me. "Sydney, you can join Drew for some or all of the television interviews, it's your choice—"

Drew interrupts rudely. "She's staying with me the entire time." He stares at me, daring me to challenge him. "I don't want you leaving my side. Not for one second. It's going to be an absolute shitstorm out there with us together. No way will you be where I can't see you."

"Drew, it's up to Sydney—"

"Rhys, it's not up for fuckin' discussion. That's it!" His voice is turning Boston. Drew is so anxious that he's starting to get pissed.

I put my hand in his and squeeze. "I'll stay with Drew, it's fine. That's what I want anyway. I'm too nervous to be without him." Rhys calms down some and nods his consent.

Quentin leans forward to pat my knee, which earns him a dark glare from Drew that he blatantly ignores. "You'll do fine, Sydney. I mean heck, you were literally born to do this!" He smiles and sits back as the limo reaches the front of the line. Poor Jane gives me a sympathetic smile, certainly feeling the waves of anxiety coming off of my body and the waves of testosterone coming off of Drew's.

We glide to a stop in front of the theater. I take a deep breath, wincing from the pain in my belly.

"Are you okay?" Drew asks, eyeballing me suspiciously. I'm sure I look pale and scared.

"Of course. Your fans are waiting babe." I give him a big fake smile. I might as well start faking it now, since I'll have to do it for the next thirty minutes straight on the red carpet. He gives me a sour look, like he doesn't quite believe me, but turns and exits the car when the door is opened.

The roar from that erupts from the crowd when Drew steps out is deafening. His family so is lucky that they got to skip this and go straight inside. Flashbulbs are firing off in a rapid staccato. Drew waves then ducks down and extends a hand to me. I say a quick prayer that I don't fall down, grabbing his hand as Drew guides me out of the car.

Oh. My. God.

If I were claustrophobic, I'd be dead by now. The carpet is wide, but it's surrounded wall-to-wall by people with cameras. In random places, workers are directing the guests to the different interview areas along the edges. Behind the swarm of cameras are bleachers full of screaming women. Hundreds of them. Waving papers and photos of Drew and signs, *Marry Me!*, *Mrs. Forrester!*, *I Love You!*, and all of that nonsense.

I get hit in the face by the bright lights and people start screaming even louder. I thought this was a tiny independent film! The magnitude of Drew's celebrity is starting to sink in.

Drew threads his fingers with mine and smiles at me, his fake Andrew Forrester face ready to go. Leaning down he whispers in my ear. "I love you baby, let's do this." He squeezes my hand and we begin to walk.

The sharp eyed reporters closest to the car figured out who I was the second I exited the limo. I hear "Sydney Tannen", "Sydney Tannen is the redhead", and "that's Sydney Tannen" exclaimed up and down the line of photographers. That causes the already frenzied crowd to up their excitement to subatomic levels. Now they have a name for their mystery woman from the Adam Reynolds incident at Verve.

Every two or three steps someone asks us to pose for them. Each time, Drew puts his arm around my waist and either smiles for the camera, or smiles down at me. I do my best to just smile and not look like a pregnant girl in pain. There's a lot of smiling going on.

A few lucky fans have scored spots along the red carpet. Drew greets them politely with his Andrew Forrester the actor persona, signs their papers, and poses for a few photos with them.

He tilts his head down to me again, whispering comforting words in my ear. I keep smiling and nod. I don't want anything I say to Drew to be overheard by anyone so I choose to keep quiet.

People are screaming my name now too. Begging me to pose for them or look at their camera, or even sign their papers. I'm not signing any autographs, it's weird. I wave awkwardly instead.

Jane guides us to the first interview showing us where to stand. I have no idea how the reporter is supposed to ask us anything, it's so loud with all of the screaming.

Drew puts his hand on my lower back and we move into position next to a super skinny blonde woman who wears way too much makeup.

She introduces herself and what show she's from and starts throwing questions at us before we can blink. Who am I wearing? How did we meet? Am I the unknown female from the club? Was I dating Adam Reynolds? Have I seen the movie yet? Before she can even ask a single question about the film, we're pulled away by a girl with an earpiece and continue up the carpet behind Jane. Drew clenched his jaw and squeezed my hand too tight when the Adam question came up.

He's never going to let that go.

By the time we finish posing in front of the step and repeat we're almost to the end of the carpet and I'm exhausted. My face hurts from smiling so much, and my abdomen is killing me. We've done about five interviews and posed for thousands of photos.

Drew wanted to avoid the whole are they or aren't they dating speculation, so he told me he planned to kiss me in front of the cameras when we reached the end of the red carpet. Go big or go home, typical Drew style. Personally, I think he wants to kill any talk of me dating Adam Reynolds, but this is his premiere. I'm going along with what he wants even though I would prefer not to have our private moments captured on film.

He turns toward me and gently tugs my hand, the signal he gave so I would know when he was going to kiss me. Drew puts one arm around me and pulls me in close. He brings his other hand up to caress my face. I notice the Andrew Forrester mask is gone and I have my Drew back with me.

The crowd starts to scream even louder than I thought was possible. He leans down and presses his lips to mine softly, keeping it tame for the cameras. Drew ends the kiss and grins at me, and I can't help but grin back.

Drew is amazing on film. It may have been twelve years since I've seen a movie, but that doesn't mean I can't tell the difference between great and brilliant. And my boyfriend is brilliant.

A Soldier's Burden is about an Army Ranger, Roger "Rogue" Hillston, and how he struggles to deal with the friendly fire death of his best friend by another man in their regiment.

I am captivated by the powerful emotions he gives Roger. Drew is beautiful up on the huge screen. I can see why people love him so much. He's rugged, intimidating, and handsome as the tormented soldier.

Truthfully, if I had seen him like this before meeting him, I would have been too scared to talk to him. He's literally and figuratively larger than life.

Drew keeps a death grip on my hand for the entire screening. He seems stiff, almost nervous for me to see his work. Or maybe he's like this for every premiere and just hates watching himself on film.

My mother loathes watching herself to the point that she used to escape to the lobby after the lights went out. Drew has nothing to be nervous about, the movie is enthralling and his performance is hypnotizing.

When the credits begin, the audience jumps to its feet and applauds loudly, people whistling and cheering. I try to stand and clap right along with them, but the shooting pains are impossible to ignore any longer.

I was so absorbed in the film that I had been able to push my stomach pain out of my mind for two hours. But now, as the director begins to thank the crowd and start his speech, I realize that the pain has intensified significantly.

I lean close. "Drew, I need to use the ladies' room. I'll meet you in the lobby."

He grabs my wrist. "I'll come with you," he says quietly but firmly.

I give him an exasperated look. *I can't go to the bathroom by myself?*

"No, you have to speak next. Five minutes. I'll see you out front." He looks unhappy, but he knows he can't leave the theater. Drew offers me a stiff nod and a frown and reluctantly releases my arm.

I give him a quick peck on the cheek and duck out, grateful that we were able to request seats near the back. The other stars are sitting front and center, but I wanted to be up near the doors in case

I had an anxiety attack from walking the red carpet with Drew. I needed to be able to slip out unnoticed.

Hurrying, I cross the empty lobby as fast as I can in a floor length gown and stiletto sandals. A chill creeps down my spine and I break out in a cold sweat, my nerves taking over. Just as I push through the door to the women's bathroom a sharp pain shoots through my abdomen, leaving me bent over, breathless.

Oh god.

I squeeze the tears from my eyes and duck into a stall, leaning against the wall for support. It takes a frustratingly long time to get my gown out of the way to use the toilet. When I stand up, I see blood. Not a lot, but any blood is enough to send a paralyzing wave of fear over my entire body. Not a stomachache.

My baby. Drew's baby. I need to get to him, now.

I burst out of the bathroom, sweating and almost doubled over from the pain. I'm sure I look dreadful, but I don't care. All I can think of is getting Drew to take me to the hospital to save our baby. A disheveled older man stands in front of me, blocking my way to the theater.

"Sydney, are you okay?" He's uncomfortably close.

"I need to get..." Another shooting pain takes my breath away. I groan and put my hand on my belly.

The man touches my arm and I get the creeps. Even in my distress, I register that something is off. How does he know my name? I feel like I know this man, but from where?

Confused, I watch as he pulls out a knife and slides it into my side, clutching me in an embrace as he eases me down to the floor. Strangely, my first thought is how he's not dressed nicely enough to be here.

I sink to my knees and fall back on the carpet with him and hear him whisper, "I've never stopped loving you, Sydney."

I can't manage any words. All I see is a bright light around his face as it dims to nothing.

CHAPTER 24

I need to turn off my alarm clock. The beeping is giving me a headache. When I try to roll over I feel a sharp burn in my arm. Reaching over to rub where it hurts, I find tubes and tape around my elbow. Panic starts to creep in, needling it's way into the edges of my fuzzy mind.

I try to open my eyes, but they feel heavy and sticky, like they're glued shut. I wipe them with my unrestrained hand and look around. It's dark in the room, but there's a small light glowing next to my bed. Wait, not my bed, it's a hospital bed. Then I remember. The cramping, the movie premiere, the blood—the creepy man. I let out a cry and sit up.

Pain! Intense pain! That's my only thought. It overrides anything else in my confused brain. *Make the pain stop!*

"Shhhh, Sydney, you have to stop moving honey." I feel strong hands gently push my shoulders back into the pillow. Drew is here with me, he'll make the agonizing pain stop.

"My side hurts," I moan, panting from the discomfort. "Can't breathe." Drew caresses my face and kisses me on the forehead, combing back my sweaty hair with his big hand.

"I know it does sweetie, relax. I'm getting the nurse." I vaguely register that he's pressing a red button on the side of the bed.

A middle aged woman in pink scrubs comes rushing into the room and straight over to the machines on the side of the bed opposite Drew. "You're awake," she says brightly. "I'll check you real quick and let the doctor know." She starts reading the beeping screens and pushing buttons. I can't help it when another moan escapes my lips as she lifts a bandage on my right side, just below my ribs.

"She's in pain, give her something!" Drew snaps in a loud voice.

His angry tone breaks me from my agony and I swing my head around to face his side of the bed. I take a good look at him. To say he's a mess is to go easy on his appearance. He has a day's worth of stubble on his handsome face, his eyes are wild with dark circles underneath, and his hair is sticking up in all directions. He's coming unraveled. I can see it happening right in here in this hospital room. This must be what Leah saw when he couldn't find me after the party at Verve.

"It's right here, Mr. Forrester," the nurse says patiently. She removes a syringe from her pocket and puts it into the tube on my arm. "There, you should feel better already," she says as she tosses the used needle into a red bucket.

Yes, yes I do feel better, and sleepy.

"I'll just go get the doctor sweetie," she pats my hand and leaves the room.

I must have fallen asleep after the nurse came in because it's light out now. I'm able to get a better look at my surroundings. I know I'm in a hospital, but it looks more like a posh hotel room with a hospital bed in the middle. There's a white board on the wall opposite me that says Cedars-Sinai Medical Center at the top, with my nurses' names scrawled underneath. There's a big screen TV in the corner of the room, a massive dark wood entertainment center around it. Next to that is an open door that leads to what looks like a guest bedroom. I can see that the bed in there is unused.

Drew is sleeping on the tiny couch next to my bed. He's lying on his stomach with his face smashed into the cushion, his long legs falling off the other end. He looks so miserable, and it's my fault. I didn't tell him about the stomach cramps, wouldn't let him go to the bathroom with me at the theater.

I suck in a sharp breath and cringe in pain from the memory. *My baby!* The worsening pains all day, the blood in the toilet, the cramping. What happened to my baby? Our baby, a piece of me and a piece of Drew. I start panicking and crying hysterically, clawing at the blankets to see between my legs. The baby has to be okay!

"Syd, what are you doing? You're scaring me." Drew is awake and attempting to calm me down. He doesn't want to hurt me by forcing me down, but he doesn't want to let me thrash all over the bed either. He's standing there with his hands on his head, unsure of himself, looking as if he might literally pull his own hair out.

"Stop it, Sydney! You're hurting yourself." I've twisted around so much that the I.V. has come out of my arm and is hanging on my skin by a piece of tape. I don't care, I need to know. Drew must decide that he can't watch me anymore because he wraps his hands around my wrists and holds me to his chest as I sob.

"The baby?" I cry softly.

I hear Drew crying with me and I know. Our baby is gone.

CHAPTER 25

"Miss Tannen? Is it okay if I come in and ask you about the assault?" A tall, middle-aged man in gray slacks and a dress shirt with a badge on his belt knocks on the door of my hospital suite and tentatively enters the room.

Drew jumps up from the couch and dashes over to the door. "Do we have to do this now?" he barks at the detective. The officer flinches back at the unexpected hostility of Very Angry Andrew Forrester getting in his face.

"Drew, let the man in," I say from the bed, my voice hoarse from all of the crying. I know I'm going to have to do this eventually. I just want to get it all over with so I can go back to New York and mourn our loss in peace.

"Sydney—" Drew begins. His overprotective tendencies have been in thermo-nuclear overdrive since the attack.

"Please? I just want to get past this." Drew backs off of the detective just enough to turn his head in my direction. "Please?" I repeat, my eyes filling with tears.

Drew's shoulders drop and his jaw clenches. "Fine." He turns back to the officer. "Come in then," he says rudely, refusing to move so the graceful older man has to walk around him.

"I'll leave my partner outside if that will make you more comfortable," he says to me, choosing to ignore Drew since he figures, *correctly*, that he won't do much more than yell. "I'm Detective Henry Keating, my partner, Detective Paul Black is out in the hall.

We've been assigned to your case." He takes a chair from the side of the room and pulls it over next to the bed to sit.

I struggle to sit up so I can see him better, wincing in pain from the knife wound. "Jesus, Sydney. Just stay still. You don't have to move around to talk." Drew is still so upset by the situation that he pretty much snaps at everyone and everything, even me sometimes. He leans in and helps me adjust the pillows.

"Thanks." I refuse to be as outwardly angry as Drew, even though inside I'm falling apart.

"So," begins Detective Keating, pulling out a small notebook and reading from it. "The man who attacked you is Peter Stubbins. He's the same man who broke into your bedroom twelve years ago and was arrested, then tried to break in again the following week." I begin to feel lightheaded as he speaks.

"What?" Just when I thought Drew couldn't sound any angrier, I'm proven wrong. "The same man from twelve years ago?" Drew's body is rigid and he's gripping the side of my bed so hard I can see his knuckles turning white. I notice bruises and scrapes covering his hands but the detective answers before I can ask about them.

"Yes, the same man. Like I said, his name is Peter Stubbins. He's evidently been obsessed with you for a very long time, Miss Tannen. He has a wall in his apartment full of cutouts and photos of you from magazines, some new and some very old. It appears that he personally took a lot of photos of you as a child." Detective Keating gives me a sympathetic look.

"He was able to get close enough to take photographs of her, broke into her bedroom and assaulted her, and was still out on the streets? He nearly killed her!" Drew roars across my bed at the detective. I shrink back at his hostility, cringing into my pillow.

"Mr. Forrester, you need to stay calm. Yelling won't help, and it seems as though you're frightening Miss Tannen," the investigator says to Drew.

"Calm? You want me to be calm? I'm feeling the exact fuckin' opposite of calm right now! In fact, why don't we go outside—"

"Drew," I wearily put my hand on his before he does something that gets him arrested. Like punch the detective assigned to help us. "You have to let the man talk" He swings his hardened glare over to me and his eyes soften. "Please, baby. I know this is hard. It wasn't your fault." Drew's tired eyes widen and I see them glisten with guilt.

His mouth opens as if he's going to say something, then closes as if he changed his mind. With a tight scowl he huffs. "Alright, Sydney." Drew drops onto the couch, then glares at the detective. "Don't upset her."

Detective Keating continues where he left off. "There were no photos of you from after you left Los Angeles. He lost track of you when you disappeared. The only recent pictures he has are from magazines printed in the last week since the interview on *Late Night Report* aired."

He looks back down at his notebook. "Stubbins lives near the theater where the attack occurred. It's our belief that he saw the live reports either on the news or internet that you were there, and immediately drove over to find you. There are no cameras in the theater. We're still interviewing witnesses to piece together the rest." He folds up his notebook and tucks it into his shirt pocket.

"So, Miss Tannen, what happened in the theater? In your words." He sits back in the chair and waits.

"I...I went to the bathroom. I wasn't feeling good." My voice cracks, *the baby*. "W-when I came out..." I swallow and squeeze my eyes shut, trying to stop the tears. "He was in front of me. He...he told me he loves me." I choke and the tears break free, running down my cheeks in tiny rivers.

"He said what?" Drew whispers, his face now a dark shade of purple.

"Mr. Forrester, please. Let her speak," Detective Keating pleads with Drew.

Drew's big hands clench and unclench and he gets up to pace the room. I notice again that his knuckles looked scarred, bruised. He's been hitting someone or something. A lot.

I refocus and keep talking. "He grabbed me and slid the knife in. It was cold." I shiver from the memory. "He...he held me to him as I fell." My shoulders shake from emotion. "That's all I remember."

Wiping my face with the back of my hand, I look at Drew. He's walking the room again, his hands clasped on top of his head, a ticking time bomb of violence. He wants to hit something, badly. I've seen my dad do the same thing when he's about to lose control.

"Babe," I call to him. His head whirls around. "Can you get me a Sprite or something?"

Drew's face relaxes into a fake smile. "Sure Sydney. I'll be right back." He stalks out of the room in a cloud of fury.

I turn to the detective. "I'm sorry for his behavior detective. This is very hard for him."

Detective Keating pats my shoulder softly. "It's okay. He's not the first angry family member I've ever dealt with. He's not even the angriest." He gives me a weak smile. "I have to speak to Mr. Forrester next. I'll do that in the other room if you like. So you can rest."

"Sure, detective. It's better that I don't hear his version of events right now. I can't handle much more stress."

"Leave the stress to me, Miss Tannen. Mr. Stubbins is in custody at the Los Angeles County Jail without bail. He'll get way longer than the two years he served for breaking into your home when you were a child."

Drew comes back into the room with my drink. The detective asks him to step into the spare bedroom and they close the door.

I can hear Drew yelling from my bed, even when I try to drown him out with the TV. My poor, tortured protector. He couldn't save me from an obsessed man. He couldn't save our baby. He feels as if everything is completely out of his control. I hear him say that he thought I was dead, and I start to cry again. Somehow, all of the crying combined with the pain medicine wears me out, and I'm able to sleep.

Later in the day, Drew is on the phone with the chief of police of Los Angeles, and the presidents of both the movie theater chain and the studio that produced his film, yelling at all of them for their failure to keep the city safe and the building secure.

He thinks he's doing this all out of earshot in the other bedroom of the hospital suite so I won't have to worry, but once again, he doesn't realize how far his voice travels when he's pissed off. I'm sure that everyone at the nurses' station can hear him in agonizing detail.

During one call, an attendant was cleaning the suite and Drew's earsplitting anger was suddenly coming from the other side of the closed door. The poor woman was so scared she dropped her supplies and took off.

I told the doctors that I was already bleeding before I was stabbed and the surgeon confirmed that the knife didn't hit anything vital to the survival of the baby. Drew still feels responsible for what happened. I've told him it's not his fault. It's my fault for ignoring all of the signs. The obstetrician that examined me said the fetus most likely had something wrong with it and wouldn't have survived either way. That doesn't make either of us feel any better.

Thank god the press doesn't know I was pregnant or that I miscarried. I couldn't take it if I had to see the pity in everyone's faces or discuss it with anyone besides Drew and Leah.

As far as the world is concerned, the obsessed stalker that had been arrested for breaking into my parents' home and threatening me as a child was the same one apprehended at the theater for stabbing me.

He nicked my liver and some surrounding tissue was torn but the knife narrowly missed my diaphragm and lung. My wounds were repaired surgically and I was released three days later with no lasting injuries. That's the official story that Rhys released to the press.

Drew's family came from the theater to the hospital to visit while I was still unconscious. He told them they could catch their flights home to the East Coast as planned. My sweet defender didn't want them to see me after I woke up and was told that the baby was gone. They didn't know about the pregnancy and he wants to keep it that way.

My mom and Leah flew out to stay with Drew at the Sunset Marquis. They didn't want him to be alone, and Drew didn't want any of his other friends to know anything more than what the media was reporting. Of course, he slept on the couch in my fancy hospital room every night, so they ended up in the huge villa by themselves.

"Hey Mom. You just missed Leah." She looks tired when she comes into the hospital room after the doctor leaves.

"Hi baby." She sits next to my bed and clutches my hand in hers. I see my mom's eyes glistening with tears. I told her about the baby the night we were on the *Late Night Report* together. She's devastated over the loss I've suffered.

"Where's Drew?" She must have noticed that he's not in the adjoining bedroom.

"Leah and I made him go back to the hotel for a workout, Mom. The anger radiating off him is causing me to feel worse. I didn't tell him that though, I just told him he needed a break."

She smiles. "Your father was exactly like that. I always loved that about him, to tell you the truth. Something about those bad boys who want to protect you by punching people is so hot." My mom giggles at the memory.

I laugh and then flinch when it hurts. "It is hot, isn't it? But right now, I need to heal. I can't listen to him spout off violence on everyone. It's not healthy. He needs to let it out and fight. His main exercise is some sort of cage fighting that he does with a few guys from his gym. He hasn't worked out since we left New York, I'm sure all that pent up testosterone has him about to explode. He's been prepared to punch every single person that walks into this room."

"Your dad came by when you were in surgery, Syd," my mom says calmly. How in the heck can she drop a bomb like that on me when I just told her I need less stress so I can heal?

"What? Daddy was here? Why didn't he stay to see me?" I'm happy that my dad wanted to see how I was, but disappointed that I didn't get to see him.

"He didn't want to add the stress of a reunion on top of everything else, Sydney. Call him when you get home, there's plenty of time to rebuild with him. He's not going anywhere. He just wanted to be here to support you and Drew right now."

"Did Drew meet him?"

"Yes, and they really bonded over their inability to keep that psycho away from you. They're very much alike, Sydney. Drew's a good man, I can see it." Mom's gorgeous features are tired and sad looking. "He loves you very much."

"I know Mom. He does. He thinks this is entirely his fault, but it's *my* past that came back. It had nothing to do with him."

Drew will always think that what happened was because of him. Will he ever think otherwise?

"Honey, it's no one's fault. You couldn't stay alone and in hiding forever. We all still think you did the right thing by living your life. Not one of us thinks you were better off before, even considering the attack." My mom is tearing up a little. "You were so unhappy and alone, Sydney. I'm just so glad you found Drew."

"Me too, Mom. He's my everything."

I haven't left my loft in twelve days. Where would I go anyway? The press has been blocking my street since Drew and I got back from California. He keeps calling the police to break up the mob, but they just keep coming back.

What's the point?

The news of the attack has been the top story since it happened over two weeks ago. We're here at my place instead of his brownstone because at least here we're eight stories up from the madness instead of street level where people can, and did, ring his doorbell at all hours. Drew has his newly hired security in the lobby and in the hall outside my front door to keep everyone away.

I'm sitting in one of the cozy chairs by my bedroom windows, looking down at the undulating mass of reporters and well wishers in front of the building. They're like a living thing, pulsing and moving on the sidewalk like a single large creature. Traffic is snarled all the way down the street and through the intersection at Hudson. No fewer than five white news vans with satellite dishes on top are lining the road. There would be more if they could find a spot to park. I could watch the news reports as they happen if I wanted to.

As soon as we got home, Drew bought me the television I promised Brandon Eastlake that I would get so I could watch his show. I don't bother with the news. I already know what happened to me and have no desire to hear it discussed as if it's entertainment. I sigh and sink back into the chair.

I received a lot of phone calls wishing me well. Jeff Talley and Ben Walton from the Warren Hotel sent flowers. Adam Reynolds called me while I was still at the hospital. We chatted briefly while Drew stewed in the other room. Adam felt terrible about what happened at Verve and apologized profusely for Kiera's behavior. I told him it wasn't his fault and he promised to keep in touch to make sure I was okay. I didn't bother telling Drew about that. I can't deal with another fight over Adam Reynolds.

Brandon Eastlake called and asked if he could come by the hospital to see me. He stopped in for a few hours. Brandon felt guilty too, since his program brought all of the attention on me. Everyone around me is feeling responsible for something that was entirely the fault of one crazy man who is currently sitting in a jail cell.

I hear Drew yelling at someone on the phone in the living room of my loft. He pretty much yells at everyone these days. I listen to the one-sided conversation.

"I said, when I cahn make it!"

"Yeah, anothah week. That's what I said!"

"What is it that you cahnt undahstand?"

"No...No...I fuckin' said no!"

Full Boston. He's really mad.

I hear him coming down the hall to the bedroom and turn to face the doorway. When he sees that I'm not in the bed, he stops dead in his tracks. His head whips around the room until he finds me by the windows.

"Sydney, you shouldn't be out of bed." He walks across the room and sits in the chair next to mine.

"I'm fine, Drew. I can't be in bed anymore. I need to get out of here. I'm going crazy." I look at him and can tell he's trying to decide whether this is a good thing or a bad thing.

He sighs and rakes his hand through his hair. He needs a haircut, a shave, and about a week's worth of sleep. "I have to be at three more premieres for *A Soldier's Burden* this week and on the set in two weeks to start production on *Downtrodden Masses* in Vancouver. One of the premieres is here in New York, but one is in Chicago and the other is in Miami. I've pushed them back as far as I can. It's in my contract, Syd. I have to be there. It's a limited release independent film, not a huge blockbuster. I can't leave the people who financed it hanging."

The tortured look on his tired face makes me feel so bad for all of the stress I've caused him. I need to make this right.

I reach out and take his hand in mine and stare at our intertwined fingers. "I know you have to be there. I'll have Leah stay with me while you go to Miami and Chicago."

He starts to protest but I stop him. "Go Drew, walk the carpet, answer the questions. We have to be normal again." He raises an eyebrow. "Okay, as normal as we can be. Then when you have to start filming in Vancouver, I'll go with you. Maybe getting out of here would be good for us." I glance up at him through my eyelashes and see his surprised expression.

"You'll come with me?" he asks softly, as if speaking too loudly will scare me into changing my mind. "I didn't think you'd want to go. I thought you'd be done with that part of my life after what happened at the premiere."

"I want to be with you, Drew. I love every part of you, even your work. Your film was beautiful, you have to continue to act and I have to be with you. What happened was not because of your job. It was because of a crazy man who was obsessed with me. He knew me long before I met you, Drew. Besides, I don't think time apart would be great for us right now. I need you to get through this, and you're too nervous about me being alone. So, can I come with you to Vancouver?"

Drew holds his arms out and I accept his invitation. I crawl up into his lap in a tight ball, and he wraps his arms around me. We've been so physically distant these past two weeks, both of us too afraid. Me afraid of reminding him of our loss, Drew afraid of hurting me. His strong embrace feels like home.

"Please come with me babe, I'd go crazy with you thousands of miles away. I need to know that we're okay." He kisses my head and rests his chin on my shoulder.

"We're definitely okay." I turn to face him and he kisses me gently. "I haven't been to Vancouver in a long time. I wonder what I should pack?"

For the first time in fifteen days, we both smile. I start to think that maybe we'll be okay. Even though we lost a lot we still have each other. My heart warms at the thought, me and Drew and the whole future in front of us.

Then I remember that his co-star in Vancouver is Kiera Radcliff and my stomach does a triple flip down to my toes.

She is going to be a big problem. I just know it.

ACKNOWLEDGEMENTS

Who do you thank for helping you take an idea, a dream, a random jumble of images in your mind, and helping you put it down in a way that others can enjoy it?

First, I have to thank my husband, Brian. Who gladly let me spend all of my free time hunched over my laptop while the rest of my obligations fell to the wayside. He picked up the slack without complaint, allowing me to make this book a reality.

I also want to thank my friends and family, who were my first proofreaders. Letting me shove copy after copy in their face for review while I begged for feedback, nervous that it wasn't good enough.

I also need to thank my awesome Betas, Heather DeLuca, Amy Woods, and Krystal Wiles-Austin, who gave me honest opinions even when they stung. You helped me give people what they want and to see past my own stubbornness to make the changes that needed to be made.

Lastly, I want to thank whoever wrote the worst romance novel I had ever read. After stopping halfway through, too disgusted to finish, I challenged myself to write something better. That's how I came up with the Famous Series. I also want to give a special shout out to Tina Reber, whose Love Series inspired me to write about a hero who isn't a complete douchebag and that nice guys can indeed be sexy.

ABOUT THE AUTHOR

After growing up in New England, Heather Leigh lives just outside of Atlanta, GA with her husband and two children. Her favorite things include traveling, chocolate and of course, the Boston Red Sox.

LINKS

Follow me on the social media for contests and release dates

https://www.facebook.com/HeatherCLeighAuthor

https://www.heatherleighauthor.com

https://www.goodreads.com/goodreadscomHeather_Leigh

https://www.tsu.co/HeatherLeighAuthor

https://twitter.com/HeatherLeigh_8

http://instagram.com/heatherleighauthor/

BOOKS

The Famous Series

Relatively Famous

Absolutely Famous

Extremely Famous

Already Famous (Drew's POV)

Suddenly Famous (a novella)

Reluctantly Famous (a novella)

Sphere of Irony Series

Incite- Adam Reynolds

Strike- Dax Davies

Resist- Gavin Walker (2015)

Wreck- Hawke Evans (2015)

Ricochet

Locked & Loaded

Friendly Fire

Extraction Point